Girl Alt Delete

Jill Marie Denton

BookLocker
Trenton, Georgia

Copyright © 2023 Siena, Jill M

Print ISBN: 978-1-958889-99-2
Ebook ISBN: 979-8-88531-516-6

Published by BookLocker.com, Inc., Trenton, Georgia.

Printed on acid-free paper.

The characters and events in this book are fictitious. Any similarity to real persons, living or dead, is coincidental and not intended by the author.

BookLocker.com, Inc.
2023

First Edition

Library of Congress Cataloguing in Publication Data
Denton, Jill Marie
Girl Alt Delete by Jill Marie Denton
Library of Congress Control Number: 2023908764

When it comes to me,

It'll never be.

Go ahead, keep your misery.

The despair I bear,

It's more than my share.

Go ahead, forget the heart in there.

"Lily" by Second, from *One Night Stand,* 2018.

Undisclosed, 2022

Not a soul, not even my wealthy boss, knew where I was hidden. I was untraceable. Mine was a life of secrecy, seclusion, and isolation. Everyone was safer that way.

The incoming text message cast my bomb shelter of a bedroom in an explosive flash of pure white. The air raid siren notification tone pierced through sweet dreams of endless zeroes and ones.

Five people on the planet had the ability to interrupt what little sleep I managed to steal. They paid me handsomely for the courtesy. As the display came into view, though, I groaned. It was just after two in the morning, forty-five minutes after I'd set the damn thing down.

Good Lord, what now?

I sat up with a wince, the phone gripped tight as I adjusted to the infiltration of retina-shattering light. My boss's name sat at the top left of the screen. As staunchly professional as ever, she'd typed:

```
A press release is in your email box. Post it and
disable comments. Take down the homepage modal
for twelve hours. Remove any SameSite cookie
embeds. Activate notifications to A-tier
subscribers and give them four hours to view.
Release to B- and C-tiers for four subsequent
hours, then release to all levels after that.
Reply when the release is live.
```

I was glad for the lack of pleasantries so early in the morning. With a sigh, I rose to my feet, stretched to the sound of popping joints, and rolled my head over my shoulders. I'd just walked away from my computer. I was returning to it for some press release?

I should double my rates. These girls run me ragged.

Convinced I wouldn't see more sleep any time soon, I made a pit stop to my coffee pot. Two scoops of shade-grown Chiapas plus sixteen ounces of glacial water formed the black satin elixir I craved on mornings like this. They came more frequently than ever.

I'd been overworked ever since she sued that ex of hers. That's when my contract was modified to include the "twenty-four, three-sixty-five" clause, and that's what allowed me to move across the globe and into this clandestine hideout.

I followed my morning ritual, stirring the coffee in precise swirls before carrying the broad mug of inky tonic to my floor-to-ceiling office window. Tugging back the heavy curtains revealed a magenta and black sky swirled with emerald and azure. These magnificent views were one of the many perks I now enjoyed. Quiet was another, as was crisp air that never turned oppressive. The winters were tough, companionship was nonexistent, and the landscape was rugged, but I'd had enough social interaction over the years to sustain me.

Besides, my phone never stopped chiming, and between video calls, online meetings, and YouTube video editing, I saw plenty of the outside world. I wanted precious little of it. It was a mess of betrayal, disappointment, and litigation.

Aren't I a ray of fucking sunshine this morning?

Settling into my desk chair, I slid my readers on and opened my email. Sure enough, the press release was there and waiting. The boss's newest pet project was headed out on tour and ticket sale info was included in the fine print. They were nine hours ahead of me and already hard at work planning. My job was much simpler. I did exactly as she asked before safeguarding the website, as always.

For the five whose lives were more important than my own, flawless online presence was everything. This work was my sole reason for existing. No one outfoxed me.

I shot out a reply email to the boss and set my phone down, scrubbing my face with chafed palms. I'd had to shovel out the morning before to get to my drop spot. Once the delivery copter pilot tossed my payload onto the powdery snow a mile west of my hideout, I had less than an hour to get to it before the deep freeze outside turned my glass bottles into grenades. I paid way too much for Californian kombucha to have it explode all over the organic produce and grass-fed proteins I had on reorder.

I began the daily task of delving into the internet's deepest recesses as my phone chimed again.

Much obliged. Add a case of the Yards seasonal ale to your next drop and bill me for the whole order. Consider it a holiday gift.

Damn, Moneybags. That's quite a boon.

With an impressed brow lift, I sipped from the mug again before typing a reply.

I'd say thanks but it's not my style. It'll be two weeks before the charge hits. Just snagged a drop yesterday.

Her response was speedy.

Don't I know it, and was that a literal or figurative 'snag?'

I couldn't help snickering. It was a legitimate question.

It took a criminal to sniff out others. My boss understood that better than anyone. Instead of occupying some jail cell, I was holed up in an appointed sanctuary, working around the clock to keep her and her second family from being victimized the same way I'd been. I did it proudly, vehemently, and immaculately, by whatever means necessary. She'd saved me. I'd earned this.

It was mine to snag. I'm reformed. Hadn't you heard?

The air horn echoed around my expansive office again.

As your legal representation, I'm relieved to be reminded. Two interviews today, a photo shoot and appearances over the weekend. Ears to the ground.

I responded in seconds.

Aye, aye, captain. Over and out.

I'd be busy indeed. Hell, the boss always was. I was just following suit.

Chichester, PA, 2015

I pulled into the parking lot of the suburban café and parked in the first handicapped spot as instructed. After hanging the borrowed placard from the rearview mirror in the loaner Buick, I stepped out into the midday sun. A garish sign hung in the coffeehouse's window, shamelessly touting their overpriced autumn specials. Like the burgundy leaves on the banner, I'd also fallen from grace, destined to crumble underfoot as a progressive world passed me by.

I hadn't ventured out in weeks. This was way too risky. Curiosity was a fierce mistress, though, as was desperation. I was running short on funds and favors. If this didn't pan out, I would earn a one-way ticket to a women's only resort with very high walls topped with barbed wire.

Three hots and a cot, but with no shot at bail this time.

My heart trilled in my chest as I swung the glass door open and stepped inside. The humid air was laden with the scent of cloying spice and roasted beans. A laptop case on my shoulder weighed me down as I meandered through the crowd. Most were fixated on their cell phone screens or on the vapid conversation adding to the din of the whirring blenders and grinders. The barista was slinging espresso on ice at light speed but she was no match for the well-appointed twenty-somethings on abbreviated lunchbreaks. They tapped their toes, muttered under their breath, and crossed their arms in passive aggression as the minutes wasted by.

I set up shop in a far corner, closest to the windows overlooking the lot. After tugging my laptop from my bag and affixing the screen shield to guard against prying eyes, I fished out my earbuds. I placed one in my right ear. Hard rock swept over my senses as my left ear kept vigilance over the crowd. I logged in and accessed the VPN, which connected me to an ISP in Denmark while I opened my RFID reader. Disguised as a wireless mouse, it sat unassumingly alongside the silicone keyboard. Hiding in plain sight, I got to work.

Within seconds, I had access to every cell phone, tablet, and POS terminal in the facility. The thirty-four-year-old brunette lingering by the barista's station was perusing shoe sales while she waited for the six-dollar fat-free drink she'd just purchased with a Visa card opened in her husband's name. The couple dressed in staunch black suits stirring blue packets into their coffees were taking a break from pharmaceutical sales pitches aimed at doctor's offices in the tri-state area. They'd done quite well this morning based on their contract-logging program's database. The barista, their name purposefully misspelled by an overly creative parent, had clocked in at five that morning and hadn't clocked out for a break yet. I sympathized just enough to peek over my shoulder at the tireless drink-slinging.

Like the sales reps, this café was also kicking ass today. There was over four hundred bucks in the till and another six hundred in card swipes since they'd opened. They only had five muffins, four-point-eight pounds of espresso beans, and enough organic almond milk for seven large drinks left.

I hope this place clears out before the nut milk's gone. I can't handle abused cow juice.

With recovered focus, I combed through the data. I was here for a very specific piece of intel, something not yet on display. I checked my spangly new smart watch. Ten minutes had passed. I'd been assured I wouldn't have to wait long. My patience was already waning. The crowd's anticipatory energy, fueled by their procured caffeine, was ramping up my pulse and paranoia.

Every second I spent in public, even wearing this ridiculous wig and polyester getup, put me in peril. I'd chosen the lesser of two evils. The other option had been to expose my safehouse. That idea was unacceptable. I relied on few and trusted even fewer. This offer sounded promising, but my throat was more exposed with each passing second.

Come on, come on. Don't waste my time.

I kept panning for gold among the patrons as the crowd began to thin. The barista was finally able to take a breath ten minutes later when the whistling milk steamer and toaster oven fell silent. I fought the temptation to pack up everything and carry it with me to the counter. Nothing looked more suspicious than that. Instead, I locked the screen and kept the RFID active, keeping the setup in my peripheral vision as I sought out a stimulant of my own.

I'd lucked out. There was enough of that almond milk remaining to swirl into a twelve-ounce drip. I preferred the tonic black, but this café's beans were mass-market, over roasted, bitter little briquets. The corn syrup-sweetened almond milk was a necessary concession. Before a second sip, I already regretted ordering anything. I could've brought a superior brew with me, from a company that understood humanitarian scruples and provided their employees with livable wages.

How would it have looked to bring your own coffee into a multi-national chain? Shut up and drink it, you hoity twat.

I sipped again after a sigh of defeat. A moment later, a pop-up box flashed on screen. The RFID had a new signal, twenty yards to the east. It was a strong signal, too, undoubtedly from a transponder.

I chanced a glance out the broad windows. A silver midsize sedan with dark tinted windows parked alongside the Buick I'd commandeered for the day. The engine was running with the car's flood lights on. My hair stood on end as I clicked to accept the incoming signal.

Hello there. Whatcha got for me?

In seconds, a black screen with white text displayed an endless string of ones and zeroes.

Jackpot.

The rows of numbers, translated by my panning eyes, became a giant run-on sentence, detailing the transgressions of a private practice doctor in Cinnaminson. The quack was in the back pockets of every known mobster and racketeer in Philly. He'd evidently grossed four million so far in exchange for unscheduled, unsanctioned surgeries ranging from extractions to reconstruction.

Seems intense for a DO to do in-office. Risking your license, doc?

The physician was active on the state's medical licensing board website. A deep dive into his insurance claims and billing revealed referrals to surgeons for his recurring client base. There was no evidence of legitimate billing for anyone rumored to be part of the city's criminal underbelly. Humoring myself, I double checked, then triple checked my findings.

Nope, no record of insurance-paid, in-office surgeries. Gotcha, doc.

The RFID signal cut out as I extracted the last of the data. I watched as the sedan pulled from the space exactly three minutes after arriving, exiting the lot, and merging into traffic on the four-lane expressway.

My work here was done. I tossed what was left of the mediocre coffee in the bin on the way out.

* * * * *

"You went in person? That was stupid. What'd you get?"

I reclined in my threadbare office chair with the burner phone propped on my shoulder. My newly painted toes slid onto the simple metal table I used as a desk. I'd opted for a kinky pink polish, a shade somewhere between ballet flat and flamingo. It matched my victorious disposition.

"Doc's been up to no good. Looks like he's in deep, too. That yacht in the Caymans and the beach house in Brigantine are mortgaged. Guess four mil just doesn't go as far as it used to."

"Phew," the female voice breathed into my ear. "Is his laundry all hung up?"

"Yep. Three outlets want the deets."

"Let me guess, DigitalDive, NewlyMinted, and HackNSack. What's the top bid?"

"Hack's got two-twenty in. Next highest is the Dive at two-ten. I'm giving them five minutes to top that, then we're sold."

"Eighty-twenty split?"

"Since when?"

"Since this was my lead and since you're my indentured servant. How's the OS on that smartwatch?"

I muted my scoff. "Whatever. I'm the one doing the dirty work."

"Quit arguing."

"It's my style."

"You're obnoxious. Eighty-twenty split. We're t-minus four minutes."

The computer app tracked bidding while we waited in silence. I waggled my toes, hoping the gel coat would dry as flawlessly as the retouched ad model promised. When a loud ding erupted from the computer speakers seconds later, she chimed in instantly. "DigitalDive?"

"No, actually," I murmured, leaning in close. "Newly's got two-fifty on the table now."

"Nice. Those bastards will tap the quack for everything he's got."

I snickered. This type of work wasn't my greatest achievement. It simply furthered my goals. Since I'd departed from my most recent employer under unfavorable circumstances, I wasn't left many options. This partnership wasn't my proudest move, either, but I did what I needed to keep communication alive with this ally. She'd taken on the cost of my maintenance, and it wasn't cheap.

Expense-wise, this suburban studio's monthly rental wasn't the problem. My tastes and habits were another story. I'd grown accustomed to a certain lifestyle. A single sip of that caustic swill at the café was proof of that. I had a grander goal, one involving disappearing off the grid entirely.

That, and my artisan goods obsession, took serious scratch to accommodate.

Three more minutes passed by in silence as I held my cell to my ear, somehow managing to not smudge the polish in the process. Once we were done, this burner was destined for the scrap heap. Despite our tumultuous history, I knew the caller was trustworthy. Cell phone carriers, not so much.

The female voice in my ear chimed at the five-minute mark. "Do we have a winner?"

Punctual as always, you stunner.

"Indeed. Congrats, NewlyMinted."

"Splendid. Always a pleasure doing business with you."

"As always. *A bientôt, mon rêve.*"

"*Oui, mon ceil du nuit.*"

The phone line cut off as a single tear crested my lower lid.

Her night sky.

I could barely believe it. Was she genuine, or just excited because we'd scored our biggest payout ever? Either way, she almost never called me that anymore. Those words were worth far more than the fifty grand I'd just pocketed.

Undisclosed, 2016

I reached the top of the snow-dusted ridge as the sun reached its apex. Being this close to the Arctic circle meant I only had a few hours of sunlight left. I'd been hiking for hours already. A wireless bud tucked into my ear, playing the newest release from a metal-core band, was my only company.

The air whipped around me as I crested a snowdrift. The sight in the basin before me was well worth the trek and the blisters. I sank to my knees in both reverence and exhaustion. I finally had a clandestine nook to call my own, and what a nook it was.

The twenty-two-hundred square foot, single-story stronghold was finally complete after a year of waiting. It was no normal homestead, though. Shaped like a broad warehouse, but with walls of solid concrete, the structure disguised itself as an outbuilding for a utility company or a waystation for scientific exploration. Posted warnings dotted the snowy scene in vibrant yellow, lending an air of danger to chase off the riffraff. The angular roof covered in solar panels faced east to capture what sporadic sunlight I'd experience out here, and a twelve-foot satellite dish, custom made by a blue chip's government support division, ensured I'd be well connected to the world beyond this valley.

I rose to my feet with a shit-eating grin, recollecting how dirty my hands had been in negotiating for that satellite access. A little inside intel, courtesy of an ousted and jaded contractor with diplomatic immunity, had done the job beautifully. I paid off the informant, then resorted in a little anonymous and cutthroat bartering. Rather than facing some serious white-collar litigation, I kindly gave them a chance to stay sparkling in the public eye.

The term "blackmail" was so ugly and cliché. I preferred calling it "alternate dispute resolution."

The final hundred yards to the shackled doors were the lightest of the entire trek. Home beckoned me.

Once the physical locks were removed, I shoved the door open. Beyond was a broad rectangular space adorned with black faux leather furniture, squat modern tables, and impressionist art. It felt like a designer condo in Manhattan. I shrugged off my snow boots, setting them in the bespoke brass bin beside the door. I left the alpaca knit cap pulled over my auburn mane and my cross-body backpack in place while I explored. I couldn't bear any further delay.

The two extra bedrooms were decorated simply. Muted greens and brilliant whites draped over the modest beds and covered the bare walls. Knowing these spaces were for guests I'd never welcome, I tugged the doors shut.

The kitchen was a much grander sight. I'd splurged here, namely on dark-lacquered maple cabinets, an Italian coffee and espresso station, and Wi-Fi-enabled appliances. Pecanwood parquet flooring and honey-colored paint reminded me of a farmhouse kitchen in my distant past.

The master bedroom and adjoining bathroom took my breath away. White marble, alabaster porcelain, and brass fixtures shined against the dusty blue walls. Imported Greek tiles rimmed the tub and completely covered the walls within the massive corner shower. Immaculately aseptic,

I exhaled a slow, appeased breath. I'd never have to cower behind a filmy shower curtain again.

The enormous bed was as inviting as I'd hoped. Low to the ground and adorned with foot-thick down bedding, I was tempted to hop in for a quick test drive. Duty called, though. I needed my office set up as soon as possible. The boss was patiently waiting for me to return to work. I had two hours of free time left. The rumor mills, gossip sites, and social media maelstrom never stopped, and certainly not for fame of the boss's caliber. I'd already have one hell of a backlog to deal with. I'd been off the job for hours, hiking from the closest outpost to my new home.

Four monitors, a firewall-protected laptop, and all the peripherals I'd ever need were up and running in short order. The plush curtains were opened to display a rapidly darkening sky as my time off grew shorter. Fortunately, there was just one thing left to do.

I popped open the front door against the bitterly cold wind. My toes tingled in the seconds it took to capture a single photo of the ridge beyond. The blackening sky was painted with a technicolor swirl as twilight lost its battle to the impending night.

With a quick swipe, I sent the photo to my greatest inspiration and former co-conspirator. It would serve as the only clue to my new location. I didn't dare hope for a reply. Forevermore, my night sky would be the one beyond my doorstep.

In my office, surrounded by the scent of fresh paint, I snapped the flip phone in half over my knee, pulled loose the SOC chip, and tucked the whole unit inside my breadbox-sized Faraday cage, just in case that phone's signal somehow survived. That secretly acquired and covertly operational NASA-grade satellite was my only terrestrial connection.

The compound's generator whirred to life as the sun set, keeping the air around me balmy and my equipment running. I settled into my plush office chair, lifted my knees to my chest, and took in my new surroundings.

I was finally done running. I was home.

Whitehall, SC, 2012

Another life ruined.

I hid my eye roll as insincere words tumbled out. At the wicker patio table alongside immaculate gardens, I felt the breeze grow stagnant. "I'm sorry, Mrs. Stuyvesant. I wish I had better news."

"No, no," the aging society woman managed, patting my hand where it rested on the table. "You did what you were paid to do. It's not your fault he's a..."

Her attempt at a stiff upper lip was interrupted by yet another deluge of crystalline tears.

He didn't deserve her anguish. I knew it. She knew it. Her heart was broken nonetheless, and I'd been the one to break it, just like I invariably would. I'd known her husband's guilt even before hearing all the details. Experience in the business was to blame there.

"What you asked for, it's all here," I murmured under the din of her sobbing, sitting forward to grip her frail fingers and move them onto the legal envelope resting between us. "You don't have to open it now, but please make sure your attorney receives everything. You'll have no issues getting every cent of alimony he owes you despite the prenup."

"Oh, *fuck* the money," she wailed, covering her face with her palms. The massive champagne diamond mounted on her finger winked in the noon-day sun. "My marriage, my life, my reputation, it's all a *farce*!"

I'd expected the weeping, the dripping mascara, even the dramatics, but nothing could've prepared me for the godless language. Clarabelle Stuyvesant's biting revelation could've been an actual punch. It would've broken her fingers, but my shock would've been the same.

"Mrs. Stuyvesant, I'll be on my way. If you or the attorney need anything else for your case, please reach out."

"Thank you, dear. I wish…" she paused, shaking her silvery-coiffed head. "I'm glad you were successful in your endeavors."

"Thank you for giving me the chance to give you the peace you deserve."

I rose from the bespoke seating before dipping my head to the soon-to-be single, and extremely wealthy, ex-Mrs. Stuyvesant. It was possible she'd acquire this mansion, plus half the county's land, in the front-page-worthy divorce proceeding.

It was yet another notch in my belt.

I waited for the houseman to open the side gate, which he did with a flourish. Sweating in his wool ensemble, he gifted me a prim smile and nod as I followed the crimson stone path to my waiting Tesla coupe in the driveway's front circle. My lips peeled back in a grin as I approached my driver's side door, glancing back at the aging three-story plantation house.

One down, two more to go.

* * * * *

I pulled between aging twin police cruisers in the precinct's lot as the sun disappeared over the horizon. The day had already been exhausting, but this final stop was a necessary evil. Sheriff Phillip Daly had a wicked sense of humor and almost no patience left for me. I couldn't blame him. I made his life a living hell.

I filled my days investigating the cases the cops didn't have time for, ones they couldn't nail down, or those on the fringe of legality. His scraps were my salvation. Showing him up, doing my job well and earning myself a little notoriety, though, put me in a lofty spot on his shit list.

Being a public servant also meant his coffers were stretched much thinner than mine, but his pension and health insurance were securities I wasn't afforded. Having the official title in a town like ours meant he was respected in ways I'd never be. It was a trade-off, but this uncomfortable alliance worked for us.

His building's lights were off. The precinct's receptionist was evidently done with her Friday shift earlier than usual.

Five minutes, tops. He's on the way.

Regardless of how insane his workload, the sheriff had a woman to return to, an obligation outside the navy-blue getup. The wife wasn't to be tangled with. I went to school with her, was faced with her verbal assaults multiple times, and knew she was a dirty fighter. His obeyance to her draconian rule was to blame there. How they hadn't killed each other yet, I didn't understand.

Thank God I'd evaded, or rather ignored, the expectation of continuing the Daly name. Phil had cast a long shadow over me in our old family home.

Sure as shit, his state-issued SUV pulled into the lot, stopping dead by my bumper. With a twisted smile in the rear-view mirror, I waggled my fingers at the new arrival, disrupting what little predictability he had left.

I watched him pound a palm into his steering wheel, mumble something I presumed obscene, and launch from the driver's seat, rounding on my door like a tiger. He gestured wildly to the sign three feet from my fender, indicating the space was reserved for the sheriff.

Shame it's not illegal to take his parking spot.

I didn't touch the window, the blaring air conditioner around me muting his voice to a rumbling growl. "You learned to read in second grade, same as me."

With him blocking me in, all I could do was lift my shoulders with an innocent look, peek again in the rearview mirror at his humming SUV, then show him my docile eyes again.

A guttural groan escaped as my door was deftly tossed open. "What the hell do you want now? Maddie'll have my balls in a vice if I'm not home for dinner."

"Your problem, not mine," I replied, tugging my door shut. "More parking in your lot would help. Back up so we can switch."

Short strides carried him back to his ajar door. Tires squealed as he backed up against the rear of the lot, giving me a few inches to make my escape. I pulled perpendicular to the cruiser to my left, just enough to let him slide in before backing up and boxing him in. When I emerged and approached his window, his forehead was on his steering wheel.

I almost felt bad for him. Almost. Maddie was a terror. Watching this diligent public servant succumb to such a tyrant made me want to cause more tension. Maybe then she'd finally cut her losses and dash. They hadn't spawned yet, so I could only hope. They'd already have to split custody of that obnoxious, clumsy mongrel they'd somehow agreed on.

He climbed from the front seat, crossing his arms over his broad chest. "I hope you have a legitimate reason for being here, not just to push what few buttons I have left. It's been a hellish day."

"Did the Stevenson cat climb every tree in the neighborhood again?"

"You know, your antagonism is about as welcomed as your Brussels sprouts at Thanksgiving," the sheriff muttered, his amber eyes narrowing on me. "Why you bother with that muck, I'll never understand."

"I could say the same about your wife."

"I assume there's a point to you being here. Spit it out. Now."

"Aww, don't hate me. I just need a protection order fast-tracked."

"Oh, did your soothing, comforting disposition finally catch up with you?"

I couldn't help but snicker at that one. "No, but once Mr. Hollings closes his joint accounts, his common law husband is going to go looking for that shotgun. I'm sure a protection order is easier to handle than murder charges."

He exhaled, his expression softening. "So, your investigation..."

"Turned up some serious shit," I interjected. "Mr. Hollings will be here in the morning to sign everything. He's pressing charges. And once he turns over the evidence, you'll have a few counts of child pornography to file in addition to the solicitation stuff. Sorry, Bro."

Phil lifted his campaign hat from his mop of chestnut hair, pushing crooked fingers through it. "Damn it, damn it. That bastard's been lying since day dot."

"Yep, and his hubby isn't having it. He's safe for now but won't be for long. I put him up at a hotel a few towns over, rented him a car, and gave him a burner phone to use."

"I owe you," he sighed. "And I hate owing you."

"I'll call Maddie and tell her I'm the reason you're running late. She can yell at me."

"Not enough."

"Ugh," I winced, gritting my teeth. "Fine, and the mutt gets a case of premium food. Deal?"

"Much obliged. And your other investigations?"

"The business I was looking into, they're dead in the water. Seems Dawkins was promising millions to business owners, millions he never had to begin with. It's a shame he already had so many on the hook. I reported him an hour ago. And Mrs. Stuyvesant's going to own Whitehall in short order. That disgusting husband of hers's been sniffing up every skirt in the tri-county area. He deserves the financial rape he's about to get."

He laughed aloud this time. "How you hide this darling personality from your clients is beyond me."

"Not all of us gets to be the good guy, you know. It takes nefarious types to dig up dirt. Technically, we're on the same team. The law just doesn't help everyone the same, does it?"

He rolled his eyes. "Don't I know it. Just, do me a favor and stop being such a bitch to Aiden, would ya? He hasn't learned your ways yet. So seriously, either go out with him or don't, but the dicking around with him is getting old."

I shrugged, looking away. "Why do you care? It's none of your business."

"You make it my business when you practically dry hump my deputy every time you step foot in the precinct. I know you've hooked up with almost everyone in town by now. Just quit dangling yourself in front of him if you're not into him. It's cruel."

What a prude.

"I'm just flirting, and for the record, I was *trying* to avoid being my normal self with your closest coworker. Fat lotta good that did me, huh? You're still all pissy about it."

"Oh, this was for *my* benefit?" Phil chortled, shaking his head at me. "Thanks for nothing."

"Fine, I'll just screw him and get it over with. I hope you'll appreciate hearing all about how amazing it'll be at the water cooler the next morning."

"It's gotta be better than 'I've been trying everything' or 'tell me what to do to bag her.' What's worse? Giving him tips on how to seduce my stepsister, or listening to him gloat about how great it was?"

"You know, you're really selling him right now. He legitimately hits you up for tips? So sad."

"Not everyone is as confident as you, and no one knows you better than me. Well, except Chey, but she's not going to help him."

"Nope, not likely," I muttered.

Chey was my best buddy in my younger years and the sister I'd never been granted. Her dropping out of community college and entering the convent in the next town over meant she no longer had any interest in her former friend's shenanigans. I couldn't help believing that my antics were the reason Sister Mary Margaret came into existence. She no doubt prayed for my sinning soul even now.

But there was only so much to do in a small town like ours. If sneaking out and having sex was the worst of it, that wasn't so bad, right?

Phil's baritone cut through my thoughts. "Let me get out of here, would you? Your wallowing to my wife will only buy me so much time. You coming to Dad's for dinner Sunday?"

"Ugh, I forgot. I really wish I didn't feel obligated to."

"You'll probably save him a lot of grief if you don't show."

"In that case, I'll be there with bells on, unless I'm bagging your buddy, that is."

"Sooner rather than later. Seriously. And I don't want any details."

I chuckled, punching his bicep. He winced, though I'm sure he barely felt the impact to the solid muscle below. "Don't forget the protection order. He'll be here first thing to sign on the dotted line."

"I'll get it started. Thanks for convincing him to leave that asshole for good this time."

"Eh, the evidence did that for me. Love you, shit stain."

His arms gathered me up instinctively for the briefest of moments. "Love you too, whore bag."

He tipped his head affectionately and smirked as I escaped to my car. I pulled from the lot, bringing up Maddie's cell number on my new iPhone. Swallowing hard, I pressed the green call icon.

* * * * *

I contemplated my conversation with my stepbrother as I made my way to Whitehall's miniscule downtown plaza. Phil was becoming a dirtier fighter every day, his wife's conditioning no doubt. Of course, he'd bring up my deficiencies when all I'd asked for was a favor for a client. He saw through my armor better than anyone.

The tumult of destroying the relative calm of the citizens around me made life outside work much less lustrous. I exploited more people than I befriended. I'd learned to from such a young age, it was like second nature. The depravity, dishonesty, and deceit I saw made it hard to even try to be honest, let alone vulnerable. I was always in research mode and ready to engage, even when they didn't see me coming.

My reputation preceded me. I was either the loosest girl in town or the most courageous, the edgiest or the crudest, depending on who I'd buttered up that day and how much dirt I'd unearthed. Friends and enemies were synonymous in a town this small, and even in the outskirts, rumors were just loud enough to rumble underfoot if an ear was pushed to the ground.

Those who didn't take my work seriously learned a brutal lesson in short order.

The instinct to listen to the words on the wind, the suspicions echoing between the thin walls of the local watering holes, and the ability to objectively call out the worst of the worst was how I turned a small-town existence into something I felt proud of, but it certainly didn't help me build relationships. My last date had been two towns over, with a rando I'd met on a dating app. Regardless of how charming he'd seemed online, his stories focused on how many chainsaw injuries he'd survived and how many beer cans he could smash against his forehead. It hadn't worked out.

I'd even dabbled with ladies, driving over state lines to avoid any potential clientele. I'd messed around with enough cheerleaders and field hockey players in high school to know the routine. Flatter her, then ask open ended questions so she fills the silence. Constant eye contact was critical. Keep her drink filled. Empathize with whatever stress-inducing minutiae was on the docket. And most importantly, when she showed even the slightest sign of intoxication, make sure to ask twice for permission to taste. It was always worth the effort, though. Women were inherently more supple, impulsive, and detached. In other words, they were perfect for dalliances.

Diligent men like Aiden Yates, my brother's newly minted deputy from Durham, were everywhere in towns like these. Like forgotten landmines in Eastern Europe, one wrong step and they blew up in your face, hurling commitment and obligation sky-high like shrapnel. Once that chaff embedded into skin, it was impossible to pick out all the remnants.

So many of my high school friends had kids now, and they were burdened beyond reason by their pint-sized antics and endless need of attention. Their spouses rarely pulled their own weight, let alone enough responsibility to allow them an hour to hang out with me, the uninvolved, unattached, wild child of Whitehall.

I'd keep the banner waving if the fortifications stood against the cannonballs of adulthood. So far, the ramparts were holding fast.

By the time my thoughts circled back around, I'd navigated to Commerce Avenue, Whitehall's main street. Dewey's, the dirtiest dive bar in town, served burgers to die for, but the only health food store in Jasper County, waiting on the opposite corner, built the freshest salads. The debate haunted me as I parallel parked near the intersection. It had been a hellish yet productive day for me, breaking up two marriages and a business partnership in a little less than ten hours. A greasy indulgence seemed like the best way to close out a successful Friday, but my conscience screamed so loud that I found myself wandering through the market's sliding glass doors yet again.

The ding-dong chime above my head lifted the lovely shop owner's eyes to mine. I saw Georgia more than my own family most weeks. Her greeting was always warm and sincere. "Hey, stranger."

"Long time, no see," I called over my shoulder, already perusing the chilled case. Four salads remained between the partitions, nestled among squat containers of artisan cheese, hand-smashed guacamole, and chunky citrus salad. I snagged the last roasted garlic Caesar. My conscience screamed again as it chilled my palm. I huffed at myself and exchanged it for the only remaining bowl of berry-topped greens with sunflower butter vinaigrette.

"Glad I put a few of those out this morning," the late-thirties transplant from Florida told me as I set down my dinner on the counter. Her eyes, slate with sapphire swirls, brightened as they lifted to mine. "No one but you seems to know what sunflower butter even is, or if they should bother trying it."

"Philistines," I muttered. "Wouldn't know health if it socked them in the jaw."

"Tell me about it," she chortled, laying a seven-grain roll on top of the salad. "Eight-fifty. But hang on. I assume you want some of that kombucha you told me about, too? It just came in right after you picked up your lunch salad."

I couldn't hide my zeal as Georgia stepped away to the nearby drink case. "You're too kind. No one in this shithole town cares about gut flora or antioxidants."

"Except you," she grinned, the faintest blush creeping up her cheeks. "They only had the pomegranate tangelo available for rush order. That'll work with your salad, though."

She placed the heavy glass bottle into my awaiting palm. The beauty was small batch, non-GMO, and made with an emperor's green tea base. It was only slightly less attractive than the shopkeeper beaming at me. I'd discussed the merits of the start-up California company with her days before. She'd remembered every word and came up big.

"Hello, lovely," I cooed at the hand-blown beauty. "I have special plans for you tonight."

"Let me know if it's good. I'm still not a fan. I'm looking to have my mind changed."

"You didn't like the blueberry açai one I recommended?" I took out my credit card. "That's the mildest one I've ever had."

"I really did try. It just reminds me of carbonated balsamic vinegar."

"It'll have its day in the sun someday. A few more hipsters need to embrace it first. Oh, and can you drop off a case of that organic, free-range dog food to the police station?"

"Treating the Sheriff's puppy again?"

"The slobbery monster is costing me a fortune, and the dog's not a cheap date, either."

She snickered as I swiped my card. Those enchanting eyes focused on mine again, a touch of shyness thinly veiled within, as she passed dinner to my waiting hands. I made sure to graze my fingers over hers, and just as I'd anticipated, she froze at my touch, the hitch of her breath barely perceptible.

But I'd learned to notice the littlest things. This reaction was one I always enjoyed.

"I hope you can get behind kombucha, Georgia. If something makes you feel good, inside and out, it's worth trying, right?"

Her dusty blonde brows nearly touched. "Are you still talking about the kombucha?"

With a grin, I leaned over the counter. "What do you think?"

"I'd like to think you only visit so often to keep me in business, but maybe I'm wrong?"

"Very much so," I murmured, tipping my head, and softening my gaze until she finally exhaled the breath she'd been holding since our touch. "Has anyone shown you around our little town yet? You've been here over a month. Tell me someone's been generous enough to offer you a walk under the blooming magnolias."

"I'm looking at her. And I'm closed on Mondays, as you know."

"I'll come get you at four. Wear comfortable shoes and be hungry."

Georgia beamed and nodded as I edged toward the door.

"Oh, and one more thing?"

She turned back to me with a dust rag clutched in her fingers. "Yeah?"

"Thanks for moving here."

* * * * *

"Siri, what time is it?"

The cheery voice replied instantly. "It's twelve-oh-six AM."

With a stretch and guttural yawn, I pushed my tall leather chair away from my desk. I'd finished dinner and traded my contact lenses for glasses three hours before, but I'd been too buried in work to notice the pitch black outside my open window.

The last drops of rose-hued refreshment rushed down my throat. If Georgia could order me a case of this stuff a week, I'd be thrilled. In the meantime, I'd have to settle for her supply of Islandic spring water and fair-trade Sumatran coffee to keep hydrated.

The empty bottle clanged in the aluminum bin by my desk as a strong breeze carried floral fragrance through the open window. Early spring finally graced South Carolina with some sympathy, the winter colder than any on record. I'd never needed a snow shovel before and hoped to never need it again. At least the condo complex's landscaping took care of the streets. My late-model, fully electric coupe was far from practical on winding county roads, but it got eighty-nine MPGe, turned heads, and spoke volumes in a town like this. I had prominent clients to impress, with whom high-level negotiations often took place. The half-dozen designer suits, high-priced leather bags, and imported heels also helped cement my status. I'd grown to love high-dollar attire.

I knew the part I played. No thirty-year old PI should look frumpy, especially not one as extroverted and ambitious as myself. And no one suspected that a small-town girl investigating her neighbors was moonlighting as a hacker.

With the local investigative work now as done as it could be, I craved some new gateway software, but I needed to cover my tracks. I couldn't acquire it through legal means. A German IP address would get me through the gateway company's firewall, but I'd need a server somewhere else to access the financial database. I'd make it look like I paid for their service, though I had no intention to do so. The three monitors surrounding me flashed with a red warning message as I tapped at the backdoor of the database's online repository. The password I managed to find on their ethernet denied me even the slightest glance.

Damn. Time locked. Figures. How secure's the front door, I wonder?

I scratched my cheek and pushed my glasses back up my nose while double-checking the company's ethernet for anything juicy. They'd certainly anticipated someone with a modicum of skill in hacking, or the more illegal form of it, dubbed "cracking." The schisms in their armor were so slight, any novice would've passed over them.

My obsession with breaking into some of the most sophisticated and clandestine niches on the internet gave me a few advantages. This company was about to hand over a one-way ticket to the dark web in exchange for some washed Euros. I just needed to break in surreptitiously. The feds combed for this type of activity constantly. I couldn't have them in my hair.

My eyes passed over lines of code. Indian Devanagari script baffled me, but a bootlegged app from Pakistan let me translate anything I didn't understand into binary. The left monitor blinked, then the Indian phrases on it shifted into an endless series of zeroes and ones.

Come to mama. Where are you?

I skipped over the numbers, tucking my thumbnail in my teeth. Patterns were everything. There was one hidden here somewhere. All I needed was a set of at least eight characters that repeated a few times, ideally with some numbers, capitals and punctuation marks nestled in. Every key stroke of every employee was here.

Thankfully for me, this company spent a whole lot more on marketing than staff security training. Any idiot knew that sign-on validation should be unique for every single person, every single time. I quickly realized the database had a single password, an old one, used by multiple employees.

Yu09s30ul. Interesting.

A quick Google search of the company reflected some curious facts about that repeating set of characters. The company started in 2009, Guanyuan Yu was the lead developer, and most of the repository's assembly team were from South Korea.

A database built in '09 by a guy named Yu, with a team from Seoul? How droll.

It took seconds to find one of Yu's employee's records, including their user ID and IP address. Remoting into his office's computer from the comfort of my study was child's play, as was locating the repository. I copied the translated characters carefully and was gifted a truly beautiful sight in return.

Financial records generated, millions of them, along with names, dates, transaction histories, addresses, exchange orders, and wire instructions. It was a treasure trove, a goldmine for a would-be thief.

I didn't need to steal anything here, though. I needed to add some falsified ones to them. This cracking was for a good cause.

Five minutes later, I dipped out of the repository and ensured I couldn't be tracked backward from the source, deleting and replacing along the way. It was a shame most people didn't understand how difficult it was to permanently remove something from the internet. It wasn't as simple as recalling an email or deleting an embarrassing social media post. It required hacking, and most of the time, the effort was barely legal.

Tonight, I'd successfully broken into the financial records of millions. Illegal didn't begin to cover it. Interpol would have a field day with this. But, as a safeguard against those more talented than myself, I multi-layer encrypted the way in. The company workers would notice the added steps but wouldn't know who initiated it. No doubt they'd assume some higher-up created additional precautions due to corporate decisions they weren't privy to.

I made it so even I would have a hard time getting back in. I'd never need to. I never walked the same path twice.

It was finally safe to use the gateway program, the one I'd just broken international law to acquire. It seemed a small price to pay to finally grow my expertise in my truest obsession. Soon, I'd have a decent crack at discovering the truest, basest filth on the internet.

I was a modest cracker, but this was the path forward. In no time at all, I'd have greater access to the depraved, twisted souls hiding in the darkest corners. Soon, I'd be circling on the white-collar dickheads calling their private investments "charity donations," the sex traffickers running their businesses like popsicle stands, and the social media mavens kiting their endorsement money to offshore arms dealers.

There were so many criminals that the boys in blue just couldn't take on, and so many they knew nothing about. All my dreams were about to come true.

I will be the next esTre11aN3gra.

Whitehall, SC, 2012

Georgia lived above her modest market in a two-bedroom apartment. A high school friend of mine grew up in the same place, one I hung out with several times a week during our junior and senior years. As soon as she graduated, her entire family skipped town, glad to follow their daughter as she began her cross-country trek to Oregon's state university and its mountain views.

I'd been so jealous of their familial bond. That stung more than their unapologetic escape. They hadn't belonged here. I felt startlingly similar most of the time. Maybe that's why we got along so well. Hooking up with her the night of the graduation ceremony as one last hurrah of sorts probably hadn't been the best idea. Her parents arrived in the middle of things and caught us red-handed. I'd lost my best friend and my favorite bra that night.

She didn't say goodbye. Their car was just gone. It hurt, but I understood their reasons.

Pulling up alongside the building now brought her sudden departure to mind. It also reminded me of all the awesome things we'd shared, like illicit secrets and jars of salsa on her roof on cool nights. We'd endlessly pranked the popular girls who didn't understand our shared love of heavy metal. I'd never forget the way her parents welcomed me into their fold, allowing me to stay over when the bitter memories of my mother's death drained me emotionally. Mom had married Phil's dad just in time, then she left us all behind. Hell, maybe she died to avoid the same caustic wit and old-fashioned beliefs that Phil acquired so handily from "Pops."

Perhaps her sudden departure was why I didn't take life so seriously. I had something to prove, years of good to do, but my existence would end without input or permission. Life would come to an abrupt stop whenever it damn well pleased. I'd fall victim to circumstance at some point, but only if I was lucky enough to not be killed by something I saw coming.

I released a breath and shook out my palms. Georgia was owed much more than my melancholy. A few hours of frivolity were well overdue.

As if on command, the gregarious strawberry blonde emerged from the side door of her shop. Clad in low-top Converse and a gauzy top over narrow jeans, she was clearly looking forward to warmer days. April had been nice so far, but the snug camisole underneath the sheer layer made me wish it was just a touch warmer.

Her love of natural food and ayurvedic yoga did wonders for her body. It was doing wonders for me, too. I'd be admiring her all day.

"Hey," I called out through the open passenger side window. "Looking good. You ready?"

"Heck yeah," she answered, approaching my gunmetal ride with a lifted brow. "All electric? Nice."

"Hop in."

Georgia slid into the leather seat beside me. A whiff of her skin sent me on a walk through the woods, on a path hedged by fruitful honeysuckle. The fragrance bewitched me completely. I tipped my head away, inhaling deeply to capture what I could before I grew nose-blind to its draw. I'd have to keep my distance or risk making a rookie mistake.

"Where are we headed?" she asked sweetly, turning those jewel-toned eyes on me as she buckled the seatbelt over her modest chest.

"It's a secret. I'm not sure if you've been there before, but I doubt it, based on what you're stocking these days."

"Are you taking me to a potential supplier?"

"Maybe. It'll be up to you, but I think that, once you see their love and effort, you'll want to help them out. I'm hoping you'll humor me and at least pretend to enjoy some time outside on such a lovely day. I think you should see just how beautiful this little town really is."

She graced me with another million-watt smile, coaxing her hair back over her ears with two manicured fingers. The glint in her eye made my heart race. "You can take me anywhere."

I slipped my narrow black sunglasses on. "I'll hold you to that."

* * * * *

A few hours later, we returned to the farm market from the fields. The familiar cashier gave us a thumbs-up, but we couldn't mimic the gesture. Our arms were laden with the best their acres had to offer. Aromas of earth and grass tickled my nose.

"What a haul," Georgia gushed, her lips curving into a proud smile. "It's way too much, but the radishes are perfect, and this arugula was too pretty to leave behind."

I nodded at the head of cabbage nestled in my right arm. "I can't wait to make a small batch of sauerkraut with this. Maybe I'll use some of that black garlic salt you've got."

"I want a jar of it when it's ready. I hope it'll be fermented in time for an Independence Day dog." Georgia laid her bounty on the counter so the teenage cashier could begin sorting. "You were right, this place is great. Do you know the owner?"

"Yep. That's my family's house right over there," I answered, pointing out the open barn door and across the gravel lot to the two-story sage green farmhouse across the road. "I stole handfuls of berries off these plants as a kid. And some nights, I'd just sneak over here and hang out with the corn stalks. They're better listeners than you'd think."

Georgia leaned in conspiratorially, flooding my senses with honeysuckle again. "I used to sneak toads into the house and put them in the bathtub, convinced they'd drown in their holes when summer storms blew in. I scared the shit out of my mother a dozen times before she learned to check the shower before stepping in."

"I wish I'd thought of that. My mom had a bad heart to begin with, though, so maybe that would've been a bad idea."

"She *had* a bad heart." She repeated, shooting a forlorn gaze out beyond the broad doors. "Is she gone? Is that still your family's house?"

"It's my stepdad Mike's house now. Mom's been gone almost twenty years. I didn't think I'd move back to town after college, but here I am. The company I interned for didn't keep me on, so I ended up right back in Whitehall, just in time to see the town get its first health food shop."

"You keep my lights on, and you seem to be doing all right, with that fancy car and all. Your mini backpack is Kors and my products aren't the cheapest in town."

No pity for me, and no sorrow. Much obliged.

"But they're the best," I argued, chancing a passing caress of her forearm. "I'm glad you're here. You make my small-town existence much easier to handle."

"You're sweet," she admitted sheepishly, turning back to the cashier to hide her reddening complexion. "I'm happy I chose Whitehall."

Women are such simple creatures. It's almost unfair.

"I got this." I nudged her gently, wrapping my arm around her tiny middle to lay a palm on her hip. I handed my card to the cashier with the other. "Add in a bag of that kettle corn and a bottle of the blackberry cider, please."

The cashier nodded and turned her back to us, headed for the supply shelf as Georgia eyed me. She remained in my embrace, her lips inches from mine. "I could've paid. You drove us out here."

I released her before I gave too much away. "Don't worry, you'll have a chance to pay me back. We're going to put dinner together with our finds, and you're going to show me how to make that sunflower butter vinaigrette."

"Then you won't come see me anymore," Georgia murmured as she edged back against me, flashing sad puppy eyes.

"Oh, Georgia, I'll tell you a secret." I met her stare brazenly, knowing she was ensnared. With sultry eyes, I brushed strands of rosy hair off her shoulder and watched her lashes flutter. "You are worth so much more than your recipes. I'll show you."

* * * * *

The sun had long disappeared beyond the skyline as I regained consciousness, lying on the wrong side of a firm mattress. I rubbed my pollen-laden eyes, sad to realize I'd fallen asleep with my contacts in. They itched like hell.

Georgia curled against me like a housecat, her fair skin glowing in the moonlight streaming in through the open window. Her silky mop of hair splayed across our pillows. The scent of her perfume lingered on my skin and her linens.

She looked so peaceful. Waking her would've been a sin. I'd already spent too many hours in respite with her while work was waiting for me back home. I had an open investigation to handle, and that gateway software was more complicated than I'd expected.

A little too carefully, I edged off the bed and went on a scavenger hunt for my clothes. They were tossed about, intermixed with hers, and it took five solid minutes to find my second sock. I rinsed and toweled off quickly before returning to her room. A quick glance at her camisole, thrown lazily over the footboard, reminded me of how fun it'd been to sweep it off a few hours before. The memory of the evening, the sun setting outside while I tasted the salt of her skin and the honey of her tongue, brought an automatic grin to my lips. She'd been every bit the dulcet lover I'd hoped for.

Get out before you lose another hour to her charms.

I left a note next to her phone, my number scrawled on it, and a well wish for a good Tuesday. I had no need for her number. If she decided to reach out, awesome. If not, ours would simply be a shopkeeper-customer relationship. I fought the urge to scowl at that thought.

Edging through her door and down the tight staircase, I escaped to the side street. I knew the path well. The last time I'd made the trek, over a decade before, I'd slept with a different upstairs tenant.

I unlocked my car as Dewey's across the street let out its last few intoxicated patrons. Among them was a familiar face, the deputy sheriff, laughing and shouting farewells to a fellow officer I recognized from the precinct. I watched for a moment as Aiden stumbled a bit, edging toward the street corner with a cell phone in hand. His ebony hair, cropped short, glistened like his milk chocolate forehead. A dopey grin was etched on his angular face as he blinked hard at the cell's display.

"Hey," I called, crossing the quiet street. "Are you calling for a ride?"

Aiden's onyx eyes lifted, the faintest glaze in them a telltale sign of his enjoyable night. "I was working on it. Where'd you come from?"

"Across the way," I gestured noncommittally over my shoulder. "I can run you home, save you a couple bucks."

"For real? It must be my lucky day."

I tucked my thumbs in my pockets, tugging down the waist of my jeans enough to grant him a sneak peek at my navel. "Mine, too. Come on, then."

I stepped to his side and escorted him across the street, nestling his massive, tattooed arm in mine as he chuckled drunkenly. He nearly tripped over the manhole cover. I worked to keep his towering frame upright.

"Sorry, I guess I let Donnie buy one too many."

"There's no need to apologize. Everyone's entitled to a fun night, right? And you said it's been lucky."

He eyed me, a sly grin tugging up his bristled lip. "It's getting more so by the minute."

"Well, if you're looking to get even luckier-"

The words barely made it out before he spun me into his chest. I glanced up to see his full lips part as his gaze narrowed beneath strong brows. I nodded in silent acquiescence.

Wasting no time, Aiden swooped in and stole the kiss he'd apparently sought for ages. The pent-up desire felt a little like rage as he forced my back against the car door, the handle biting into my lower back. His tongue carried barrel-aged flavor into my mouth as our limbs tangled around each other. The heady murmurs rumbling in his chest stirred my blood, and before I could think better of it, I snuck my palms under his tee to feel his core muscles tighten.

His breath hitched as he nestled his lips below my ear. "Your place or mine?"

The words, thick with lust, washed over me like magma. A pant was all I could muster as his nails brushed against my collar, tangling in the soft auburn waves I'd pinned back. My eyes rolled back as he ground his hips against mine, the whiskey on his breath amplifying the heat I felt emanating from his lap.

"Yours," I finally croaked as his tongue traced the curve of my jaw.

"Penrose Place," he murmured against my neck. "Unit fourteen."

"Ten minutes," I replied, pulling my face back and blinking hard against the blood pounding my temples. "Can you make it?"

"Can you?" His charcoal brow lifted as his rough palms squeezed my hips. I watched his carved biceps flex and forgot completely why I'd avoided this in the first place.

* * * * *

Two hours later, I finally pulled into the rented garage outside my condo's door. I pushed the ignition button and sat back, well and truly spent. Georgia and Aiden had wrung me out like a dish sponge.

Terribly dehydrated and tender in all the right spots, I plugged my car into the charger stand, flicked the button to lower the garage door, and climbed the stairs to my third-floor hideout.

I'd forgotten to leave on any lights and nearly dented my knee crossing the dense carpeting to the floor lamp. Wall switches were completely occupied by tech; the surge protectors monopolized by the security, proximity and motion alarm systems keeping me surreptitious. My cell number was unlisted, and I scrubbed online records constantly. My PO box was in the next town over. My door had three deadbolt locks. A wide-angle camera captured my front entry. Aside from my stepbrother and his father, no one knew my physical address or where to start looking. This was Whitehall's Fort Knox.

My IP address was even more secure, scrambled and encrypted multiple times an hour. Sometimes the computer in my condo was in Antarctica, sometimes it was on a desolate island off Peru, and it had even made appearances on a freighter headed to San Fran from Thailand.

The entire world was connected by a thin wire called the internet. Any dot along that endless line was a place to hide my antics. If no one knew where my equipment was, then no one knew who I really was or what I spent hours of my life doing. My idol did the same, tiptoeing over the border between notoriety and secrecy. They were the epitome of an online vigilante. They'd been at the top of their game for years. I followed in their footsteps like a stranded puppy.

No one knew more about *esTre11aN3gra* than me, not that there was much to know.

They were elusive, enigmatic, and always a step ahead. They were the greatest champion of digital vengeance. They poked their head out, only to unleash clandestine truths, then retreat into darkness before anyone could make a positive ID. Their retribution was swift and unavoidable. They exposed the worst, the most indecent and disgusting in new and creative ways with each passing week and I, for one, couldn't wait to see what they'd uncover next.

A few sites claimed *esTre11aN3gra* was multiple people, a kind of watchdog organization, that worked together under the moniker. How else could so much work be done in such a short time?

Doubtful. Too many participants meant too many potential points of failure.

Those who fancied themselves experts claimed the online entity was an international spy; a covert operative assigned with exposing corporate fat cats and undercover political scandals.

Then why did they bother with celebrity cases and social media investigations?

A few others claimed my idol was only doing the work under contract for undisclosed and mind-boggling amounts of money.

That's possible, but who would pay for dirt on a nobody? esTre11aN3gra *hunts everybody.*

I had no doubt that *esTre11aN3gra* was a single person, a Bengal tiger stalking the perimeters of the dark web. I only wished tigers hunted in pairs and that I could be *N3gra's* mate. I imagined they led a much more exciting existence than I did.

Ever the pragmatist, my hideout was purely functional female. My condo's living room was a blank canvas aside from a bland beige couch, huge flat screen on the adjacent wall, and an archway to the idle kitchen. I had little use of the spaces outside my office. I only needed an occasional stint of sleep in the equally unadorned bedroom, morning trips to the dryer to retrieve clean clothes, and dashes to the plain bathroom for obvious reasons.

I was tempted to skip out on work, and to abandon the gateway software, to seek out the super-thick king bed I'd splurged on, but as I passed the office door, the siren call beckoned. With a huff, I sat on my plush chair, wheeling to the three-screen display and powering on the CPU.

My phone chimed as the monitors flickered to life. Grabbing it from my purse nearby, I swept a finger across the screen. A text waited for me.

Hey, kid. Whatcha hiding from the small-town cops nowadays?

I chortled, opening the keyboard to reply to Bryan, the only gay man I'd ever fallen in love with.

Same old. Tapping into financials, perusing unsecure Cloud accounts, catfishing local pervs. Whatcha doing, darling?

It took a few seconds for my phone to chime again.

Working too much to have a life of my own. You have a moment for me, or are you neck-deep in some snatch?

I touched the green phone icon. Within seconds, my college buddy picked up, greeting me in that fabulous high-pitched squeal I knew all too well.

"Oh, my love! Your mouthpiece does work. Maybe you could try using it more often, hmm?"

I scoffed, sitting back in my chair. "You're always too busy wooing lumbersexuals to bother with me, Bryan. I barely saw you when we worked together."

"You were busy perusing for company of your own, as I recall. And it's awfully late. I assume not much's changed."

"You know me too well. To what do I owe this pleasure?"

"I've got a saucy lead, my dear. I figured you'd want to hear first."

I sat forward. He had me, hook, line and sinker. "Our black star?"

"Indeed, precious. Ever heard of Anderson-Hilliance?"

"The venture capital firm? Of course. The co-founder of Cyvestment is headed there as a consultant. I've been watching him. Where he goes, big money follows. Why?"

"What if I told you they called on thirteen of the brightest from our alma mater to fill positions at their brand-new Philly office, all at once and without a word as to what they'll be working on? No disclosure on their titles, their starting salaries, nothing. Radio silence from the largest private investor firm in internet development."

Easing against my backrest, I tossed an ankle up on my desk. "Suspect. Thirteen MIT grads? Even if they don't hire them all, that's still too many. No mobile game, social platform, e-commerce site, or IT project needs that many hands at once. Unless..."

"Ah hah! And now we're getting to the good part."

"Shit. They're looking for them. Or are they hiding trying to hide? These grads are from the cyber security program, yeah?"

"Comp science, security, and programming. That's gotta mean Anderson-Hilliance is up to no good, or they're out to bag a big catch."

"Damn," I puffed. "This venture capital company's investing millions in its own work? I bet *N3gra* is already sniffing at their hydrant."

"Guaranteed. I'm running some spyware now and phishing their existing employee base. If there's a crack in their armor, I'll find it."

"If there's no crack now, there won't be going forward. They're bricking up their systems. That wall will be six feet thick by morning."

"Odds are, *N3gra* will find a way in, even if we don't."

I couldn't help but sigh. "They always do. If only I knew how."

"If only any of us knew. And in the meantime, tell me, who occupied your evening, my love?"

Bryan was MIT's finest underground web scout, but his biggest weaknesses were scuttlebutt and snack cakes, neither of which were good for his health. He dug into the rumor mill so deep, he practically buried himself in wood pulp. I loved being on his good side. His deets were always delicious.

He kept my secrets, as I did his. I needed a confidante, someone to share my most intimate cracking secrets and obsessions with. Not only did Bryan share my love of all things borderline-illegal in the cyber universe, but he also had a set of skills that he himself kept hidden from his family, friends, and numerous hookups.

"A lord and a lady occupied me tonight. Not together, though that would've been hot."

"You are such a whore. I love it. Who was better?"

"She was like apricot jam, sticky fingers and all, but you don't care about that. You want to know about the stud. He must spend hours a day in the gym. He lifted me off the floor and tossed me over his shoulder like a Neanderthal. I wasn't sure I'd be walking right after he was done with me."

"Good Christ, girl. Was he my type?"

"You know, I'm not sure. Are you into dark chocolate these days?"

His hearty chuckle warmed my soul. "Oh, darling, I've never turned down dessert in my life. And I'm officially jealous of your social life. How sad is that?"

"Can't help wanting to keep my dance card full. There's not much else to do around here. I'm either consulting the betrayed or getting laid."

"That's almost poetic, Lizzie. It's time for you to move on to bigger and better, to get outta that one-horse town. You know that, right? Going home just wasted your potential."

"Moving back to Boston is out of the question. Even if I could afford it, if I ran into anyone from Midas, I'd be less than cordial. Their owner-slash-resident dickhead spread the word on me overnight. I can't believe you can stomach that asshole Monday to Friday."

"You're not as hated as you think. And for the record, he just didn't like your delivery. He's intimidated by tough chicks. It's a hit to his machismo and all that." Bryan huffed above the sound of a cabinet door slam. "I'm stress-eating. Talk me out of it."

"And I'm guessing it's said asshole's fault?"

I heard another sigh, this one more guttural. "Got it in one. Sixteen-hundred online records. Sixteen. Hundred. Two-hour deadline. Me and a noob. That's it."

"That's inhuman. I'm kinda glad I told him where to go when six more months unpaid was his final offer."

"I had free housing and a trust fund. You didn't. I'm earning that sixty thou a year now, though, let me tell you. If I'd gone into private practice, I'd be wearing Gucci and Vuitton, too, rather than slumming it in Tom Ford."

"You poor baby. It's sad that Tom Ford is Boston's idea of slumming it."

"Who are you telling? You know, Anderson-Hilliance's field office might just pick you up. Just don't use Midas as a reference and you're golden. Toss your name in with those thirteen, I dare ya."

"The field office in Philly? I'd have to reinvest in winter wool. Besides, my female dalliance opened a decent naturalist shop. I can finally get organic kale and artisan kombucha in Whitehall."

"Lizzie, you are a trainwreck and I love you for it. I'll let you know how this spyware works but keep an eye on our little star's movements. It's only a matter of time until something big turns up."

"Oh, I will be. It's gonna be a long night."

"For both of us. Night, darling."

"Night, handsome. Thanks for the intel."

I hung up and tossed my phone on the desk. Slipping out my contacts and sliding on my glasses, I hunkered down for a long night of ten-key and decoding, hot on the heels of *esTre11aN3gra.*

Whitehall, SC, 2012

Morning dawned as I pawed at my half-lidded eyes. Aside from the twelve-square feet of space I occupied on this huge bed, the world outside was freezing, unwelcoming, and borderline cruel to the sleep-deprived. An icy wind wailed over the squat balcony outside my bedroom's sliding glass doors, a not-so-subtle reminder that spring was still just outside South Carolina's grasp.

Rolling over with a huff, I brought the comforter up over my shoulder to obscure the harsh reality of the world outside. Grabbing for my phone before instantly tucking myself in again, I yawned deep and pressed the circular button.

"Siri, good morning."

Her familiar response rang out in my quiet condo. "Good morning, Lizzie. May I tell you what's in the news?"

On my back again, I set the phone on my chest. "Yes."

Another chime rung out as I forced fingers through my tangled hair. I nearly dozed off again as Siri rattled off my morning review.

"Today is April twenty-seventh, two-thousand-twelve. Here are the top news stories from your feed. On Capitol Hill, President Barack Obama's healthcare reform is being argued. Is it constitutional? The US economy is holding steady as Wall Street holds its breath. And in entertainment, *Pottermore* is unveiling its e-bookshop today, *The Hunger Games* breaks another box office record, and noted Canadian filmmaker James Cameron is the first person in fifty years to visit the Challenger Deep, the deepest point on Earth, at the bottom of the Mariana Trench. For more news, tell me to go on."

"Siri, play my music."

"Playing your channel."

An unfamiliar hard rock song's percussion erupted from my speaker as I rolled off the mattress, planting both feet on the frigid plank flooring. With a grunt, I trudged toward my coffeepot, already sputtering to life on the kitchen counter. The unwashed stoneware mug from the day before greeted me, as did the decades-old teaspoon I'd left inside. The tarnished bit of silver was the only remnant I had of a simpler time. I held onto it for dear life.

Every morning until I grew too heavy, Mom lifted me onto the counter alongside her percolator. She let me add a heaping spoon of sugar to her cup and stir the inside perimeter ten times, counting with each revolution, until I learned to both adore coffee and count without using my fingers.

I took mine black, but I still stirred the onyx potion ten times with that same spoon every morning regardless. I'd convinced myself years ago that the process cooled it enough to enjoy quicker, though I knew the argument was a sham. Being sentimental wasn't smart for an objective seeker of justice, and Mom had been gone too long to still be maudlin about it.

With another yawn from the depths of my soul and a douse of caffeine on route to my nervous system, I retreated to my office, my cell phone churning out heavy guitar as I carried it along. Plopping on the chair and spinning to the monitors, I noticed the processes I'd initiated hours before had run to success. The pop-up detailed a search of the state's sex offender registry. Multiple records matched my criteria. Pulling up my latest customer's file, I combed through the results, sipping and slogging through the details with my glasses pushed up my nose.

By the time my broad mug was empty, I'd turned up enough to justify continuing the quest. The construction business that contracted my services did way more research on their hires than state law required, but their reputation in town was immaculate. It needed to be. They conducted renovations and upgrades to some of the most expensive and historic buildings in the county, and their contractors were often left unattended to perform services. Propriety was the name of the game.

Their projects included the Stuyvesant estate, also known as Twin Willows. I shook my head and smirked at the events of the prior week. That cheating geezer made my job so easy. He practically hung himself out to dry.

I had little to no patience for charlatans, especially those whose hypocrisy dripped off them like acid rain. Isaiah Stuyvesant's aisle seat on the first pew at the Methodist church was reserved for him every week, he sponsored the county's only women's shelter, and he funded the police department's athletic league. My brother never liked the guy, skeptical of that polyester smile the debutant pasted on while posing for media photos. But Phil lacked the internet skills and free time for such dirty work. Bro was also beholden to legalities. I didn't share that obligation and had technical ability in spades.

The fact that Isaiah Stuyvesant was a sugar daddy to a half-dozen college girls in Charleston was enough to get the missus a divorce and a sizeable alimony. The fact that he also paid off a prominent congressman to shelve a complaint against a massage parlor he frequented was something else altogether. And that massage parlor was forging their practitioners' licenses, as they'd done numerous times over the years. The business licensing's online repository had been scarily easy to infiltrate, as had the online records of the trade school that'd allegedly issued massage certifications to ten illegal immigrants without qualm.

Of course, they'd done nothing of the sort. The documents were faker than Stuyvesant's alibi. That school would never participate in something like that. They'd lose their accreditation instantly and would never risk lawsuits. I knew that better than anyone. That same school issued my PI certification when I moved back home.

Out of curiosity, I dipped back into the business licensing website for South Carolina and searched the construction company's records. Daly Contracting was established thirty-one years ago in Jasper County, and had no records of delinquent renewals or outstanding judgments. The company was founded by Michael Lee Daly of Whitehall.

Hi, Pops.

I snickered at the screen, picturing the graying man's judgmental eyes peering at me over his hand-tooled dining room table. I only called him that to his face, and only because it got his goat. I'd been hell on Earth as a teen. He'd done what he could to rein me in, including enlisting his faultless son to corral his misguided stepdaughter. The old sap had probably sworn to keep me in line while my mother laid on her deathbed, grabbing her frail hand and promising her he'd keep me safe and secure while her body shut down one organ at a time. He'd been pitifully outmatched.

And I wasn't much better nowadays. At least I'd made sufficient effort to coexist in this small town. In the intervening years since Mom's death, I'd become an uneasy ally.

After an unfortunate encounter and subsequent conflict mediation, I became his office's PI. I helped him hire and retain the best talent with some subtle investigating work. That lined my pockets with his money and capitalized on his insecurities about the integrity of mankind. It was a win-win. As a result, we both entered strict NDAs to keep our business dealings professional. Mine included a clause prohibiting disclosing my identity to any of his employees or partners, and his included one to keep his investigation tactics and my geographic location to himself. I searched for anything incriminating on his potential hires and employees while he kept our affiliation a closely guarded secret.

His only child, the incorrigible sheriff, was also in my pocket. After trying to quell my teenage antics, Phil backed off. Being a few years older than me wasn't enough to convince me that he was worthy of my respect or obeyance. Years later, the badge he'd earned made me second-guess my attitude toward him. I stayed just shy of intruding on his work. Impeding and interfering with an officer on duty meant my hard-earned cash would have to be spent on bail rather than the newest tech. Giving him hell was a benefit of my status as stepsister and his back-pocket investigator, though.

I closed the state's licensing site, navigating to the Mexican consulate office. At least I could find his new hire's next of kin here. If he had any claims against employers, or if they had legal issues with him, evidence would abound here, too.

Sure enough, once I tapped into the system using a borrowed user ID and password, I found a slew of allegations from a previous employer in Nevada, leveled squarely against Mike's interviewee. They included misuse of company property, timeclock violations, labor disputes, and inappropriate conduct. A log detailed that misconduct, an interlude with the company owner's teen daughter, in explicit detail.

Damn. I'm surprised her daddy didn't chase him across state lines.

I logged out after capturing screenshots, resetting that borrowed password to safeguard against the next hacker in line behind me. A little photoshop work on the screenshots hid any defining details from view. A quick crop job and paste into an email with Mike's company's email address at the top completed the task.

I started typing the body email, then deleted it to restart. I started anew, then deleted it all again.

I sat back with a huff. When my eyes closed, I saw my mother's face, eyeing me exhaustedly in our family kitchen. Her listless words flooded my mind.

Come on. You don't have to love him. Just be nice. He's doing his best. Have a heart.

When my eyes reopened, I exhaled a tenuous breath. My fingers passed over the keyboard as I thought about the wisdom I missed out on, having lost her too soon. I completed a cordial yet dryly proficient email before her visage completely disappeared from my mind's eye.

I clicked the send button and closed the browser before I thought better of it.

Sitting back, I rubbed my palms over my eyes. Even in my memories, she was sick, frail, and devastated. Her voice was a whisper that echoed between my adolescent ears. The healthy woman's face, the good times, and the affectionate smiles she'd gifted me were all gone now. Only bitter recollections and battle scars remained.

* * * * *

The midday sun finally warmed the air enough to coax the chill from my bones. It was a short trek from narrow road to gravesite, one I'd made weekly since I'd returned from college. I owed her this much.

The cone of flowers I'd left the week before was still propped against her headstone, the lily stems inside devoid of petals and dried by exposure. From the look of the site, no one else had stopped by or bothered to tidy up. After sweeping away the strewn petals, I lowered to a crouch on the grass. I snagged the forlorn bouquet and traded it for a bundle of ivory honeysuckle, smiling as best I could as I eased back to read the stone.

Susan's name, birthday, and a snippet of a poem were inscribed on the marble I'd had installed the month after I moved back to Whitehall. The prior marker was a simple flat tile, one Mike selected from a catalog at the last possible moment. He'd prioritized their finances. I hadn't been consulted.

Upgrading it without his consent or input created radio silence between us in the days that followed. That calm was welcomed after he'd slung some of the worst insults I'd ever heard my way. I'd tossed back a few of my own. Phil watched with horror as his only family devolved into utter mayhem over a dead woman we all loved. It was Phil who negotiated a truce once he'd seen the stone for himself.

I flashed back for an instant, my stepbrother's skeptical face reappearing in my mind as we gazed upon the stone together. He wondered aloud why I'd omitted her date of death. The tinge of skepticism, of impatience, and of judgment still lingered in my mind when I pictured his ignorant expression.

I remembered my response in explicit detail. I repeated it aloud.

"No one needs to know when you died. They only need to know that you lived."

I sighed and lowered my eyes to the sunny blooms, their scent bringing me back to Georgia's embrace the afternoon before. "Sorry, I should've said hi first. Hi, Mom. And I hope it's okay that I brought honeysuckle today. I know lilies are your favorite, but these were so beautiful, I couldn't resist. It doesn't look like anyone's been by lately. Mike said he'd come once the weather warmed up but..." I trailed off with a headshake.

Why am I not surprised?

"I'm tired of trying to fool us both. He won't come. I should just stop bugging him about it. I'd like to think he's given up on this because he watched you die, buried you, then moved all your stuff out of the bedroom.

But I did that, too, and so did Phil. And we… well, I guess it doesn't matter, does it?"

I laid out a towel, setting my backpack on it as an anchor. Carefully dropping to the cloth, I dug through my bag for my phone, cueing up her favorite bluesy rock tune. The sound carried on the tepid breeze, tangling with the sweet blooms' scent.

"I guess you wanna know what happened with the cases I finished up last week," I began, taking out an egg white breakfast sandwich from the downtown coffee shop and a bottle of artisan water from Georgia's shop. "Success on all three, fortunately for me, but unfortunately for everyone else involved. Two marriages are done, and one business is kaput. It's too bad I can sniff these people out so easily. Maybe one day I'll be able to do the type of work that helps people rather than tears them apart."

The sandwich was mediocre at first bite and tolerable the rest of the way. I'd have been better off stopping by the natural food store. Before I thought better of it, I was picturing Georgia's smiling face, then her bare shoulders, then the curve of her hip, then the way her throat trembled when my lips snuck in for a taste.

I shook my head violently, tucked my trash back into my bag, and crossed my legs out in front of me. "I told you about the health food store that opened here. The owner, Georgia Harris, she's from Florida. If you listen to her, she'll tell you she left because of the tax laws, but I think she ditched town to get away from her ex or something. It seemed sudden. I know that's why Phil's deputy Aiden left Durham. I saw them both yesterday. And I know, I know. My reputation precedes me."

The blossoms rustled against the marble as another breeze swept through.

"Aiden needed a ride home. It wasn't planned, I swear to you, but Phil told me he was interested in me. Well, he didn't say that in as many words, but still. It was fine. He'll make a great partner for someone else. But Georgia, she was lovely. She rescued a turtle in the Gooding's field. She was afraid a tractor would run it over, so she put it in the basket they gave us and carried it out past the fence line. The little guy wouldn't climb out of the basket, so she left it there and made me carry everything back to the barn in my arms. She made me do something and I didn't argue."

I could only imagine the smirk Mom would've given me at that. I'd railed against brushing my teeth for a solid week once just because she harped on me. She never checked my toothbrush. If she had, she'd have found it damp every single day that week. I waited until her bedroom door closed to get the job done.

"I didn't argue," I repeated, in awe of the simple fact. "We didn't argue. It was so nice not having to fight for once, not having to be ornery. I'm not sure why I let my guard down, but I did. I hope that wasn't a mistake."

A low-flying blur of crimson flitted overhead, casting a shadow over the wild blooms by my feet. I glanced up to watch the wide-winged cardinal swoop into a nearby tree.

"Mom, I seriously think I'm spinning my wheels." I exhaled, my eyes closing as my heart clenched relentlessly. "I just want to be something, to be someone you'd be proud of. You did so much good. I have dreams and goals. I'm doing what I can in Whitehall. I just know I could do more, could be more, if I stepped up. I can't be afraid to fail again."

I wanted so badly for her voice to ring out from behind the marble, to echo around me, to tell me that I hadn't failed in Cambridge. Not getting hired post-internship isn't a failure to most, but it was a slap in the face to me. I was magna cum laude while Bryan graduated forty-eighth in our class. We interned in adjacent cubicles. He was offered pay and I wasn't. My advisor had gone to bat for me. It still hadn't been enough. My outburst at the president of Midas hadn't been my best moment, but my blood roiled so loudly under my temples that I barely heard the venom I spat.

"I ran back here with my tail between my legs, and I've spent the past few years in between others'. What should I do?"

The air stood still around me, around us, as I waited. The words I needed most never came.

"I'm headed out, Mom. Maybe a pint of full-fat ice cream and some sitcom reruns will mellow me out. I'll be back next week with a healthier meal and lilies like usual."

I rose with a sigh, gathered my stuff, and escaped to my sedan as the cardinal swooped back toward Mom's grave, settling with a ruffle of feathers on the top of the arched marble.

Guilt wrung my heart out before I could put the car in drive. Instead of stopping at the convenience store for an indulgence, I pulled to the curb outside Georgia's modest shop. Inside, I found her only hire, Carrie, behind the register. I'd never seen her here on a Tuesday before.

I grabbed my usual salad, still craving that vinaigrette, though I'd damn near drank a cup of it the night before. Setting it on the counter, I slipped off my bag. I waved off the roll, knowing my breakfast sandwich already exceeded my processed carb allowance for the day.

"Eight-fifty," Carrie told me. "I'll need to manually input your card. The machine's down."

I arched a brow. "Is Georgia okay? I can't believe she'd let that thing be broken for long."

The twenty-something brunette shrugged, taking my card and swiping it. "She called me in. There's some emergency, apparently."

"Is she upstairs?"

"Her car's gone. You need a receipt?"

"Nope, but let her know I was asking for her, would you? I hope everything's all right."

Carrie nodded kindly and handed my card back. "Will do. See you tomorrow, probably."

"Yeah," I replied apathetically, biting my lip as I retreated. "Take it easy."

"You too, Lizzie."

Back behind the wheel, I chanced a glance to the market's second floor. The interior lights were off, the curtains drawn to block out the afternoon sun. With no one partying at the bar across the street and the workday in full swing, the shopping district's silence was eerie. With a lump in my throat, I drove back to my condo, eager to put the bizarrely emotional day behind me as soon as possible.

When I pulled into the condo's lot and circled back to my garage, what little spunk I had left fizzled instantly. The heavy door was dented in, the siding marred by smears of what I hoped was chocolate pudding.

And on the side of my rented garage, in garish red spray paint, a sickening message greeted me.

BITCH!

Whitehall, SC, 2012

"How many times do I have to say it? I have no fucking clue. You know how careful I am."

"Sure do," Phil commiserated, reclining on his well-worn office chair's backrest. It tipped back with a whiny groan. "I know about your precious privacy, but someone with an axe to grind clearly knows where you live."

I rubbed my palms over my face. This guest seat in front of his state-issued stainless-steel desk was marginally more comfortable than a folding chair. Lower back spasms vied with a burgeoning migraine as I grunted. "You and Mike, that's it. Seriously, Phil. That's it. I'm unlisted. The condo complex doesn't sell personal data. Solicitors aren't welcome, and I used Bryan's card to pay the yearly fee for the garage."

"All's good with Bryan?"

"Why would a gay man fly down here from Boston to paint a worthless insult on my garage and then leave? He's called me worse to my face. And before you ask, I spoke to him last night. He was at his place, snacking away a stressful workday. His cell pinged to his apartment. I already checked."

Phil's eyes narrowed only a second. "You don't trust anyone, do you?"

No answer was worth my time.

The sheriff laid his forearms on his chair's armrests, his fingers twisting over his middle. "And not a single companion ever went back to your place? Not in all the years you've been back?"

"Nope. I barely touch anyone in town anymore anyway, and I always go to theirs or get a place for the night. I hide my online identity, too, so no one's finding me that way, either."

"Don't I know it. IP addresses, multi-layer encryption, blah blah blah." His pissy little hand gesture boiled my blood, but I let it pass. Phil was my best hope. "You're protected in your little online hidey-hole. Fact is, someone sniffed you out. There's no damage inside your place and you're sure nothing's missing?"

"Nothing. They didn't get past the physical locks."

Phil swept his meaty fingers through his tousled mop. He looked exhausted. "So, tell me what you've been up to the last day or two, then. Let's start there."

I sighed, sitting back. "I worked late Sunday night and got up around eleven yesterday. I worked a few more hours at home, then picked up Georgia Harris outside her market around four. We spent an hour and a half at Gooding's, in the fields rescuing turtles and picking produce, then went back to her place. I was there until one in the morning or so."

He jumped in before I could finish my recap. "Gooding's, really?"

"That's what I said, and we didn't go out again once we were back at her place. I left alone around one, like I said."

"I should ask what you were doing, but I'm afraid you'll actually answer."

I sat forward, tipping my head with narrowed eyes. "Why is the sheriff afraid to hear facts? We. Had. Sex. Multiple times. That was only after a dinner we prepared together, a healthy one of no interest to you. And the sex was good, Phil. Really, *really* good. Clothes everywhere. Screams of ecstasy. A big wet mess. I think a little's under my nails still if you want a..."

He sat forward, mimicking my pointed gaze and lowering his tone though his office door was closed. "Fuck you, Lizzie."

I could only grin, oddly proud of my ability to make him squirm.

"So, you left around one. You went straight home?"

"That was my plan, yes, but I was interrupted. Or rather, I found a fun alternative."

"And now I'm really scared. What did you do?"

"Aiden," I murmured, crossing my leg as I sat back. "At long last. Aren't you relieved? He was leaving Dewey's and looking for a DD. I decided to play good Samaritan and offered him a ride. He offered me one, too, and since you insisted, I took him up on the offer."

His head stayed dipped. "The dalliance was at his place, I assume."

"Yep. No pleasantries were shared, so it took about an hour. I was back home by two-thirty. Bryan texted then called me. I worked an hour or two, then slept until about eight this morning."

He lifted his thin metal pen, fidgeting with it as he sat back. His left ankle perched on his right knee. "And this morning, I know you sent a file over to Dad, but you left the house at some point."

"Yeah, I finished his request, sent the email, and headed out to have lunch with Mom. I stopped at Calla's on the way. I grabbed a breakfast sandwich there and didn't speak a word to anyone."

"And Biddle's?"

I shook my head. "No, no need. I found some honeysuckle on the road."

"You always get her lilies," he murmured, his expression graying. "And you still go every week."

"Twice a week, at least. Tell your dad he's behind a few hundred visits now."

"I'll bring it up, but it won't do any good. Any stops on your way home?"

My phone buzzed in my jacket pocket. Bryan's name displayed on the screen. I swiped the red button. "I pissed myself off at the gravesite. I was going to stop for ice cream."

"But you didn't," Phil interrupted, eyeing the pocket my phone was tucked into. "Too many calories, right? You grabbed a handful of vegan, non-GMO, free-range ice cubes instead, probably."

"I hate that you know me so well."

"It comes with the territory."

"The best cubes in town are at Natura Foods. Carrie was working. She told me Georgia needed coverage. It was a last-minute thing. It's not like her to abandon work."

"So, your liaisons are our prime suspects, then, unless some long-scorned lover came back into the picture."

"Doubtful. And what reason would-"

Before I could finish the thought, the sheriff pushed his chair back a foot from his desk and rose, his eyes locked on the precinct's door beyond the glass wall of his office. His deputy had just arrived, suited up in a navy uniform that held onto his towering frame like sausage casing.

Phil edged around his desk, swinging open his door. "Deputy, a moment please."

Aiden nodded once at the receptionist, a mousy little thing in narrow hornrims, before obeying Phil and skirting through his office doorway. His charcoal eyes settled on me as he swept his campaign hat off.

The day had warmed up enough to merit wearing a white eyelet sundress. I crossed my leg, cupping my knee with both palms. His breath stuttered as he positioned his hat over his middle, turning away from my provocative gaze. "Yes, sir?"

"Reports show you were west of the city limits this morning on calls. Is there any chance you changed course, or any reason you'd have made a quick run north?"

My brow arched instinctively.

Wow, Phil. I'd be touched if it wasn't your job to be so accusatory and suspicious all the damn time.

His second-hand man's expression didn't falter. "No, sir. I filed the cases as I processed them. The records are there." He chanced a glance back at me. "What's going on?"

Phil retook his seat, resting his forearms on his paper-strewn desk. "Someone hit Lizzie's place earlier today and did some property damage. I know you two were together last night. I'm just-"

Before Phil could finish the sentence, Aiden was crouched beside my chair, anxiety ebbing off him like radiation. "What? You're good, right? Were you home? Why didn't you call us immediately?"

His look was too sentimental and too demeaning, but I did what I could to soften my tone. "I'm fine, and I did. And here I am, filing a police report. I'm a big girl. Lay off."

Only then did Aiden exhale, his eyes darting to the floor below his knees. "Jesus. I should've gone to yours instead. I should've stayed."

"She wouldn't have let you," Phil tossed in, lifting a sheet of photo paper off his desk, and holding it out for his deputy. "So, this wasn't your work, then?"

He stood again, hovering over Phil's desk. With the picture of my garage in hand, he let out a startled snort. "What the fuck? Absolutely not. This is some petty shit. I've got better things to do with my time. Apologies for the language, sir."

"Understood and thank you, Aiden. That will be all." Phil told him, snagging back the paper and eyeing his door. "I'll come find you and fill you in on proceedings once we're done here."

He didn't want to leave, that much was clear, but when Phil's disciplined frame stood tall and his expression soured, his deputy finally swept his hat back on, tugged the door open, and snuck out without a second glance in my direction.

"Lizzie," Phil began, dropping back onto his office chair. "You have a reputation in town, one you should be more ashamed of than you are. But you're not ashamed of anything, are you?"

I snickered, holding my tongue.

"Fine. So, how many of your conquests would be willing to risk getting caught spray-painting and throwing dog shit around your property in broad daylight? Aiden's right. This is a petty move."

"Georgia's the only one, then, right? That's what you're implying, that I hurt her feelings, slighted her, and made her jealous? That'd be a shame if it wasn't so pathetic."

"Whatever, Lizzie. The only question is, how'd she know where you live?"

I could only shrug.

"She followed you to Aiden's, then to your condo. That must be it, right?"

I shrugged again. "Poor thing. It probably broke her heart."

"And you pity her for catching you messing around with someone else five steps from her front door. You are a piece of work. You know that, right?"

"Not all of us can be as righteous as you, Sheriff," I retorted, slipping my backpack over both shoulders. "We went on a date. We slept together. That's it. No promise of commitment, not even a promise of a round two. It was a hookup. You've done the same before. Quit being so judgmental."

"I was a teenager. You're a grown-ass woman. This is shameful."

"Luckily I don't give a flying fuck what you think."

He rubbed his face with both palms, a guttural groan of malcontent sneaking through his fingers. "I hate that I feel obligated to help you. Tell you what, you can go handle this with your jilted one-night stand, or you can leave it up to me. Fingerprint analysis is underway. I'll be getting results back shortly. We can either go at this legally and press charges, or you can find her, settle this like adults, and maybe avoid a messy legal proceeding."

His last sentence hung in the air as I escaped the precinct's doors.

* * * * *

I approached the entrance to the upstairs apartment, swallowing back bile. Carrie's sedan was still parallel parked on the street where it had been hours before, and there were still no signs of life in the second-floor abode.

Against better judgment, I climbed the narrow staircase to the familiar door. Wringing out my palms and putting on my PI face, I pounded on the wood below the brass-ringed peephole.

Silence.

I released a breath and stepped back. "Georgia?"

Silence.

"I know you're home. Let's just deal with this."

Silence.

I tried the doorknob. A twist and shake made the door shimmy. The deadlock I knew to be on the other side wasn't secure. I pulled the glass-shattering tool from my bag and set the tip in the peephole's cavity.

"I'm worried about you. I'm going to break this if you don't open up."

Silence.

I checked left and right, released a fatigued breath, and rammed the pointed edge into the tiny circle of glass. It splintered into pieces, cobwebbing in the hole. Using a pointed metal-tipped nail file from my shoulder bag, I cleared the glass pieces and popped out the metal disk that held them. I leaned in, squinting to take in the space beyond. It was dark, quiet, and as clean as it had been the night before.

Damn, is she in the wind?

With a shrug, I jammed the file into the knob's keyhole. I'd picked tougher locks than this one before, though never at a fling's place. My break-ins were mostly at the offices and rented condos of the rich and salacious, the places where mistresses and dirty ledgers found their place.

Breaking and entering in a traditional sense wasn't my favorite, as the cyber method was much easier to cover up, but I wasn't sure Georgia's emergency wasn't a medical one. Under the guise of concern, I jimmied the inner mechanism until I felt a click, then twisted the freed knob ninety degrees.

I took one soundless step inside, my head on a swivel for any signs of life. The shades drawn against the sunshine outside glowed, barely illuminating the nearby retro-chic chairs and glass-topped table we'd occupied the night before. She'd righted the room and wiped down the kitchen since then. We'd been too busy tasting the meal off each other's lips to prioritize cleaning up.

After a quick check of the remaining rooms, I was disappointed to not find my prey holed up in a closet or behind a shower curtain. She'd clearly left, and not in a huge hurry, as I'd been led to believe. Shoes were lined up as they'd been before, with the low-top skids the only pair missing. The air felt vacated, not vengeful.

Returning to the living room, my eyes skipped back over to the table. In place of dinner dishes was a stack of paperwork. Beige manila folders with blanched sheets tucked inside them were topped with a formal document of stark white. It was a contract, complete with signatures and a notary seal. The private lending firm info, the proposed investment, and specific repayment terms were all there. Georgia's autograph in blue sat above one belonging to Douglas Dawkins.

That letterhead belonged to Dawkins Investments, Inc.

Fuck me.

Under the contract was a handwritten letter, crumpled but pressed flat again. Today's date was scrawled at the top. The words blurred in my vision.

Dear Ms. Harris, Apologies for disappearing, but someone in town is out to ruin me. I had no choice but to close shop and move on. I'd hoped to see your business flourish, to see this town wrap its arms around you, but I am no longer in the position to invest in your dream. Since the banks in town will want to see years of records, of success on your part, to finance a fledging business, you'd be smart to seek out a town with a more diverse, cultured, and moneyed demographic. Investors will be easier to find there. I wish you all the best. And a word of wisdom, avoid the Daly family and their wayward daughter at all costs. ~ D. Dawkins

I couldn't help crumbling the letter in my palms.

That spineless bastard.

There was no more damage to be done here and no more havoc to wreak in this woman's life.

As I stepped over the threshold, I prayed she'd give chase, that she'd see I'd saved her so much tumult in the long run. Maybe then I wouldn't have to avoid my favorite shop in town. And maybe then, all the work I'd done exposing Dawkins wouldn't have been in vain.

I was met with enduring silence as I escaped with my heart clenched mercilessly in my chest. All I could do was flee. Somewhere deep inside, I knew I'd never set foot in that apartment again.

Whitehall, SC, 2012

The night passed painfully slowly as I tossed and turned in bed. Not even the prospect of chasing *esTre11aN3gra* could coax me out of my misery. I parted the curtains, trying to count the stars. I wiggled each toe independently just to see if I could. I counted heartbeats as they thundered in my ears.

I'd miss her salads, her kombucha, and her cheerful greetings. Perhaps more disturbingly, I'd miss her scent, taste, and the promise of more.

After six exhausting hours of so-called rest and a pitstop at the florist, I parked by the familiar curb. Mom's grave was exactly as I'd left it, the honeysuckle fluttering in the early morning breeze. A groundskeeper toiled a few rows down, trimming back hedges that threatened to conceal the surrounding stones.

On sullen steps, I made my way across the grass to her final resting place.

"Mom, I'm leaving."

There was no voice on the wind. The only sound was the whistling breeze between the neighboring headstones.

"It's time. Bryan, my friend from college? He told me there's some suspicious stuff going on with a company I've been following-slash-stalking for the past few years. He's been vishing but hasn't turned up anything solid. We think the online vigilante we admire is circling them, too. What if I applied? I graduated MIT at the top of my class, and I can do whatever job they assign me. Do you think they'd hire me, too? Maybe they'll let me in on a few of those secrets they're trying to bury. Maybe it's something huge and I could expose it from the inside."

I exhaled, closing my eyes, trying desperately to hear anything. There was no reply.

"I'm surviving here, but I came back because I had no place else to be. You're the only reason I haven't left already, but this isn't enough anymore. That makes me such a selfish daughter, doesn't it?"

Silence.

I sighed, tipping my head back to enjoy the split second of sun peeking through the dense clouds. "I'll still come back, I'll still visit you, and I'll make sure your site's well taken care of. I'll pay someone if I have to. I just need to chase this. I need to do some real good for as many people as I can. You did so much good. I'll never be able to beat you there, but I'm going to try. Will you forgive me if I move to Philly?"

Another breeze carried the scent of springtime to my nose. Maybe the walking trails in Pennsylvania would be flooded with honeysuckle, too. I was imagining strolling through them already.

"Mom, I'm going. I need to either find and help that online vigilante I admire, or I'll become an even better version of them. I have a gift, a goal, and I want to do better things with my life than dig up dirt on the neighbors. I'm doing this. I hope you understand. I'll always be your daughter, and I'll always love you. Whitehall just isn't for me anymore."

I exhaled, having said my peace. I felt my heart sink as the silence enveloped me. I was fleeing a ghost, heading toward an enigma. I'd only driven through Philly a handful of times on my way to Massachusetts. Before Anderson-Hilliance opened a field office there, the city hadn't even registered on my radar.

I wasn't scared of a new place. Failure, though, was terrifying. I'd spent years interning thanklessly for Midas in hopes they'd keep me on. Instead, they insulted me by offering me a shitty position and telling me it was for my own good. I feared this Philly move was another red herring.

After spending a few hours researching last night, digging into Hilliance's extensive funding, their lust for technological improvement, and their seemingly limitless drive for progress, I couldn't help but feel the pull. If I could glean a little insider info and gain a leg up on *esTre11aN3gra,* that was a huge step forward. If they took me on, I'd be surrounded by others who loved penetrating the firewalls and hidden niches of the internet as much as I did. And I'd be able to see Bryan more often with the distance between us halved.

"I'll let you know how the application process goes. Maybe by then, they'll have called me. Fingers crossed."

I examined the headstone again. The stethoscope curled around Susan's name brought tears to my eyes. "I'm going to make you proud. You'll see."

Raw and fretful, I turned my back on Mom. Parked behind my coupe was the Sheriff's SUV, powered off with the town's top elected policeman leaning against the hood. Standing tall as I neared, he tipped his head sympathetically.

"Hey," Phil began, tugging off his broad-brimmed hat. "Another lunch date, I see."

"Sure, whatever. Look, I'm not in the mood, okay?"

Dodging past, I opened my passenger's side door and tossed in my bag. Before I could escape, Phil grabbed my Tesla's spoiler. "I'm not planning on riling you up. I just thought you'd want to know the results of our investigation."

"And it had to be here, at the last peaceful place I have left," I muttered, crossing my arms. "Go ahead and tell me it was Georgia before I lose what little patience I'm holding onto. I already know she hates me."

He brushed back his mop with crooked fingers. "You went to her place?"

"I did as you asked. She wasn't there and the place was spotless. Well, except for a flowery contract on the table. Dawkins promised her funding, then left her with a pissy, self-aggrandizing note and a warning to stay away from the Daly family, myself included. We're trouble, you know."

Phil let out a half-grunt, half-swear, tossing his brimmed hat onto the SUV's hood.

I mimicked Phil's disdain. "Damn that Dawkins and his bullshit. He cost me the best salad dressing I've ever had."

Phil took a hesitant step forward. I knew he was analyzing me. Damn him for knowing me so well. "Lizzie, this is more complicated than that now."

"Oh, do tell. I've got time to hear how much worse things can get from here."

"There's no trace of her at your place. There are no fingerprints and no witness accounts of anyone matching her description."

"She's a five-foot female. Anyone can wear a hoodie and look like anyone else. And her fingerprints would be on the paint cans that are MIA, not on my garage. Tell me the sheriff knows that much."

"Criticize how I do my job again. Try it. See how that goes."

I took a step back and held up my hands for peace. "You're right, that wasn't cool. Sorry, Phil. Look, it's been a weird couple of days."

"It was a local troublemaker. The paint isn't MIA. The cans were found in a trash bin on the next street. The kid's prints are on them, no question. He's a juvie with a record and nothing better to do."

I goggled, rolling through my mental Rolodex. "Which kid? Do I know them?"

"I can't say. They're a minor. I sent Aiden out about an hour ago. I should get a call any minute."

"Shit. Georgia's probably out looking for me, or for you. I got myself all assed up and broke into her apartment for nothing."

"That's why I'm here."

"Oh, well. I mean, you told me to go over there."

The sheriff's face stiffened instantly. "I told you to confront her, not break into her obviously empty home and rifle through her things. Your prints are everywhere. And before you try to criticize my police work again, the prints are on items that weren't on display the night before, and they're all around the shattered keyhole. You wiped them, but not well. Come on,

Lizzie. You're smarter than that. At least, I thought you were. What were you thinking?"

I felt the blood drain from my face. I'd been so angry and so callous that my PI trigger had been tripped before I'd had the chance to consider the repercussions. I'd in fact validated Dawkins's theories.

Fuck me sideways.

"Ms. Harris called us about an hour ago. There's an investigation into the scene, but I knew who was responsible immediately. You will be questioned officially this afternoon. Officer Reilly will be by after two. Between you and me, you'd better have a damn good reason for being in there or you better create yourself a decent alibi. Otherwise, everything I know will be disclosed. I'm already risking my badge being here now. I can't lie for you. I won't."

I exhaled a shaky breath, my fingers twisting through my hair as I paced a few steps away from him. For the first time in my life, sass eluded me. I had no snappy comebacks. No snide remarks felt appropriate. I could only stammer. "Phil, I-"

"We're done." He interrupted, sliding his hat back on and striding to the driver's door. "I'll expect Reilly's interview notes by the end of the day, and I owe Ms. Harris a follow-up tomorrow morning. Don't call me, my wife, or Dad. You're on your own."

I turned back as I heard his door slam shut. I exhaled a shaky breath and motioned for him to roll his window down. Once it sank halfway, I could only manage a few words. "Can I fix this?"

He shrugged, more apathetic than I'd ever seen him. "I'm not your legal counsel. I just hope the next time I see you, it won't be in cuffs."

His SUV pulled away, leaving me in its wake. The cemetery around me swallowed me whole as I sank to my knees.

* * * * *

I gave myself one hour to clean up my business. It took fifty-two minutes.

The keystroke at the forty-fifth minute corrupted the Whitehall Department of Justice's software systems, as well as the state's databank. In moments, the entire repository of phone calls, interviews, and investigations involving the search term "Daly" dissolved from their computers like salt in the wind. I was no longer findable, searchable, or locatable to anyone with the authority to do so. I ghosted into thin air.

While I was tapping into the dark niches of the internet, I tampered with MIT's records. I was no longer a graduate of their prestigious university. Just after, I also disappeared from Midas's human resources database and the accreditation board of South Carolina. I'd never been a PI, nor inquired about the program. A few more button clicks deleted my entire life.

Everything I owned that was worth saving was then loaded into my trunk and backseat. The apartment was scrubbed, all utility services were cancelled by anonymous email, and Bryan's credit record was wiped of any affiliation with my condo's garage rental. I hoped he'd forgive me in time for tapping into his accounts. A *mea culpa* to my oldest buddy was my last concern now.

My car was unregistered, my license no longer searchable. I only needed to make it six hundred miles without being noticed. Once I was hidden away in some clandestine hotel, I'd use a VPN and create a new identity for myself, one I was already looking forward to. It had to be better than this one.

With Whitehall in my rearview mirror, my only regret was not seeing Mom one last time. At this point, forgiveness was an easier pill to swallow than accountability.

Undisclosed, 2022

Without cue, I found myself riding a sunny yellow bike through an urban park. The high-rises of Center City, Philadelphia cast long shadows over the tree-lined path.

The metal between my legs squeaked reassuringly as I pedaled. A gel seat cushioned my bounces as I proceeded over occasional stumps and fist-sized rocks. My mind disconnected from routine. An industrial rock tune infiltrated my thoughts through a single bud in my right ear. I imagined myself at a concert, watching the enigmatic singer pace emphatically across the stage with an electric guitar at his hip.

I hadn't been to a concert in ages. Why I hadn't bothered to buy tickets, I wasn't sure. My mind was too occupied with the boisterous tune and winding path to overthink it.

The trail weaved between oaks and maples, their leaves beginning to shift from jade to mahogany as the days grew cooler. The crisp wind whipped my loose locks back, fanned my rosy cheeks, and challenged my quads as the path began to ascend. Ahead, obscured by flora in every direction, the foot-wide path eked ever upward.

Strange. I don't remember this trail being so hilly.

With a shrug, I powered forward. Sweat pilled above my brow, the salty beads dripping into my eyes. They stung contrarily. I lifted off the seat to add more torque to the pedaling. Only fifty feet of the path was visible ahead. The incline mercilessly continued.

Moments later, I was breathless and struggling. Never had an inner-city ride been so painful. My eyes clamped with exertion, my breaths growing shorter as the path's surface turned to cobblestone, jagged brick, and meandering tree roots. Before I could turn the bike around, the front tire slid into a crevice between graying stones. I felt gravity release its hold on me.

I flew like a condor over the handlebars. I launched head-first, my arms outstretched to break my fall. The gnarled roots and broken bricks shredded my forearms as I screamed out in shock, pain, and confusion.

I woke with a start. My forearms ached the same as in the dream. Realization set in slowly. I'd crashed onto my dinner plate on my computer desk, with my social media probe software still running. Familiar metal music poured from the speakers. An eighteen-ten-stainless-steel steak knife jutted from my left forearm. As I jerked up, the knife slipped free, releasing a stream of crimson down to my elbow.

I leapt from my seat and grabbed for anything to apply pressure. I'd already stained the silicone keyboard, but I managed to rip off a sock and stop the deluge before I ruined anything else. I'd never tried my stash of chemical-free cleaners on blood stains before. I prayed they worked as I peeked at my injury. Blood poured out the instant the sock was removed.

Shit! What now?

I removed my other sock and used it as a tie, wrapping it around the makeshift bandage and knotting it tight. With a free hand, I grabbed for the mouse and clicked on the video conference app the boss preferred.

I connected and placed the call request. Exhaling, I sat back against my office chair and gripped my forearm, squeezing as the chittering app reached out across nine time zones.

Sweet merciful, please let her have a free minute.

The sock was turning red with each passing second. How it was safer to keep knives sharp, I'd never understand. I was hours from medical treatment, and I had very little equipment here to deal with hemorrhages.

Damn my thin blood.

My eyes rolled back as the call connected. With a grateful gasp, I sat forward, still gripping my forearm. The boss's face came slowly into focus, angled from below. The camera shook as she audibly excused herself from a meeting, escaping from what appeared to be a formal conference room. Against a drab, beige-papered wall, the phone recentered on her intensely beautiful face above a black suit's collar. Ivory skin, golden curls, and eyes like tanzanite analyzed me curiously.

"What's on fire? You never call."

"This," I managed, lifting my arm and saturated socks into view. "It won't stop bleeding."

"Socks aren't sterile," she muttered. "Let's see it."

"It's still actively gushing."

"Let's see it," she repeated. "How did this happen?"

"Steak knife," I grunted, untying the sock to reveal the frayed gouge. "I fell asleep and landed on it." While the blonde analyzed, I caught the stream with the wadded cotton. "You think I need stitches?"

"That's tough to say, but let's try something first. Got a hook on the ceiling?"

"What? Why?"

"Just answer me. Do you?"

I did, weirdly enough. I'd had two installed on the laundry room's ceiling for an impromptu clothesline if my dryer went down. "Yeah, sure, not in here, though. Let me connect with a cell."

I quickly grabbed a burner phone, then transferred the call to its audio-conferencing app. She watched my every move with patience, without an ounce of fear on her face, and it calmed me in a way I hadn't experienced in years.

Mom never panicked when I hurt myself, either. I guess med school just trains it out of you.

I carried the phone into the laundry area off the kitchen, propping it on the washer. "All right, they're on the ceiling in here."

"Perfect. Got any twine, rope, or something stronger than dental floss? And you'll need either a tampon or a pad, whichever you use. Grab that stuff, plus a clean cloth and duct tape."

Who am I, MacGyver? Am I dodging death or building a prop plane?

"Jesus, okay," I mumbled, dashing to the closest drawer. Inside was a roll of kitchen twine. In the bathroom were the requested tampon and a fresh washcloth. I ferried everything back, still clutching the sock against my arm. "Is this good enough?"

"Yep. Keep your arm above your heart for ten seconds, then let go of that sock and let's see what happens."

I followed her commands without question. Once my arm was lifted and I'd counted with the Mississippi method, I dropped the sock. It landed with a wet slap on the tile floor. Blood eked out, though the flow had slowed encouragingly.

"Good. You are clotting, just not quick enough," the boss commented. "Unwrap the tampon and stick it against the cut. Take that clean cloth and wrap it around to hold it in place, then wrap the tape around the whole thing to keep it secure."

I huffed involuntarily. Frontier medicine was more than I'd bargained for. The tampon was effective though, and once I had the clothed arm mummified with silver tape, I held it in view. "Done. Now what? Is the twine to nosh on so I don't starve to death?"

She grinned almost imperceptibly. Occasionally, I was graced with a reaction like that one. It helped dull the pain a little. "No, you ungrateful swine. It's for a makeshift tourniquet. Wrap a loop around your arm close to the elbow. Throw the twine up over the hook so it dangles down and raise your arm up. Bend at the elbow so your forearm is parallel to the ceiling. Use the hook like a pulley and pull down as hard as you can stand on that twine."

I wondered how silly she sounded to anyone within earshot, but my heart pulsing in my forearm kept that thought brief. It took three frustrating tries, but I managed to snag the hook. With my arm over my head, I grabbed the twine and tugged downward. The fiber clenched around my forearm, biting into bare skin as I winced. "You know, I could've tugged on this without using the hook."

"It's easier to keep your arm up this way, and it applies pressure in the right spot. Keep bitching and I'll be the witness to your time of death." She countered with a lifted brow.

"Terribly sorry for interrupting your meeting, boss."

Her head tipped patiently. "I can't have my most valued employee keel over in the middle of nowhere, can I?"

"I'm your most valued employee?" I retorted with a snort. "Well, I guess that'd have to be the case now. The hired help around the house is family."

"You must be feeling better. You're borderline chatty. Now, release the twine. Let's see if the bleeding's stopped."

I was certainly hoping so. The tingling in my fingers was painful. Lowering my arm and unpeeling the tape revealed a saturated tampon beneath the towel.

The boss's eyes narrowed as she peered at the injury. "Tug the tampon loose, carefully, please. Fingers crossed."

I knew her medical expertise was to be credited if this worked, not luck of any kind. With trembling fingers, I pulled the trundle of cotton away to reveal an angry, yet dry-looking laceration.

"Perfect," the doctor remarked. "If you've got bandages, use them and whatever antibiotic cream you have. Replace it hourly until the skin seals. Keep the entire arm clean. When was your last tdap?"

"What?"

"Tdap. Tetanus, diphtheria, and pertussis. The vaccine. When was your last one?"

"Um, no idea," I replied, carrying the phone to the bathroom to hunt up what few supplies may be stashed there. "Before college, for sure."

"Every ten years," she chided without venom. "I'll order you one. Have you given yourself a shot before?"

"I haven't had to, but I think you're gonna want me to."

"Good assumption. I'll give you directions. Tell me who your drop-ship contact is."

My blood turned cold. "Nah, I'm sure I'm fine."

Her expression soured. "That wasn't a request."

I turned my back to the camera, my palm shifting into my tousled hair.

Damn it. One slip-up and my hidey hole's not so 'hidey' anymore.

"Hey," the voice called out over my shoulder insistently.

I turned back with a sigh, mimicking her snide tone. "What?"

Her jewel tone eyes turned up at the corners as she managed a diplomatic smile. "Your secrets are safe with me. Haven't I proven that?"

I rested my palms on the sink's edge, leaning forward with a scowl. "Stop lawyering me. I'm not on trial here."

She nodded approvingly. "Fine. You want the lawyer? Here she comes. Thanks to me, you've never been in court and won't ever be. Furthermore, in your memory, have I or anyone I associate with caused any trauma, abuse, or deception, either malicious or accidental, through our own actions, or the actions of anyone with whom we affiliate?"

"Stop."

"Have we divulged any corporate, personal, or proprietary secrets held in confidence? Or, for that matter, have we, in any way, broken any of the terms set forth in the agreed-upon and signed non-disclosure agreements in effect since 2015?"

"Stop," I repeated in the same dry tone.

"In your memory, whenever an emergency whistle was blown on your part, how did I or any of my associates react?"

I exhaled, turning to face the phone screen again. "I've always been treated as part of the whole, as a respected ally and teammate. And with all due respect, prosecutor, I see very little reason to continue this questioning. I have no intention of breaking my own NDAs, the ones you drew up for my suppliers and contacts here. I will survive without the vaccine, and if I don't, I still won't regret this. So, as my counsel and my physician, I decline the vaccine. Am I clear?"

The blonde sighed. "You are impossible. All right, you win. Call me back if that arm swells or if a fever develops. Otherwise, get back to work."

The video cut out instantly. For a split second, I lamented my hardheadedness.

She meant well. She was my boss, too, not just my lawyer and doctor. It wasn't her fault I made careless mistakes, or that I was so resentful. I'd made her bear the brunt of my malice.

I took out my bitter anger on the closest object. The cheap burner phone exploded like a grenade when it slammed against the far wall, tossing shards of black plastic across the marble tile. Bits of twisted shrapnel dug into my heels as I stormed back to the office.

I had to get back to work. Boss's orders.

Philadelphia, PA, 2012

Selling the Tesla was the final insult. The overpriced apartment in the city, plus the exorbitant parking fees in dilapidated garages and incredible insurance cost, made keeping my baby just too impractical. Instead, I pocketed six-grand of net income and bought myself a dandelion-hued electric bicycle. Technically, I could've walked to my future employer's office, living a few blocks from the massive skyscraper's glass doors, but the draw of the newest tech and knowing the closest artisan market was over a mile away made the purchase feel wise. Plus, with so many cultural dining options in town, I'd need to burn the extra calories by peddling or face the dreaded office-chair-ass syndrome.

It was all worth it, though, if Bryan's lead was to be believed. Either *esTre11aN3gra* was in Anderson-Hilliance's crosshairs, or they were desperately trying to avoid the online vigilante. Either way, I was in on the game. I thought myself a shoo-in with a flawless record and impressive resumé, both of which showcased my real talent, creating something from nothing and deleting everything else.

The interview went swimmingly, though it had taken place at a local café rather than the headquarters as I'd hoped. I'd wanted to see the mecca for myself. Instead, I was sitting in a stained armchair, surrounded by midday clamor, entertaining a vapid HR coordinator who gleamed at me like a rising run. She was in awe of my experience and confidence, as well as the flashy ensemble I'd chosen. I'd crafted a CV worthy of a Pulitzer Prize, falsified enough references to make her swoon, and managed to convince her that the designer suit and patent leather pumps I'd worn were stretchy enough to also fit her. I'd unquestioningly lend them to her, and we could absolutely gush over the newest styles every season. I certainly did need new friends to accompany me on daytrips around the city. No, I hadn't been to The Contemporary before now, but yes, I did see why people loved this café. And yes, I'd love to show her how to tame her curls like I did mine.

I couldn't help snickering as I departed. The latte she ordered for me, swirled with tepid, hormone-saddled dairy, had disgusted me with its aroma alone, but I feigned sips as my interviewer prattled. If the dubious promise of friendship got me in the door, it was well worth the fib. I could fake with the best of anyone. It was par for the PI course. That past was firmly in my rear-view mirror now.

Philly would be blissfully unaware of that life, of the Lizzie that was left behind in rural South Carolina. I never liked the moniker Lizzie anyway. The farther I escaped from that persona, the more alive I began to feel.

I was now Serena Marie Hunter. No one, not even Bryan, would call me Lizzie ever again. He was more than willing to sign the non-disclosure agreement and every other legal document I'd commandeered from a firm's online repository and customized for my own needs. The undersigned, Serena Marie Hunter, was now in full command of her past and her future.

Serena knew four languages. Serena played tennis. Serena had enjoyed a wealthy upbringing. Serena's parents retired early due to smart investments in the nineteen-nineties. Serena had graduated from Carnegie

Mellon five years ago, making her a modest twenty-seven years old, compared to Lizzie's thirty-two years. And most importantly, Serena was a pristine, dewy-eyed yet well-trained dancing monkey, perfect for a corporate position.

A few things paralleled my former existence, enough to make the falsehoods easier to administer. Serena also enjoyed using skills in cyber security to sniff out ne'er-do-wells and those with questionable ethics. We were both active and health-conscious in our daily lives, and we were both new in town. We both preferred to start over, to reinvent ourselves, rather than dwell on our pasts or in our families' shadows, and both of us were careful about revealing our deepest secrets.

In my new one-bedroom apartment, with the scent of damp paint stinging my nose and new carpet cushioning my steps, I felt more alive than I had in years. Being Serena was going to be awesome. I'd added bold stripes of stark white to my auburn locks and started wearing green contacts to enhance the dull brown. I was proud of the new mossy tone, with flecks of emerald and honey hidden within, and how it twinkled with intrigue when I pretended to take interest in whatever drivel the HR rep hurled in my direction. Before this new life could continue, though, I needed a real cup of coffee.

Maybe I'll find a worthwhile café partner, but I doubt it. Until then, I savor alone.

With the fresh brewed black magic on its way to my veins, I snuck back to my office-slash-bedroom. I slipped on a pair of headphones and sat back in my new chair. With gently closed eyes, I absorbed every snooty French word thrumming my eardrums. This was one of two languages I now had to learn to be Serena. I had Spanish on lock. I'd be learning sign language shortly. Maybe no one would ask me to translate, or maybe I could excuse a lack of knowledge as being "rusty," but risking it exposed me to potential fallout. Instead, I chose the simultaneously difficult and rudimentary task of learning two languages in as many weeks.

My brain repeated the guttural syllables.

Juh swee. Tooh ehh. Vouze ett. Noo sum.

I sighed and sat up, rubbing my temples as the droning continued. I closed the transcript of the lesson and reclined, resting my ankles on my simple metal desk to settle in. The unadorned room, secured by closed-circuit cameras with live feeds to my phone, three newly installed deadbolt locks and a motion sensor, was just safe enough for relaxation.

Sometime between listening to conjugated verbs and math terminology, my phone vibrated violently on the steel. A car horn blast exploded from its tiny speaker. I launched forward, nearly tumbling out of my chair as the headphones clattered to the carpet below. With a grunt, I rubbed the fatigue from my eyes and grabbed for the blinking screen.

Who's got a restricted number?

I turned on a cell tracking app, opened the corresponding program on my computer, then accepted the call. Within thirty seconds, I'd know who thought themselves so important that they'd keep their number restricted from the public.

I slapped on a phony smile to lift my voice an octave. "Hello?"

A brisk voice erupted from my earpiece. "Good afternoon! May I speak with Serena Hunter, please?"

"This is she. May I ask who's calling?"

"Oh, very good afternoon to you then, Serena. This is Joy from Anderson-Hilliance. I'm calling with an update on your application with us. Do you have a minute?"

The effervescent HR clone. Nice. They better offer me six figures.

"Absolutely. Fire away, Joy."

"I'm happy to report that you've passed the preliminary interview stage and can move on through the process."

Process? Am I working for them or running the place? How hard is it to get a job around here?

"And what would that entail?"

"A few managers will meet with you for a final interview. You're expected here tomorrow at two p.m. sharp. Please bring your resumé, CV, references, and remember to dress for success. I hope we can depend on your arrival as scheduled?"

I bet they hired those MIT plebs without qualm, yet I have all these hoops to jump through.

"Absolutely," I uttered, the phony smile stuck firmly in place. "I'll be there. Thank you for your call and the continuing consideration."

"Oh, it's my pleasure! See you tomorrow."

"Enjoy your evening," I managed as I swiped my finger across the screen.

With a sigh, I sat back, rubbing my eyes with my palms.

One more day of whoring myself on a street corner to become a corporate lackey.

* * * * *

The stark, antiseptic entry of Anderson-Hilliance's tower at 17th and Arch was an abstract masterpiece. I was instantly infatuated. Sharp white angles of laminated wood formed the security desk and partitions between seating areas. Two massive escalators stretched from the atrium lobby to the third floor, with grand acrylic art installments above, their spinning shapes whirring in the circulating air. High-dollar, six-foot high HEPA filters kept the air crisp. The ultra-modern, low-profile seating in ivory surrounded a squat table of thick, gray-streaked marble. Gentle harp music coming from everywhere and nowhere made me feel like I'd wandered into a modern art museum.

I'd been admitted into the skyscraper via speaker just beyond the broad glass doors, tinted against prying eyes. At the security desk, a bored guard the size of a linebacker validated my carefully forged ID against the handwritten schedule on a metal clipboard. Sufficiently satisfied, the dark-skinned twenty-something gestured to the waiting area.

"HR will be down for you shortly. Have a seat," he paused, looking down at the sign-in sheet again. "Miss Hunter."

"It's Serena," I corrected sweetly, my brightest smile on display. "There's no need to be so formal."

Clearly caught off-guard by my not-so-subtle flirtation, he shyly beamed. "As you say, Serena. Have a seat."

I felt his gaze press against my back as I strode toward the adjacent seating on my four-inch stilettos. I chose a spot facing the window so he could continue his gawking without shame. I observed the passing commuters outside, on their way to jobs they'd already secured while I waited to perform a song and dance for management.

I had to start the game early, shameful though it was. Buttering up the physical security was yet another stop in infiltrating Anderson-Hilliance, one physical or virtual firewall at a time.

I bet esTre11aN3gra *is the kindest person on the planet to people's faces and a backstabbing harpy when their backs are turned, too.*

I waited two minutes before Joy's exuberant voice rung out behind me. "Ms. Hunter? Thanks for being punctual."

I stood, tugging down my lipstick red pencil skirt before taking her hand with the warmest smile I could muster. "Ah, Joy. Thanks for your call and the interview invitation."

"Oh," she turned rosy with a chortle. "Of course. That suit is even prettier than the one you wore to the café. It's perfect silk! Is it Chanel?"

She's got a good eye. I'll give her that.

"Mm hmm," I murmured in agreement. "Two seasons ago, though, so nothing to write home about, I'm afraid."

Her azure eyes slipped south to my ankles. "But those are new Louboutins! Wow. I can't wait until we go shopping together. I need pointers, bad. You're going to save me. I just *know* it."

I smiled and lowered my gaze, hoping to seem humble. She certainly did need help. That suit was off-the-rack, gaping at the knee with a top button two inches north of her navel. The style in brushed wool was antiquated and dowdy on such a prestigious professional.

"You're too kind," I managed, lifting my leather briefcase from the floor. "I'm ready if the interviewers are."

"Right this way. May I call you Serena? We like first names around here."

"Of course," I replied easily, following behind as she navigated to the escalator. "This building is spectacular. How long has Anderson-Hilliance been here?"

Six weeks this past Tuesday.

"Almost two months now," she replied, stepping onto the first ascending stair before turning to face me. "Our CEO just loves Philadelphia and couldn't wait to open an office here. Apparently, this city's like his second home."

It's his first home. He was born here before he went to Cornell in '94. That's where he met Timothy Darren, your newest consultant from Cyvestment. Get a clue.

"Oh, that's interesting," I added, reaffixing that cordial smile. "I never spent much time here, but the city seems charming so far."

"It's a melting pot for sure. No disrespect to your hometown, but it's so much better than the suburbs of Pittsburgh, I promise you."

I mean, sure, I guess.

I kept my face neutral as she stepped off the escalator ahead of me. The third floor was the end of the line. I glanced around to see a rectangular open area surrounded by ceiling-high pane doors, frosted to shield the office's tenants. Vertical bars of brass formed handles on the immense glass.

"This way, Serena. Please watch your step. They installed the thickest carpet in these offices, I swear." She stepped to the door straight ahead. Her full name, Joy Saracco, and "HR Partner" were carved into a gleaming nameplate to the left of the entry.

I managed a polite chortle as her broad glass door swung open. Beyond, a vast rectangular office with plush carpeting like freshly fallen snow reflected the intense sunshine flowing in from the broad windows beyond. The room was quiet, despite the horns and conversations I knew were ringing out on the streets thirty feet below. An L-shaped mahogany desk was positioned on the left wall, with two modern aluminum chairs pushed against it. Near the right wall was a broad conference table and six high-backed, soft-cushioned chairs around its perimeter. Standing between me and the table were three of the most stunning faces I'd ever seen.

I held back exclamations as I was suddenly face to face with the top brass of Anderson-Hilliance. Far left, with his palms tucked into his pockets, was the illustrious Timothy Darren, in all his upper-class glory. His impeccable grey suit and bespoke black shirt with a mandarin collar would've seemed pretentious on a lesser man. To his right was Andrew Hightower, as powerful in appearance as his name implied. The navy wool and flirtatious coral polo underneath spoke of a wealth I hadn't seen since my time in Boston. Both sported stylish coifs of chestnut hair and the tanned skin of workday golfers. They could've passed for brothers, with pairs of eyes nearly the same shade of aquamarine.

And farthest right, taking a few steps forward to stand alongside Andrew, was a woman I didn't recognize. As she came into focus, her height and prowess entranced me. With almond-shaped eyes and a thoroughbred's onyx mane, she reminded me of a geisha, but her golden skin and broader cheekbones made me question her breeding. On towering silver heels and wrapped in snug, crimson silk like I was, I felt my libido stretch to its limit. She was a cinnamon hard candy, and I was suddenly craving a spicy treat.

Joy stepped to my side and gleamed. "Serena, this is today's interview team. First, our CEO, Andrew Hightower. Drew, Serena's the hard rock fan I told you about."

She included that in their pre-interview briefing? I mentioned it so casually.

His eyes lit as he stepped forward and offered me a broad hand. "Ah, yes. Have you been to any concerts here yet?"

I gripped his palm while I paged back in my memory. The rock band Second had been through the area the month before. They'd sold out the show, and I'd seen the live footage. That would sell my lie enough. "Second, over in Camden. I only get to a few a year, but I can't miss one of theirs. And they're from here, so the shows are extra special, right?"

"They owe the Philly crowd for sure. I was front and center at that one. I swear I'm still sore from the pit." He rubbed his arm with a wince and a wink in my direction. "I slid under the radar. Everyone was too busy thrashing into me to care who I was."

"You should've seen him the next morning," my other male interviewer interjected, stepping forward to place a palm on his boss's shoulder. "Mr. Metalhead here needed two huge cups of coffee and a palmful of painkillers to get through the muster meeting. Hi Serena, I'm Timothy Darren, the COO, but I'm just Tim around here. My mother calls me Timothy when I'm in serious trouble. Hearing it puts the fear of God in me. Anyway, welcome to Philly. Still taking in the sights?"

"Thank you, sir," I replied automatically, admiring his banter, then taking his hand when it was offered. I managed two quick pumps before he retracted it. "I've been sightseeing a bit. People are particularly proud of living here."

Boston was bigger, more interesting, and more friendly, but don't say that. Hell, he's letting me call him Tim, and Andrew Hightower, the third richest man in the country, is now Drew? This is surreal.

"They sure are. It seems to me that you enjoy the finer things. There are lots of hot spots here. I can point you to some boutiques, or you can do the designer shops at King of Prussia."

"Oh, I'm already on that," Joy chimed in from my left. "And Serena, this is Tsumugi Iruma, our CXO. Serena is our coffee aficionado, the one I met at The Contemporary."

Su-MOO-ghee. Su-MOO-ghee. Eh-ROO-ma. Got it.

"Ah, yes," Tsumugi took three elegant steps forward on those lofty heels, tied elegantly around her ankles and calves. Her hand was a fine plane of porcelain with ruby-tipped nails, placed before me like a tribute. "A pleasure, Serena, and please call me Su. Joy showed you her favorite spot, but she and I disagree on where to find true quality. I assume an enthusiast such as yourself has a grinder at home?"

Her tone was like imported sake, satiny and smooth with just a hint of exotic charm from the last bits of a Japanese accent still lingering around the edges. Her eyes narrowed sweetly as a smile tugged her fine lips toward the ceiling. My palm clutched hers as gently as I could manage, and I prayed it would stay dry enough to not tip my hand. "Of course. Javaphiles know the value of whole bean. I'm grateful for your input. My tastes are refined beyond the casual chain places."

I winced inwardly as the words escaped. That comment sounded Lizzie-esque. I released a breath as the two men's brows lifted in response to my curt opinion. I'd seen that half-curious, half-suspicious look a million times before.

"Not all of us appreciate the nuances," Tim added with a sweeping gesture toward the table. "Shall we get started? We've only got the swill from the chain place here. That's my unrefined taste for you, but I can offer you a spring water instead?"

Yikes.

I managed a polite head bow and followed the trio toward the table. "I appreciate your time and the offer. Where shall I sit?"

"Here," Joy told me, pulling out the chair at the head of the vast stretch of polished oak. "You're the guest of honor, after all. Shall we start with the formalities?"

* * * * *

Back in my apartment with the sun below the horizon, I paced the fresh carpeting in my living room. I'd already tugged out more than a few strands of hair and consumed an arsenal's worth of caffeine. It was going to be a long night.

I thought I'd had it in the bag. I was fine on the walk to the office building and in the lobby. I was a perfectly composed corporate wannabe in a trim suit with a killer briefcase. That is, until I was sharing a meeting space with two of the internet's most notorious showmen and a Japanese firecracker with a body like a swimsuit model. When Joy told me I'd be interviewing with a couple managers, I was thinking senior vice presidents or area directors, tops. The idea of meeting the top brass for a job interview felt ridiculous then and now. It was no wonder why she'd hidden that truth until the last minute.

Searching the web for Andrew Hightower and Timothy Darren resulted in millions of articles, editorials, pictures, and opinion columns on their prowess, but nothing had prepared me for how congenial and fraternal they'd be. Apparently, the effervescence Joy showed me was contagious, because the interview felt more like a panel television show than an interrogation. I'd spent so much time preparing antiseptic responses to benign questions that I found myself flummoxed on how to answer their casual inquiries.

Question one was, "When you cook, what's your go-to meal?"

Lizzie preferred capitalizing on others' culinary talents, so Serena offered an answer. Mother's pasta primavera, with the freshest veg available, was basic enough to learn on the fly if challenged.

Question two was, "What did your family think when you told them you wanted to move here for work?"

I didn't have an issue answering that one. Lizzie's mother, buried back in Whitehall, had been neutral on the matter, so Serena's reply was the same. The parents didn't have an opinion on the choices I made. I was a big girl and could make my own decisions.

They also asked, "What made you leave your first job?"

I answered that one honestly, as Lizzie and as Serena. The summer had ended, and I couldn't balance the workload of a multiple-degree education with answering phones at a bank full-time. It wasn't confessed at the table, but banking had been the perfect environment for eavesdropping and for learning the ins and outs of financial systems. It had also allowed me to dress above my station and to flirt shamelessly with attractive cubicle mates.

The rest of the questions passed by so fast and were answered so easily that I lost track of what I was saying, the gray area between Lizzie and Serena seeing constant foot traffic. I was careful enough to not contradict my resumé, but laissez-faire enough to feel awkward when I passed through the sterile lobby and down the city streets after we'd concluded.

Su hadn't said much, but listened calmly with occasional nods and reassuring, polite smiles in my direction. I'd done everything in my power to keep my wandering eye at bay.

All three interviewers were top tier as far as sexiness went. The internet and tabloids were convinced that Tim and Drew were single, and Su's ring finger was bare. When I reached my computer desk, before kicking off my heels or starting on my coffee binge, I pulled her up on every search engine. Tsumugi Iruma was listed as the Executive Experience Officer of Anderson-Hilliance everywhere I checked and had an impressive pedigree. She was from a prominent Japanese family. Her mother was a fine-looking woman wrapped in lustrous silk. Her father held a seat on the Kyoto Prefectural Assembly, as he had for years, and he'd been a prominent financier before accepting the government position. With two master's degrees, one from Kyoto University and one from UCLA, plus all the HR accreditations available, Su was a marketing and human relations powerhouse. No wonder she kept so close to the cuff.

Finally, I tired of pacing endlessly and collapsed onto my office chair. I was worn out physically and mentally. All I could do was waste the hours until I heard back from the obnoxious HR butterfly.

The overnight hours passed too slowly as I paged through internet sites, listlessly researching *esTre11aN3gra* and their latest escapades. In the past twenty-four hours, they'd sidelined a half-dozen sex traffickers and exposed their dark web exchanges to the world. Even my finest cracking software couldn't penetrate the sites the vigilante had unearthed. The superhero had bricked up the wall behind themselves so well that no one would use that corner of the web ever again.

Damn. So impressive. Let's see how secure AH is nowadays.

I scrubbed a bit more as my music playlist restarted from the beginning. It had already been through two cycles as I toiled at the keyboard.

I'd seen the inside of Anderson-Hilliance now, in all its opalescent glory. Physical security was minimal, so I poked a bit at the cyber security forming a perimeter around their operations. Their main site featured snippets of their investments toward software development, cutting-edge encryption for international commerce, and online security systems for personal data protection. Their client base was impressive, spanning from government agencies to local businesses with a few thousand employees. It all seemed above board. AH was simply interested in investing in projects to keep data safe and the world entertained as the internet began infiltrating our everyday lives. A quick search fueled by a foreign, multi-layered, and clandestine account led me to the employee login area. This wasn't my first attempt to break in. I was hoping it would be my last.

I'd learned the company's username creation system by activating an RFID reader inside my briefcase hours earlier. The little beauty recorded everything on their local network in short order. I'd also learned Joy's username was as obvious as I'd expected. Using the "Forgot Password" link and a little tinkering into her personal email account, I snuck through AH's backdoor.

Tapping in as a member of HR wasn't ideal. It wouldn't show me company secrets. In fact, accessing as an HR superuser revealed less than I figured. I cursed the federal laws that so stringently protected employee data. There were no staff lists, nor any identifying info about anyone. All I found were useless reports with data pulled from other sources across the web. Their staff was more concerned about their reputation at Forbes and Kiplinger than was useful.

There must be more than this. AH has been in business for years.

I poked around for hours, scouring every crevice and digging for anything I could find just inside their firewall. Nothing. It was scrubbed cleaner than a show dog's ass.

I sat back, slipping the designer readers off my nose before rubbing my eyes with damp palms. Even after employing all my dirty tactics, I'd only found a picked carcass in the desert.

After daybreak, while studying the company, its senior leadership, and their mission statements so I'd pass for an interested candidate, my cell finally rang. "Restricted" once again appeared on screen. Connecting to my tracer app confirmed it was Anderson-Hilliance, the same number that contacted me the day before. I prepared my spriteliest voice for Joy, who I knew would be far too jubilant for the hour of day.

"Hello?"

"Ah, good morning, Ms. Hunter. This is Joy from Anderson-Hilliance. Do you have a moment for me?"

"Of course," I replied, mimicking her upbeat tone. "What can I do for you?"

"Truthfully, I'm calling to see what you can do for us. We're prepared to offer you a handsome starting package. May I go through the details?"

"Yes, please."

As Joy detailed my six-figure starting salary, benefits package, retirement matching, and peripheral hardware allotment, a grin split my face. I accepted without qualm.

"Wonderful!" Joy proclaimed. "We'll expect you this coming Monday. Please report to our main office's lobby at seven in the morning. I'll be conducting the usual day-one pleasantries and your handoff to your supervisor, who'll show you to your new office space."

Wait, what?

"I'll have an office space? I figured I'd work remotely. That's the norm in the industry."

"Senior leadership likes a communal work environment, so Anderson-Hilliance bucks tradition and has its cyber security and encryption teams on-site for open collaboration and transparency. I hope you'll adapt well to our unconventional workspace. We're proud of it. I think you'll fit in perfectly."

I gripped the phone a little too hard, the rubber case twisting in my grip. I could transform into Serena, with her endless smiles and daft optimism, for a few hours at a time. Now I'd be expected to be on stage all day, like a method actor masquerading among their sources of inspiration.

Big picture. I'm gonna find esTre11aN3gra.

"I understand. I'll be there as expected. Is there anything else I need to know?"

"I don't think so. If you have questions between now and Monday, send an email to joy-dot-saracco-at-hr-dot-Anderson-Hilliance-dot-com. I answer my emails frequently. Oh, and Serena?"

"Yes?"

"Between you and me, I'm so glad the executives chose you. You were my favorite candidate."

Whitehall, SC, 2007

Maddie shipped in every pink rose south of the Mason-Dixon line. They exploded in tufts at the center of every tulle-wrapped table, filled the giant brass urns lining the edges of the event hall, and adorned the three-tier cake so it looked like a stacked bouquet. Even the tablecloths were trimmed with blushing blooms. It looked like a princess had been born and every florist on Earth fought for a place at the celebration.

It also reminded me just how precious the bride felt, sequestered in her perfect world of blonde hair, bleached teeth, and old wealth. The Umber family had more money than God and the resources to smear it in everyone's faces. I was at least partly convinced that, with Phil's newly achieved Sheriff status and my father's lucrative contracting business, this marriage was one of joining Whitehall's great houses as well as joining hearts. Madelyn Eustace Umber-Daly would be the town's favorite bride.

This garish display was proof of her tenuous grasp on reality. My stepbrother's first gift to her was a pink rose, plucked from the Stuyvesant's briars at Twin Willows and placed delicately above her ear. Ten years later, she was still infatuated enough with the cloying buds to destroy the sinuses of everyone in attendance at this circus of a wedding.

The production began eight months ago, when the first of three premarital parties was held on the terrace at our family farmhouse. That scene was also adorned in endless roses and taper candles in the same blush hue.

The menu was bland and boring enough that I skipped out early, nursing a headache from the canned country music roaring from the rented speakers.

Whitehall's eighteenth-century bed and breakfast hosted her second party. The illustrious inn was her family's pride and joy, but had proven perilous for my stiletto heels, leaving me teetering precariously on thinning rugs and cracked floorboards. I'd stayed long enough to be seen and to try to talk Phil out of this farce while he still could. He hurled colorful curses in my direction. I ditched before his future wife tore my eyes out for disrupting her precious party.

The third soiree, I avoided altogether. The happy couple decided to have a gender reveal for their newly adopted retriever, and to name the dog their wedding attendant. They'd just purchased a custom home on a lot outside Whitehall and wanted to show that off, too. I'd heard every obnoxiously planned detail from Maddie's best friend and maid-of-honor, who'd joined me for a drink the Friday before the festivities. She needed an ear and I needed a beautiful dalliance, so the circumstances worked themselves out. Once a witness came forward, one who'd seen me necking with Sophie in the front seat of my coupe, Maddie refused to allow me anywhere near the party. Spite would've meant crashing it, but when Phil got involved, I thought better of making an appearance.

I'd gladly have followed her ancillary command and avoided the wedding, too, but Phil won that argument at their little homestead. Regrettably, I now sat at head table across from Mike and Maddie's picture-perfect parents. I gritted my teeth behind sealed lips. Maddie and Phil had tied the knot. The din of celebrants and overrated dance tunes around me brought back the headache from the first party. My stepdad and the in-laws chatted about local business while I rubbed my temples. The pain pills weren't working fast enough.

I'd sworn to Phil that I'd stay long enough for cake. I'd been tempted to dash twice already, once when I entered the church and swore the building would collapse around me, and again when Mike demanded I say a few words about the happy couple. He'd enjoyed watching me sweat over it. He knew I hated Maddie and the claws she'd dug mercilessly into Phil. He also knew I hated being the center of attention, much preferring a quiet computer in the corner or an off-handed comment made behind the scenes. Fueled by the flask of whiskey I'd snuck in, I addressed the crowd. Fortunately, the hoity audience wasn't nearly as averse in pop culture as I was, so my toast, borrowed from a contemporary comedy movie, did the trick. I mustered a few chuckles and managed to escape with only minimal barbs tossed in the couple's direction.

Yet another mob dance number started up and the vinyl flooring packed solid again. I sat back, watching lines of intoxicated partyers coordinate their steps. I garnered a few glances from those still seated around me. Not only had I worn stark black and knee boots to this spring wedding, but I'd also researched many of the families and cohorts in this very room. Some never knew the results of my investigations, while others blamed me entirely for the downfall of their business ventures and personal relationships. I ignored them entirely, skipping over their judgmental faces, safe in the knowledge that I'd only contributed to debasing the lowest common denominator. I'd have found nothing if there was indeed nothing to find.

"Graduated top of your class, didn't you, Lizzie?"

The cocktail party effect kicked in and I sifted my name out from amongst the racket. I refocused my gaze on the questioning voice seated across from me. The late-forties blonde with pristinely coiffed hair and a strand of inch-width pearls beamed at me expectantly. She'd spent a little too much time in a tanning bed recently, the chasms around her mouth even more pronounced because of it. I managed a calm expression as I poured over her words. I'd only caught a few of them, so I filled in the blanks as best I could.

"College? Yes. In high school, I was in the top ten percent."

"You attended the Massachusetts Institute of Technology, yes?"

Only stodgy old biddies call MIT by its full name.

"Mm hmm," I hummed with a head nod. "Dual major, computer science and computation cognition, plus minors in statistics and data science."

She seemed adequately impressed, silenced with subtle expressions of befuddlement and awe. Mike sat to her right, his arms crossed over his broad chest and his narrowed gaze on me. The bicep areas of his suit jacket strained as his fists clenched under his elbows.

I could read the old man like a book, and right about now, he was praying I'd excuse myself before anything "unfortunate" came out of my mouth. I was too curious about the line of questioning to give him an ounce of satisfaction, though.

"That's quite a pedigree, perhaps too much for our little town," Maddie's rapidly graying father mused. "You must be commuting to Augusta or someplace."

I managed a smile. "I have a home office."

Maddie's mother continued in her slow, southern drawl. "Oh, well, isn't that handy? I'll never understand those computer things anyway. Good thing they're not for me. I imagine your father here had quite a tuition bill for all those fancy degrees. How long will those payments last, I wonder?"

The question was directed at Mike. I bit my tongue until I tasted copper.

Deep breaths, Lizzie. Deep. Breaths. Let him answer and dig his own grave.

To Mike's credit, he glanced at me expectantly. I sighed and sat forward, reining myself in enough to answer logically, but my palms ached from digging my nails into flesh. "*Mike* didn't pay for any of it. I earned grants and scholarships. I was offered a fellowship my last two years. An internship covered some living expenses. The loans I took, I'm repaying."

"We were thrilled when South Carolina University offered Maddie a full scholarship. Harland here was instrumental in the renovations of their library, after all."

The metallic taste coated my tongue completely now. The Umber Literary Repository was the only saving grace of USC. I'd dipped in digitally a few times over the years, but its namesake was an old coot with rampaging eyebrows and a permanent scowl. He sat judgingly at his wife's left, his highball glass nearly empty.

Without that generous donation to the university, their dimwitted daughter wouldn't have been accepted to their veterinary program. Her GPA was in the bottom twenty percent of her graduating class. Sure enough, after two years of struggling through rudimentary liberal arts classes at USC and declining externship opportunities because the hours weren't "agreeable," Phil proposed and her parents suddenly decided that college wasn't that important after all. She could be the wife of a highly regarded, pensioned public servant, and live comfortably without having to administer pentobarbital to terminally ill shih tzus.

I now prayed for euthanasia over continuing this charade.

"And how long have you been back home?" Maddie's mother added as my silence continued.

"Almost two years now."

"You're still dressing like a Yank, I see. Such heavy fabric, and a cape, in South Carolina spring?"

I lifted my brow at the comment. It felt genuine in its curiosity but backhanded in its execution. "It's called *style*. Dress for the occasion, not the season."

"Whose funeral is it, then?" Maddie's father chimed in. He touched the temple of his narrow glasses, analyzing me like an underperforming financial portfolio. Unfortunately for him, I had no intention of being micromanaged.

Mike's eyes widened almost imperceptibly. He felt the tide shift. He knew how fickle my seas could be and he'd seen them toss many unprepared mariners deftly overboard before.

I sat forward in my seat, lowering my tone so it would be heard by those I intended and no others. "Oh, I can think of one person whose life is ending today. The parts of his life that involve him making his own decisions, anyway."

Mike winced and his eyes closed, shoulders slumped like a man watching his favorite team lose in the last inning.

Maddie's mother's brows nearly touched, her head tipping like a curious poodle's. "It's a shame you're so callous, child. Our girl wants nothing but the best for Phillip, and today is a celebration of all they've accomplished together."

"Sure," I replied flippantly. "What she's *accomplished* is finding a patsy. Phil's her golden ticket to a life of entitlement and privilege. He'll endanger himself to keep her blissfully ignorant and sated like the sow she is. Now, if you'll excuse me, there's got to be a bar in this hotel, one that serves better than the swill on the open bar *you* so generously gifted."

I rose and made my escape as the Umbers gaped and Mike sunk dejectedly in his seat.

* * * * *

Fifteen minutes later, I was perched at the hotel lobby bar, nursing a squat glass of whiskey. This was my second round, and I'd already peddled through my flask. My arms and consciousness felt heavy, the roar of a headache replaced by a dull buzz. I could've napped on the smooth oak, but managed to keep myself upright, traipsing a finger along the rim of the glass in slow circles.

I'd never simultaneously despised and envied someone before, and I hated that it was Maddie. A sour taste replaced the copper. I sought to drown it with more Tennessee antidote. The bartender knew his place, keeping his mouth shut, my glass full, and my credit card tucked in the cash register drawer.

"Damnit, Lizzie! Can't you shelve the bullshit for one day?"

My face twisted into a satisfied smile. The annoyed, paternal voice was closer than I would've preferred, but I'd expected him to chase me down. I kept my eyes on my glass. "How is this my fault?"

Mike stormed to my side, grasping my forearm with a damp palm. I shook him loose immediately. The bartender kept a wary eye as Mike slinked back. He lowered his voice as the half-dozen patrons around us focused on the drama. "You *need* to be the bigger person here."

"And why is that?" I turned on my stool, taking him on. "I was minding my own business when Mr. and Mrs. Von-Holier-Than-Thou started antagonizing me."

"You could've replied like the woman you are, a cultured and educated one. Instead, you resorted to your old routine. You just deliver a low-blow and dash before anyone can hold you accountable. You should be ashamed of yourself. You're so selfish, just like you were decades ago."

"How would you know? You were too busy up your own ass to pay attention to anything back then, and nowadays, you avoid me like the plague. You haven't changed much either, you know."

"You mean, I was too busy working to pay for the home you grew up in and the medical bills? Work kept food in your belly. You never went to bed hungry, even when your mother was gone. *I* did that. And I still work my ass off. You're have *no* idea."

"What a shitty memory you have," I retorted. "You used her pension to keep up the house, the house *we* had before *you* came along. Her life insurance disappeared, too. She'd earmarked that for *my* education, *Pops*, and yet, Daly Contracting came into being right around then, didn't it?"

"Lizzie," he huffed, losing what little patience he'd had. I reveled in his creased brow. "I refuse to have this argument with you again. You know where the money went, and you know I worked to get here. Have some respect."

"Only when you show some for your children. Those old crows stepped all over my accomplishments, just like they judged Phil years ago for his career choices, and both times, you kept your mouth shut."

"I let you two speak for yourselves and your choices. The big mistake was giving you the chance to. I should've spoken up back there. I should've told her the truth. You have no *idea* what hard work is."

"Not all work involves backhoes and bulldozers, you ignorant jackass. I work hard for what I have. So has Phil. Hell, the worthless mooch he just married lounged around the apartment he paid for while he aced his criminal justice program and worked full-time. You think she wanted to stick an arm up a cow's ass for a living, or do you think she thought she'd look cute in a white lab coat, posing on a billboard for the clinic she'd open and then pretend to run herself?"

"Enough, Lizzie," another male voice chimed in. I recognized this one, too, from so many kitchen table arguments over the years. "That's enough, Dad. Let me handle this."

"With pleasure," Mike breathed, stepping back so Phil could take his place. "Don't waste too much time on her. Today's supposed to be for you and Maddie, not this selfish brat."

Mike disappeared from the bar as a grin split my face. The bartender, sensing calm on the horizon, wandered over the refill my drink and place a bottle of water at Phil's elbow.

The groom's tie and jacket were missing, his white shirt's collar button undone. Sweat dewed on his forehead. His expression was one of disdain and exhaustion, both undoubtedly my doing. This farce of a day had been picture-perfect to all but the Daly family.

Phil didn't chide me instantly, instead taking the water bottle as he turned toward the televisions behind the bar. He stood at my side, watching the college game on display while taking measured sips without a word. I was forced to admire his ability to handle me.

After five minutes of quiet, the bartender circled for a refill. I waved him off. I knew my reign of tyranny was at an end. Phil was destined for an awesome career in interpersonal communication and crime scene defusal. He demonstrated mastery by doing nothing at all.

He finally turned his torso, waiting patiently for me to meet his gaze. And when I did, he simply lifted his brows.

I was a flurry of words in an instant. "Oh, come on. Mike's just as big an ass as your new in-laws, who, mind you, are also arrogant and entitled. Your wife is a lazy narcissist, and you're the town hero. Meanwhile, I'm ungrateful, and about as worthless as her college credits. You can't expect me to smile and bat my eyes at their blatant insults. I don't owe them anything. But you're about to say that I make Mike's life hard because I enjoy it, not because he deserves it. He's got COPD. He's out of his league dealing with me. Blah blah blah. It's the same old chiding for standing up for myself when he starts the arguments. Does that sum it up?"

"Hmm," he murmured noncommittally, setting down his empty water bottle. "Seems to, except you forgot one thing."

"Oh, and what's that?"

"The favor you're going to do for me."

I scoffed, turning away from his gaze to refocus on the mounted TV. Georgia was destroying Samford. The undulating, red-clad crowd cheered endlessly. "I owe you nothing."

"You will once I smooth this over. I've got a plan. It's surefire, and you're too damn stubborn and curious to not hear me out. Just admit it so I can get back to the sixty-thousand-dollar party in my honor."

"It's in your *wife's* honor. The vomitous avalanche of pink proves that. Only because I'm already toasty and this game's a blowout, what's your brilliant solution?"

He couldn't hide his smirk as he faced me. "Work for Dad."

I nearly spit out my diminutive slurp of whiskey. "Hah! You've clearly lost your mind. Can you imagine? Lizzie the computer nerd donning a hardhat and drinking from a Thermos in the noon-day sun?"

"I'm sure it's someone's disgusting fantasy, but sadly, no," Phil remarked. "If you cared at all about what little family you have left, you'd know he's expanding his business. He's taking on high-dollar accounts for the affluent around here. He needs to bring on more talent, and background checks only reveal so much, you know."

I tipped my head inquisitively. "Uh huh, so I'll be digging up dirt on his potential hires, then."

"Exactly. You'll use your dastardly talents for a decent purpose, and you'll be helping the old man out for a change. I'll make sure he compensates you well. I can probably negotiate double what he'd pay for a basic search into someone's background. It'll take you a couple minutes and save him thousands in litigation if one of his contractors gets a little handsy with some rich customer's jewelry box. It'll also save us local cops valuable manhours, so it's a win all around, not that you care about that."

I faced the bar again, considering all sides. If I used my education to benefit the old man, maybe he'd finally see a computer-based profession as a legitimate one. It was also possible that I'd uncover future thieves in the process, adding to my life goal of outing the dastardly. I'd have an excuse to flex my hacker muscles and the chance to dig into systems and databases I hadn't considered yet.

And, on the peripheral of my conscience, I realized Phil had planted a seed. He'd tilled the earth, tucked the kernel into the soil, and handed me the watering can. All I had to do was accept it and watch the fruits of his negotiation grow into something mutually beneficial. He was offering a middle ground, a fertile plot in the neutral zone.

Phil spun my barstool around after a minute of silence passed. "Today, Lizzie. I do have someplace to be and a wife to undress at some point."

My lip curled at the thought, but I sighed and met his gaze. "Fine. I'm agreeable to that. I can start immediately. I'll have contracts for him to sign."

"Excellent. Nothing like a few contracts to show trust between family members." Phil's eyes rolled as he leaned in a little closer. "And what am I getting in return for restoring relations with the only family you've got left?"

"My eternal gratitude?"

"About as worthless as my wife's college credits, as you so kindly put it."

We shared a smile, the first I'd managed today. "Fine. I'll stroll back in there and apologize, you damn tyrant. First, to the old bats, then to Mike, then to the illustrious bride."

"You'll say it loud enough to hear."

"Ugh, fine."

"I mean, not just them. It'll be loud enough so everyone can hear. And you'll mean it. Otherwise, no deal, Lizzie."

I leaned back on my barstool, the edges of my liquor-induced haze sharpening too quickly for my liking. "Pick up this tab and it's a deal."

He groaned dramatically and lifted his wallet from his pocket. After trading my card for his, the bartender rung in a half-bottle of top-shelf booze. I grinned, sliding off my stool. "Pleasure doing business with you, you shit stain."

"Is that my new nickname? I'd prefer a whore bag like you giving your savior a kinder one."

I waited for him to tuck his wallet away before looping my arm through his. "Ah, come on. Imagine how boring your life would've been if I hadn't come along to screw it all up."

"It certainly would've saved me a lot of grief, and I'd have gotten much better Christmas gifts. The coffers were divided after the parents married."

He shot me a conspirator's wink and I led him back to the ballroom. "Don't I know it. You're a good apple, Phil. Don't get stupid in your old age."

"Despite evidence to the contrary, you're all right yourself," he replied. "You just gotta keep your nose clean. The deeper you dig, the dirtier you get. Problem is, you just don't know when to stop."

"You underestimate me," I debated as we crossed the ballroom threshold. "I dig just deep enough."

Philadelphia, PA, 2012

Dressed in Gucci and spritzed with artisan perfume, I strolled through the front doors of Anderson-Hilliance's downtown office at seven. Serena was punctual for day one, bright-eyed and eager. The curtain lifted on my new life, the ridiculous stage show that it was.

I couldn't wait to settle into one of those partitioned offices at the top of the grand escalator. They closed tightly and were soundproof, based on observations during my interview. My name etched onto brass would greet guests kindly enough, and that veil between hallway and office space would give me enough time to plaster on a smile.

The same security guard who ogled me endlessly the week before greeted me openly this time, a broad smile on his chiseled face. The onyx stubble was a telltale sign of a long weekend. "Good morning, Serena. Welcome, officially, to Anderson-Hilliance."

Before I could reply, a sweet voice echoed around the sterile atrium. "Julian, that's my line."

The guard snickered as Joy came into view, her petite frame descending the escalator one revolving stair at a time. I bowed my head politely and offered a hand. "Good morning."

"Serena, welcome to the family. Are you alone today, Julian?"

He responded with a more professional tone than he'd afforded me. "No, ma'am. Greg stepped away for an escort. I expect him back in a few minutes."

"Excellent," Joy responded with a smile. "Please come to my office at 9 am."

"Yes, ma'am," he replied easily, lowering his gaze to the monitors. Closed circuit images of the company's upstairs hallways were reflected on the screens.

Joy led me to the escalator. "Come, Serena. Day one always means paperwork, doesn't it?"

"Always. Fortunately, I brought my best ink pen with me."

"Let me guess, it's designer."

"How'd you know?" I responded amiably. Joy giggled as we ascended.

* * * * *

Two hours later, I'd finally signed my last legal document. The morning began with a mediocre brew and HR forms for payroll. It continued into non-disclosure and non-compete agreements, segueing into tiresome business practice and policy signoffs. The droning finally ended in vaguely worded corporate responsibility forms. By the time I scratched my initials onto the final page, the words had blurred into a fog of legalese. I was also exhausted of keeping an ever-present smile firmly in place. Joy never wavered, presenting document after document, peripherally explaining each one as I resorted to overrated, over-roasted office coffee for encouragement.

The wall clock in her office, shaped like Mount Fuji with a sun rising incrementally over its apex, rung out again at nine, as it had at eight. A simple gong rung out in the expansive office as we sat at her conference table, papers tucked into broad envelopes all around us.

"Your clock is very unique," I commented, slipping the last document into a crimson folder before handing it to Joy. "Was it a souvenir?"

"Oh, I wish," she gushed, eyeing the clock after stacking the folders in order. "I'll get there someday. It was a gift from Su. She said I should have a clock in my office."

"That's very kind. Do you lose track of time?"

"Don't we all? When I'm up to my eyebrows in computer work, I lose track of time and place. I'm sure you've been there before."

"Almost daily, though I wager our work's a little different."

"Eh, it's all work, isn't it? It's for the greater good and all that."

"That's why it matters."

A knock at the door grabbed our attention. Joy glanced at the clock again and smiled before calling out, "Come on in, Julian."

The broad-shouldered guard pushed the opaque glass door open and stepped inside with a lowered head. "Are you both ready?"

"Indeed," Joy remarked, standing primly. She grabbed all the folders, plus a set of keys from a dish on her desk. "Shall we?"

I rose from my seat, tucking my pen back into the inner breast pocket of my navy jacket. I contemplated why a security guard was needed, but I didn't have time to question it. Joy was already moving toward the door. I grabbed the handle of my briefcase and followed behind without a word.

On the descending escalator, I glanced backward, up and to the offices I was now leaving behind. I couldn't help but ask. "Where are we headed?"

"To your division's office," Joy responded sunnily. "After today, you won't need an escort. We'll finish your security clearance. Then you'll be granted access to the area once your background check, fingerprints and retina scans come back clear."

As we passed the security desk, Joy handed the folders to a guard I hadn't seen before. In a tailored suit and with a bud tucked into his right ear, he looked more like a bodyguard than a penny-per-hour front desk attendant. He nodded once and began slipping on gloves as we turned a sharp corner, headed to a darkened niche behind the escalator.

"I didn't submit any fingerprints or a retina scan," I replied as a sleek elevator came into view, tucked into the wall. "Did I miss any of your instructions?"

"Nope." She replied, pulling a keycard attached to a retractable cord from her waistband and pressing it to the reader alongside the elevator. A single beep sounded.

"But you just said I need to pass a check. I don't mind getting printed."

Joy smiled at me. "Serena, there's no need to go get printed." She slid closer to the elevator, tucking her fingernails around the button adorned with a downward arrow. It popped off into her palm. In the new opening, she inserted a key from her keyring. With a single twist to the right, a second beep rung out. "We have what we need."

I watched in awe as she replaced the elevator button, then pressed her index finger to that button and her thumb to the button above it, one with a black upward arrow on it. A third beep sounded as the elevator doors slid open.

"You have what you need?" I uttered, equally shocked and pleased at the incredible display of physical security.

"Mm hmm," she murmured, stepping onto the elevator and waving me forward. "You've touched everything and you made a bathroom stop last week, so we're good."

I couldn't keep my lower lip from dropping as Joy centered her right eye over a small glass panel above the elevator buttons. A bright green light flashed over her face before a fourth beep echoed around us. The elevator doors slipped shut and the metal box descended, though no buttons indicated the building had a basement. Julian never took his eyes off me, his arms crossed as Joy smiled vapidly at the closed doors.

* * * * *

I was back to pacing the living room carpets in my apartment again at dusk. "If I'm lying, I'm dying. They fingerprinted my non-disclosure contract's signature page and grabbed my retina scan from the bathroom mirror. They offer you a drink to ensure a bathroom trip. That's some FBI level shit."

"Wow," Bryan breathed into my ear through the phone speaker. "Equal parts thorough and paranoid, and I'm not sure it's legal, so forget the feds doing it. You said the lackeys work in the basement?"

"They've got a legit fortress under the building. My department is down four floors. It's a huge cylindrical room with desks in a ring. In the center's a globe-shaped projection monitor that displays breaking news and any incoming messages from top brass so we all can see it. It's wild."

"Sounds like the start of a Kubrick movie. Are you all expected to have a port implanted on the back of your neck once you're through probation?"

"I signed so much shit today, that could've been in there. I'm pretty sure the fine print for the fingerprinting and retina scans was. I wish you could see The Red Room. That's what they call our workspace. The tech's top-notch. And they get that each person wants a personalized setup. A check for five grand just cleared my account so I can build my own CPU, buy my own peripherals, and invest in earwear, head-mounted displays, whatever I want. The division supervisor runs a scan for Alienware and unapproved peripherals, but otherwise, we design our own systems. Oh, and no spoken convo during work's allowed."

"Sounds like they're building a faction. If they make you shave your head, bail."

"I get it, though. Nothing pisses me off more than worthless chat when I'm working. By the way, they ended up hiring all thirteen of those MIT grads, plus some other chick from Cal Tech. She's already being a bitch, too. Fifteen's an odd number, an 'obvious slight to those with imparnumerophobia, therefore providing a non-inclusive workspace,' according to her email to us all. And since I'm the last one chosen for the kickball team, it's all my fault."

"She emailed you and not HR? What a hatchet wound. Put luster dust and cornstarch in her aerosol keyboard cleaner."

"I totally will. That's diabolical."

"Have they made you walk around and pretend to enjoy meeting everyone yet?"

"That's tomorrow. I'm the subject of the morning muster meeting. Get this, the entire cast of characters convenes in the lobby at eight-thirty, exchanging pleasantries and all. Mr. Hightower, the megalomaniac he is, stops the escalator and stands halfway down. He apparently tells them all about how wonderful the company is and whatever other propaganda he's got to share, then the whole team disbands to 'conquer the day.' That's their send-off."

I heard a cabinet door slam shut behind Bryan's voice. "This is getting more cultish by the second. How'd you avoid having to muster this morning? I figured they'd indoctrinate you right away."

"I was too busy signing my life away. Get this, they have a conditional power of attorney. If you lose consciousness at your workstation, they have the right to remove you from the office and secure everything before they call for paramedics. That was one document I managed to read completely before I went cross-eyed. It's no joke in there."

"We already know they're up to no good. They gotta guard the nest and all its baby birds, Serena."

Hearing Bryan call me that made me burst out in laughter. "Seriously, what's become of me? I'm suddenly a yuppie with a yellow bike, working for the man downtown. I've learned two languages and I'm exploring retirement plan options. If I forget Def Main parameters, end me before it's too late. Oh, and it's not 'downtown.' It's called Center City here, for some reason. Philly's weird."

Bryan chortled between bites of something that sounded chewy. "Just don't lose your southern charm, you delightful slut. Any snatch on your radar yet?"

I dropped onto my desk chair, spinning it three-sixty. "Yeah, but she's out of my league in a big way. And that's me saying that, so you know it's true."

"No one is out of your league, darling," he mused. "Not schoolteachers, not clergy members, and certainly not dark-skinned keepers of the peace, as we recently learned."

I took a prolonged swig of blueberry kombucha. It was repulsive compared to the stuff I'd gotten in Whitehall and had cost me twice as much. "No doubt about that. She's an executive at AH, a real blue blood. Plus, she's exotic, stylish, and cultured. There's Japanese in there, but there's something mixed with it. Maybe she's Mediterranean, too? Not sure. I'll see her again tomorrow. That's the single benefit of this muster meeting nonsense."

"Your silver linings usually involve sex," Bryan remarked. A cabinet slammed shut behind him once again. "If I keep eating, you won't recognize me when you come up next month."

"Well, quit it, then. Have your jaw wired shut or something."

"Girl, I'm already a milkshake whore. They can wire everything shut, and I'll still figure out how to get it in me. The local creamery's got a honeydew cucumber one. It's so good. I swear I'd be skinny if the boss wasn't up my ass all the time."

"Honey, if the boss was up your ass all the time, you wouldn't be thinking about eating."

"Facts, precious. Let me go before I drag you down to my level."

"Bye, lovey. I'm gonna get to work. Go flirt shamelessly with a married man. Make him question himself. That'll make you feel better."

"Hah, it always does. Tootles, you hussy."

I hung up and flipped on my computer monitor. The sun was setting on my first day at Anderson-Hilliance, but it was far from over. I was more convinced than ever. Their perimeter was defending them against *esTre11aN3gra*. There was dirt to find. I just had to keep digging.

Cambridge, MA, 2001

A red-eye session in MIT's computer lab meant I was twenty minutes late to meet Bryan. The bistro café at the corner of Main and Portland left their patio tables out all night, knowing the evacuees from the nearby pubs would need a resting place as they drunkenly hobbled back to dorm rooms and studio apartments. Once seated, the salesmanship of the servers encouraged the inebriated to grab an overpriced burrito or bag of garlic fries before resuming their inebriated trip home. It was a brilliant move on their part, one my naturally opportunistic mind appreciated.

This devious plan worked perfectly on Bryan, who considered this spot his favorite late-night pitstop. A muscled footballer from Boston College waited tables there on Friday nights. Bryan insisted he'd capture his attention in due time. Plus, Bryan's roommate, a total bore with a bowl cut, was certainly fast asleep with his eye mask on, so my buddy was in no hurry to get back. This was a common occurrence, Bryan drunk-dialing me a little after midnight and begging me to meet him for gossip, gelato, and gaping at the apron-donning stud serving us.

As I turned the corner in a near-canter, a group of giggling undergrads brushed past me. Apparently, their evening had involved baptism in local lager. I felt the gag before I could control it, my empty stomach roiling and reminding me it'd been twelve hours since I'd shoved that organic protein bar in my face. Thankfully this café's kitchen was auspiciously tidy and served a salad I could tolerate.

Bryan came into view, perched at the patio table farthest from the eatery's door. I shook my head with a knowing grin. The longer the trip from his table to the eatery's front door, the more ogling time Bryan enjoyed. The glaze of my buddy's eyes and the droop of his lower lip told me it'd already been quite a festive night. He stank of stale cigarette smoke as I drew closer, the scent turning my stomach upside-down again. He was all smiles, though, haphazardly sidesaddle in the wrought iron seat.

"Oh, *there's* my little workaholic. How dare you, leaving me to entertain that sweet chunk of man all by myself."

"He's more your speed than mine, anyway," I snickered, planting a smacker on Bryan's crimson cheek before sitting across from him. "Ease off the vodka tonics. You're about to burst into flames."

"Girl, you know I can't. Rocco's mixes with this tonic water they get from Milan. They swear it makes the vodka 'sing.' All I know is, after a few of them, I'm ready for some Liza karaoke."

Rocco's was a notorious haunt for the bi-curious crowd, thus my friend's obsession with the place. He wasn't fully out of the closet yet, but we both knew it was coming.

I checked my flip phone as I set it on the table. No new texts meant my roommate wasn't done partying yet. Michelle had an annoying habit of keeping me in the loop. Maybe she hoped I'd join her, but her idea of being social was dancing on barstools in short skirts and soliciting for company outside the faculty building. I preferred to earn my grades, and any due respect, rather than demean myself for it.

"Whatever makes you happy, dearest," I cooed. "And what is handsome Heath bringing you?"

"Besides naughty dreams? God only knows. I can't even remember who I am when he turns those baby blues on me."

I chuckled, sitting back before crossing my right leg over the left. "How much longer before you stitch a saucy limerick on a pleather thong and hand it over, you man whore?"

Bryan retrieved a round mirror from his pocket and examined his complexion scathingly. "Something tells me you've resorted to that little tactic before."

"You know it, and for the record, it's not easy getting that kind of lingerie back in Whitehall."

Before Bryan could manage to slather on a sweet face or even speak, Heath returned to the table, alight and jovial. He handed Bryan a menu before turning to me. "Hey stranger. You need a menu, too?"

"Nah, I'm predictable," I replied, chancing a brush of fingertip over his bare forearm below the rolled-up sleeve of his white Oxford. It was firm, with silken hair like a stallion's hind quarters. I felt his muscles twitch ever so slightly. "But, you know, Bryan's always up for something new. Where's your favorite spot in town?"

Heath's eyes turned upward as he pulled back from my grasp as subtly as possible, his hands settling on his hips. "Well, when I have a few minutes between working, school, and practice, I like Rocco's on Prospect. Guys from the team always seem to be there anyway."

I couldn't completely hide my grin. "Huh, you don't say. My bestie here happens to be a regular over there."

"No kidding! It's a shame we've never crossed paths." Heath glanced at Bryan with a smile, but his gaze didn't linger long. In two seconds, he was facing me again.

I saw Bryan titter in his seat, his lips tucked between his teeth. Clearly Heath had hesitated at my touch for the most obvious of reasons. Bryan was going to owe me big for this.

"Well, I hate the idea of cutting in on your getting-to-know-you chat, but Bryan here happens to also be a big fan of the team. Maybe you'll humor his endless questions on your next night off?"

Heath's gaze slipped away from mine, redirecting to Bryan's as a pale pink glow appeared at the apples of his cheeks. "Sure, that'd be great. Tuesday night at eight?"

Bryan nodded once. "I'll be there."

"Sweet. Now, what can I get you two?"

"My usual is fine, just spring water and the arugula salad."

"And you can bring me whatever you like best," Bryan told Heath, his voice turning to honey. "Oh, and I've got the tab for us both. If you give her the check, I'll never forgive you."

Heath tugged the menu from Bryan's hand with a bashful smile. "I wouldn't dream of it, then. Be right back, you two."

As our server disappeared, my smile turned wicked. Gaping and awestruck, my friend sat forward and grabbed my hand. "You are absolutely fabulous and I *hate* you for it, but I have a date with Heath!"

I couldn't help giggling. "You sure do, and it won't be cheap. I guarantee you he's a beer drinker, and Rocco's is all microbrews. I've done what I can for you, padawan, so it's all you now."

"My Jedi master got me a stud and I didn't get her anything," he pouted playfully.

"I'm good. I've got unlimited access to the computer lab thanks to a PA who recognizes potential when he sees it, and my newest silicone bedfellow keeps me company. The longer I can avoid tapping into the coed dating pool, the better."

"Are you still pining for that ex-bestie back home?"

"I wish I wasn't," I admitted as Heath returned with our bottled waters. I twisted the cap off a little too forcefully, slicing my thumb on the jagged edge. Ruby thumbprints smudged along the ribbed plastic instantly. "One night with me was enough to send her running west. I thought we were on the same page. I guess not."

"It just wasn't meant to be. There's no harm in keeping casual. You're young and beautiful. Get someone else to buy your drinks."

"You mean, like you're doing now, without me having to sleep with you?"

He snorted, gesturing with his water bottle. Some sloshed out in the process. "Boo, it's nothing personal, but you're missing a very important part of human anatomy."

"Isn't it time to come clean? It's not that big a deal."

His grunt was guttural and his eye roll overly dramatic. "You know I'll lose my parents' money if I say a word. Once I've got some income, I'll make it official. I promise."

I poured out a little water to rinse my bloodied thumb. "I'm so glad I got that fellowship. If I had to suck up to Mike and lie to his face just to get a piece of parchment, I'd be pissy, too."

"He's gotta know you had your share of booty back home. And speaking of the fam," Bryan sipped his water with a brow lifted. "That stepbrother of yours is quite a dish. Did you guys ever…"

"Bryan," I interjected with a scowl. "Seriously. Ick. You two are the only humans I even slightly respect, and that's saying something. Besides, he's been up Maddie's ass for years. She'd have an aneurism if I showed the slightest interest in him. Ooh, actually, that sweetens the pot a bit."

"I'm almost sorry I asked. Almost."

I chuckled as Heath laid my arugula, raspberry, and sunflower seed salad down before me. He then placed a platter topped with a pile of hand-cut fries by Bryan's elbow. They were doused in white, pepper-flecked gravy, topped with crumbled sausage, fine shreds of pale cheese and slivers of green onion. It reminded me of breakfast back home, in the land of heart attacks and hypertension.

"This is my order when we lose a big game," Heath told us. "Mom's from Toronto and Dad's from Tallahassee, so this is a bit of them both. Poutine, but breakfast style, with country gravy and cheddar. I hope you like it. It's not the best thing for the love handles, but whatever. Everyone deserves a little indulgence, don't they?"

Bryan was all smiles again as he lifted his delivered napkin. "My mouth is watering. The fries look scrumptious, too."

"Stop it," Heath argued sweetly as he retreated once again, calling over his shoulder. "Enjoy!"

Bryan's voice dropped a few decibels. "I'm probably not the best thing for him, either."

"If you don't go, I'll never forgive you."

Bryan dove headfirst into the mountain of dairy and starch. "Oh, I'll be there, but he'll high-tail it within an hour, you watch."

"A microbrew does sound pretty good, if you're buying. Maybe I'll wander in and watch, if you're offering."

"Don't you dare. I tell you everything anyway."

I lifted my fork and sifted through the roughage on my plate. "You better. Oh, and speaking of dishing, you got any dirt on Gideon?"

Bryan snickered, delicately pulling a fry from the bottom only to collapse the entire pile like a game of pick-up sticks. "Oh, darling, do I!"

We picked through our meals, Bryan with stubby fingers and me with a long-tined fork, as he delighted me with tales of the software firm's misdeeds. Gideon was making a name for itself in all the wrong ways. They hired, then disassociated the country's best programmers after capitalizing on their talents. They formed litigious relationships with rival companies. They laundered money through shady investments overseas. We wondered what blunder would finally bury them.

Bryan shrugged, taking a break from his cardiac special to sip his water. "I heard there are online groups trying to sabotage them. Maybe their former employees, the ones they screwed over, are the ones behind that?"

I shook my head pitifully. "Burn enough bridges and the architect's bound to come knocking. It's hard to watch your work be desecrated from the unemployment line."

"True," he commiserated. "Word is, one's particularly motivated to burn Gideon to the ground, and a bunch of other button-down criminals out there, too. She's making quite a name for herself."

"How do you know it's a chick? I mean, I hope it is, but how are you sure?"

"They go by '*Estrella Negra*.' That's feminine, right?"

I gestured with my fork, flicking the tines toward him. "*Estrella* is feminine, so the adjective is, too. Was foreign language not required at that fancy lads' boarding school you went to?"

Bryan snickered. "The German teacher was from Bavaria. He had a swimmer's build. I learned four phrases and what brand of boxer-briefs he wore, all from the comfort of his king bed."

"Nice. I'd be jealous if I wasn't dead set on exposing your exploits myself."

"You wouldn't *dare*," he replied with a lifted brow. "I've got your number, too, sister. Anyway, back to the *Estrella Negra* thing. What kind of character needs an online persona? It's a little hokey."

I sighed wistfully. "A superhero, or someone who's afraid of exposing themselves in the line of duty. They're afraid of being misunderstood, or of being blamed for the collateral damage of the good work they do. It happens all the time. Just because they're masked doesn't mean they're evil."

"That's almost profound. You dual majoring in Philosophy now?"

"That'd be creative writing, you dunce," I fired back after swallowing a bite of peppery greens. "Seriously, were all your teachers fuckable and eager to hand out passing marks? Not that I'm bitter or anything."

Bryan belly-laughed, sitting back from his picked-over plate. "Hey, we both got into MIT, didn't we? And maybe you're right. Maybe this online good Samaritan's got the right idea."

"I think so, and the market's prime for unearthing sins. I just spent three hours applying for software beta testing work with the main players. Let's see if any are foolhardy enough to get back to me."

"Oh please, Lizzie. I'm sure you're only interested in following the rules and conducting above-board analysis. What risk would you pose them?"

"Absolutely," I replied a little too quickly. "There's no harm in utilizing my education to help a few companies with their user acceptance testing. And if I happen to find some stuff by digging in a little deeper than they expected, it wouldn't be the worst thing. It's all in the name of learning, right?"

"And I assume you'll be willing to keep me abreast of all the exciting job details and test results?"

"Would you expect any different? After all, we're both students in the field. What better way to learn is there than to share knowledge? Same time, same place next week?"

Bryan lifted his water in a mock toast. "Wouldn't miss it for the world, lovey."

* * * * *

In the junior dorms an hour later, I fenagled my key into my room's lock. The space beyond was dark and silent. I glanced to the heavens in gratitude. Michelle wasn't back yet. I prayed for a miracle in the form of a horny dalliance, one that would keep her busy until dawn.

Retrieving my laptop, I hopped onto my rickety bed. After starting up my rock playlist, I logged into the campus's extranet. My email inbox was empty. I scowled and logged off before I was tempted to work ahead on next week's practicals.

I was researching within minutes, and sure enough, Gideon was under fire from all directions. News outlets were circulating damning photos of executives sweating before masses of reporters. The company's website was utterly silent on the subject. Stocks were falling. Rivals were capitalizing on Gideon's struggles. Pop-up ads for competitor's programs lined every page I accessed like parade revelers awaiting the first float.

I shook my head as I perused the article's comments. The public was just as vindictive as the news sources. Everyone wanted blood. According to the masses, this was just another example of inexcusable corporate crime that made the rich richer and turned average Joes into hapless victims. With the company on the edge of demise, the customer support and troubleshooting departments were already laid off. Their clients, a smattering of small businesses and non-profits, were now in a tailspin.

Without much difficulty, I found mention of the Spanish-monikered whistleblower. Social media and blog sites were listing *esTre11aN3gra* as a source, but very little detail followed. It looked like a gamertag but searching for the handle on game platform databases yielded nothing. With a scowl, I started scrubbing free email sites for a user with the same ID on any public servers. Faced with zero results, I rubbed my eyes and rethought my approach.

This vigilante was undertaking a perilous endeavor, unearthing a company's dirty laundry. The libel suits alone would destroy *esTre11aN3gra* socially and financially if their identity was discovered. That made them even more elusive. I needed a new strategy and I knew just who to ask for perspective. I lifted my phone without hesitance. No one knew how to protect servers like Bryan.

With his mind tapped and the call ended, I was off and running. Within the hour, I'd found my way into Gideon's human resource database. Very little information remained. Dismayed, I perused the few former employee profiles left behind. Only three had email accounts listed. One profile showed active content.

J.Hernandez@zmail.com.

Hmm, curious. Now I just need in.

With newfound zeal, I accessed zmail's homepage. Borrowed access to a key-counter software app let me review the most common keystrokes used by that account. I typed in the email from the Gideon file. It was only a matter of time until I found the needle in the digital haystack.

Sometime before dawn, the radiant heater in the room kicked on. Winter was over but Massachusetts hadn't gotten the memo. It wasn't nearly cold enough to merit the eighty-degree heat pouring from the porcelain coils, though. With sweat beading on my brow, I cracked the window and shrugged out of my hoodie. In a simple satin bra and with hair pulled up in a messy bun, perched cross-legged on my duvet, I got back to work.

After what seemed like an eternity, I snuck into the email account. The inbox, outbox, spam, and trash folders were all empty. There were no contacts in the address book and no messages archived. Even the personal details were scrubbed, leaving behind only the account's email address as an identifier. The trail ran cold. I sat back with a frown.

Dead end. But who creates an email account only to thoroughly delete everything off it?

I was mid-tantrum when the dorm room door slid open silently. My eyes flashed up instantly. A familiar face, flushed from booze and caked with makeup, appeared in the gap. Michelle was far too young to be allowed into the bars she frequented, but I strongly doubted anyone looked at her ID when her cleavage and mile-long legs were on full display, as they were now in an olive-green mini dress.

Once inside, she closed the door gently and leaned back against it. Her emerald eyes were dreamy as her gaze narrowed on me. Even in my sleep-deprived and frustrated state, I knew that look. I couldn't help biting my bottom lip and taking in her full frame, my eyes traipsing top to bottom and back up as she tipped her head with a smile.

I just barely got my computer closed and to the floor before she was on my lap in its place. She tasted of sour apple liquor and sin. As the sun rose outside our window, opened to the spring air, I forgot all about my online scavenger hunt, instead savoring the tipsy blonde in my bed.

Unfortunately, that was the first and last chance I had to enjoy her. I heard that her upper-crusty parents arrived to collect their trophy daughter that afternoon, and when I got back to the dorm room we shared, there was no trace of the party animal. I glanced up to see the window, still cracked and letting in a warm breeze laden with raised voices. Glancing outside, the reason for her departure became all the clearer.

The yard below was the practice field. The soccer club enjoyed the green in the afternoons and the cross-country team started their morning runs by the closest goalpost. Though I wasn't interested in joining their ranks, I knew they got started early, even on weekends. Michelle and I hadn't been the only ones enjoying the early morning breeze. We'd had one hell of an audience.

She was gone before the rumor mill kicked into high gear. I was the one left holding the bag of dusty grain.

Philadelphia, PA, 2014

Across the glossy oak table, a fifth-generation antiquities dealer from Kennett with a wicked widow's peak was nursing a gimlet in his calloused fingers. The tan sweater-vest-over-plaid-Oxford was apparently "thrift shop chic," which made me sad for humanity. Eyes like charcoal drooped a bit at the corners, like he'd spent years in mourning and his face was sick of the monotony. Our conversation over drinks in this retrofitted historical pub stymied while we waited for our checks. We'd already discussed my fabricated love of pop-country, my parents' retirement plans, and my favorite vacation spots, none of which I'd ever visited. He'd clearly read my online dating profile dozens of times, every nauseatingly untrue word of it.

I, on the other hand, prepared for our date by tapping into state records. Despite the glaring evidence to the contrary, this bumpkin was indeed twenty-seven. Being a former Mennonite must've put those extra years on his hairline and complexion. My attention span was taxed, but I'd listened closely enough to learn he'd inherited his father's business as his only son. His separation from the faith during rumspringa made this a reckless move on his dad's part. He was building his client base with Center City wealth, since his own community shunned him and refused to patronize his business immediately after his father's death.

After dropping that lively little bomb on the dinner table, he deigned to ask me about my biggest heartbreaks. The server had two minutes to return with my credit card before I reported it lost and dashed into the night.

"That's quite a story," he meekly replied when my tale of woe came to an end. "It's a shame she disappeared. A few of my best friends are from my teen years."

Back in the eighteen-hundreds?

I hid my snark behind the rim of my wine glass. I'd taken to drinking Australian reds on lackluster dates. The dry tannins and lazy drinking pace kept my subconscious wise ass at bay. It also kept me guarded and sober enough to not let Lizzie and her erudite opinions slip out.

I drained what was left in two swigs. "Well, she wasn't cut out for a quiet life in a slow suburb. She belonged out west. I missed her friendship for a year or two into college, but I found other companionship in time. Some of those disappeared, too, but we move on."

"We do," he managed with a smile. I was again faced with teeth subjected to a severe lack of orthodontic care. "I had fun tonight, Serena."

"That's nice to hear. I'm glad you could get a night away from work."

The server, at long last, dropped off two black check holders. My card peeked from inside one. I added a decent tip and signed with a flourish before standing. He knocked his knee on the underside of the table when he leapt up like a dutiful Labrador.

"Get home safe. The weather's supposed to turn. They're expecting a foot out my way."

I managed a polite yet terse smile. "I'm less than three blocks from home. I'll make it just fine. Thanks for meeting me."

He nodded once as I grabbed my clutch off the table. He reached out a hand for a shake and I played the part regrettably. Without another word, I headed down a small, dark hallway in the back of the building. I knew this bathroom route a little too well. This was the third date I'd been on this month. They all ended with a retreat to sanitize my right hand and regret my life choices.

I chanced a glance at the bathroom mirror once the door was locked to outsiders. I looked as exhausted as I felt. The mossy amber of my eyes had turned cloudy, and my highlighted auburn hair was matted from hours of playing listlessly with it. The narrow black sweater dress I'd pulled on was bunched around the waist from sitting recumbent for over an hour. The boredom of this enduring stage show and the nights flooded with red wine were turning me into a crow.

Dating for the sake of maintaining an outwardly "normal, twenty-something" image was driving me to drink subpar booze in dives like this one. I needed to be seen in public, to seem social in a world of twenty-somethings, especially those who frequented this bar on weekends. A few peers from AH had been over my shoulder the entire night, perched at the bar and shooting occasional glances in my direction. I'd been able to confirm their interest every time I took out my cell phone for a selfie I never snapped. They'd vacated their stools a few minutes before my check was delivered, signaling my farce of a date had gone on long enough.

After dabbing my face with a damp paper towel, pressing out the fabric creases at my lap, and ensuring my date had departed, I made my way back into the dining room.

"Serena?"

Two and a half years of relentless beckoning almost made the name a birthright. I turned to the elevated voice, finding that it belonged to a fellow cyber security lackey, Avery, who was stationed three desks down from mine in The Red Room. He and two others from the department, the same group who'd watched me so diligently all night, now occupied a high-top by the front wall, overlooking the blustery city street beyond. They hadn't left. They'd just moved.

I buried my disappointment, digging out another beaming smile from my bag of tricks. I'd hoped to make a hasty retreat and get home in time for my favorite show's nine o'clock premiere, but as I neared their table, that goal slipped away. Serena's work was never done.

"Hey strangers," I shouted over the cacophony around us. "Don't you get your socializing in at the nine-to-five?"

Avery, the most outgoing of the trio replied. "Please. You think I'm going to risk my job for these two a-holes?" He forced chubby fingers through his mop of dirty blonde hair. "Socializing equals a one-way ticket to the Third Circle."

Ah, yes, the charming nickname for the executive floor.

To his right, Kavish rolled his ebony eyes. Whether it was a lack of patience with pleasantries or a lack of English comprehension, he limited himself to three words max and always preceded them with a pointed period when typed. Downing his beer like a tonic, his mood sullen despite the atmosphere, he seemed as irked to be a part of this conversation as I was. Like so many of his ilk, he preferred his day job as a full stack engineer over happy hour gossiping.

At Avery's left elbow was Vera, the only other female in The Red Room, and the Cal Tech grad who'd given me endless shit for being fifteenth on the team. While crass and lacking even basic social skills, she was a skilled programmer beyond her years. She'd graduated summa cum laude at nineteen and had created the foundation for AH's firewall within a month of being hired. She'd mastered C+ and C++ in high school. I'd struggled with those basics all through college. While we all contributed in some way to the whole, her talent was paramount in The Red Room's impermeability. She was also thirteen years younger than me, which seriously burned my ass. I decided Serena would be cordial, though, while Lizzie snarled in secret.

The mousey brunette with the short crop of fringe and pale eyes regarded me curiously. "Who was your plebian tablemate?"

"Douglas. Nice guy, though dull as dishwater. I guess I couldn't hide my boredom, huh?"

"Nope," Kavish interjected, gulping from his pilsner glass. "Were you trying?"

I exhaled. "Damn. Not well, I guess."

Avery lifted a brow at my uncommon expletive. "Where'd you meet Kid Dynamite? He's no techie, that's for sure."

"Online. I figured I'd try to meet someone from the outside world since I'm stuck in a basement all day. My parents are down my throat about finding someone."

"I'd have bought you a drink. Why didn't you ask me?"

Lizzie and Serena battled for a voice. I found a fair compromise, which so happened to be the truth. "You deserve better than me, or, if that seems contrived, you're not really my type. I hope you understand."

Vera stirred her squat glass of clear liquid with a black straw. "Was he?"

The bite was merited. He'd been chosen because he embodied Serena's quaint charm but certainly not her style. Vera's poignant snark was my recompense for working with intellectuals, and observant ones at that. I resorted to another approximate truth. "I was trying something new."

"He's new," Kavish supplied, finishing off the last of his beer, then gesturing at Avery with the empty glass. "Probably unspoiled, too."

Vera laughed while I donned the most sympathetic face I could muster. Avery turned crimson before skulking off to the bar with Kavish's glass and his own. "Yeah, yeah, mock the nice guy."

"And yet he keeps buying you drinks," Vera remarked to the provoker before turning to me. "Have you heard Avery's latest theory?"

I lifted my brows. "He has theories?"

"There's no way I'm the only one he blathers to about this nonsense," she answered, dropping a listless fist onto the table. "It would be more efficient to send you the texts. It's all day long. Someone's sneaking in after hours. Someone's tampering with his computer. Someone's moving his desk chair just a little."

"He thinks someone's breaking into The Red Room?"

"Evidently. He's debating turning on his webcam. I don't need to remind you of the implications of that."

I fought the urge to laugh. If Avery's webcam flicked on for a second, he'd be subject to every line of fine print in those NDAs we'd signed years before. No one on the outside could know what The Red Room hid, what the programmers within were constructing, or anything about the projects that AH had in the works. A single fleeting glance into the fortress of solitude hidden below the Center City streets would be the end of his career, his livelihood, and his future. It would also destroy his family, his friendships, and his reputation before he could apologize to anyone caught in the crossfire.

None of us dared to challenge the legalities of those documents. We'd seen AH part ways with a few of their clients under unfavorable terms. The Red Room had been responsible for subsequently destroying them across the web. Ruthless was a kind way to put those former clients' treatment. Brutal was a more accurate term.

Sweet little Serena had ruined more lives than she'd ever admit to her fictitious white-collar parents out in western Pennsylvania. It was one of many tasks she was paid handsomely to perform, without question or qualm.

I decided to let a little Lizzie snark enter the arena. "If he does, it'll be the last job he has anywhere near a computer. He won't be able to work a cash register, let alone a data system ever again."

Vera sipped a little of the clear liquid from her squat glass, then winced. "Repulsive. People enjoy this?"

I eyed her curiously after a little mental arithmetic. "Wait, is that your first drink ever?"

She shook her head as if to clear the experience of that singular taste from her memory. "And it'll be my last. What utter garbage."

I hid my eye roll and snatched the glass. "What did you pick?"

"The vodka in the fanciest bottle."

Sure enough, when the glass was within inches of my nose, I knew it was pure, uncut, high octane, and even higher class. It was exquisite, colorless, and unscented. "You ordered it neat?"

She nodded, suddenly interested in my knowledge of the subject. "Was that a bad decision on my part?"

I momentarily relished the idea of knowing something my brilliant coworker didn't. "Very much so, though I bet this is a good one. Do you mind?" I tipped the glass toward my mouth.

She shook her head and pushed a palm in my direction. "You can have it, all of it."

One sip let me know she'd chosen a triple distilled, top shelf Russian brand. Bryan and I shared enough overpriced vodka in our college days to know that much. It brought back hazy and nauseating memories, so one sip was more than enough. I'd already given up brown liquors in public, deciding Serena wasn't the whiskey-drinking sort, and my vodka days were long gone. After a few glasses of ashy red, the sip of pure fire tickled my gag reflex.

I placed it back at her elbow. "You picked a good one."

"I thought you only drank reds," Avery commented, sidling to the table. A balloon goblet of Shiraz was before me yet again. "I'd have gotten you vodka if I knew you wanted it. The bartender remembered your pick. I went along with it."

"That's very kind, Avery," I smiled as sincerely as I could. "And because you're so kind, I won't ask how you know that I 'only drink reds,' as you put it."

He pushed his fingers through his mop once again. "Um, well, it's not like I meant to. I just-"

Kavish snagged his glass from Avery's hand, interjecting. "He's a gawker."

Vera sighed and shot me a tired look. "He watches you work, too. They all do, even this one." She pointed obnoxiously at Kavish, who merely shrugged and returned to the recorded rugby match on his phone's display. "We're the estrogen in that basement. I'm the smart one. You're the hot one. They're pathetic Neanderthals. It's sad, really."

All I could do was laugh, though my chuckle sounded callous and childish to my ears.

Why you little...

I lifted my wine in Avery's direction and gifted him a tiny smile before turning on my heels and striding off. Behind me, I could hear Vera question her choice of words. It took every ounce of patience I had left to not toss that twelve-dollar dose of red all over her.

Just finish this glass and write the entire night off.

I snuck through the crowd once again, suddenly realizing I was the oldest one in the place by a good ten years. At thirty-four, even the bartender looked like a baby. Being youthful, docile, optimistic Serena was too tiresome on nights like this, especially when the only company I'd found was boring beyond words or ignorant beyond reason.

I found a few inches of real estate on the corner of the polished bar, sliding in close enough to lean on the surface. Amid the mayhem, I tipped my head down and closed my eyes, the noise around me morphing into a dull roar that lulled me into memory. A dozen years before, a night like this would've come standard with the school loans. Now I felt like a has-been, a poser, and thanks to my shitty coworker's ignorance, a stupid one at that.

I'd overstayed my welcome. The glass of red was drained in seconds and pushed across the bar toward the thumb-high pile of damp paper coasters and signed credit receipts awaiting attention from the overworked barback. Without a glance at the table I'd visited, I exited the humid bar and bee-lined down the desolate street.

The weather was as frosty as my mood. Gossamer flakes of white shimmered as they descended to icy sidewalks. I'd regrettably decided to leave my coat behind on this venture. Within seconds, I felt even dumber than Vera has surmised. The bitter wind turned my cheeks to sandpaper.

At the corner, I turned east toward my apartment building. I could see it in the distance, many of its windows alight beyond the wisps of snow. It had only been three hours since I'd set out on this ill-fated trek. I was already looking forward to thick socks, a warm drink, and some dark web scouring to soothe my soul.

On the next corner, a woman in a glossy red trench and matching pumps hailed a cab. Alone and bundled against the wind, she waited as the yellow taxi squealed against the curb. A quick blast of frigid air sent her hood backward, revealing a face I knew well. I'd dreamed about it for years.

Su.

I froze on the spot, bewitched by the sight of her gathering her long ebony hair into an impromptu twist with closed eyes. The sway of her hips as she approached the car's side door and the smile she gifted the driver dampened my palms. I continued my evening of bad decisions without a rational thought to the contrary, dashing across the street to gain her attention. I wanted a moment of her time, and perhaps, a tiny bit of her favor.

She was dropping her black leather shoulder bag to her side and preparing to climb into the backseat as I shouted her name. As if a divine entity had summoned her, she glanced skyward before scoping at street level. A touch of pity graced her almond-shaped eyes when she finally realized I was approaching at speed, without coat or shame.

"Serena?" I heard her say, lifting her purse back to her shoulder. "Are you all right?"

"Yes, sorry for interrupting your cab ride." I managed to reply, my breath calming as I skidded to a halt on my heeled boots. "If you're in a hurry, I can catch you Monday morning."

Her head shook twice, letting loose the nest of hair she'd tied back. It cascaded over her shoulders like an obsidian waterfall. "No, I'm in no hurry."

"Well, I am," the impatient cabby groused through the open passenger window. "You coming or what?"

My blood boiled at his crassness in the face of such beauty, but Su was unmoved. She simply exhaled, slammed the rear door closed, and stepped back onto the curb. Her voice, normally honeyed, was spiced with a touch of admonishment as she shouted through the same window. "Shame. I was about to tip you for your patience. I guess it's just not your night. Off you go."

A few obscenities and a gesture were left in the cabby's wake as he peeled away from the corner. A blast of horns echoed between the buildings as he swerved back into traffic, gunning it through a red light.

I saw Su's shoulders tremble in laughter as she tossed her hair back in the bitter wind. Once the spectacle had ended, her attention turned back to me. "I'm surely blackballed from that cab service. It's a good thing I so rarely need them."

"What made tonight different?" I asked, leading her aside and under the protection of a nearby awning. "Hot date downtown?"

The world spun a little slower as she laughed sweetly, revealing the slightest dimples alongside her lined lips. "Hardly, unless you consider a review of finances stimulating."

I checked my watch. It was a little after ten. "At this hour? That's inhumane."

Her face transformed into a sincere smile. "In Kyoto, it's midmorning tomorrow. My broker works all hours insofar as his commissions continue. It's been fruitful enough to merit these late nights. I only wish he hadn't needed a wet signature. This weather is abhorrent."

The three syllables that formed her hometown were uttered without a trace of an American inflection. I would've given anything to have her continue in her native tongue. She could've read from a Mesopotamian history book and I would've listened like my life depended on it.

"Ah," I managed, obnoxiously betrayed by the heat flooding my cheeks.

"I won't keep you, then. If you were planning on taking a cab, I can call on one for you. That driver may have already alerted the guys back at dispatch."

Su tugged leather gloves over her slender fingers, huddled against the building as another gale blew down the alley. "There's no need. I moved recently, into a loft just a few blocks from here. I'd considered dinner at Masa, but I've changed my mind. It'd be better if I headed home before the streets are impassable."

Masa was incredible, no question, but it wasn't worthy of Su's pedigree. The ramshackle storefront eatery served the best tamales in the area, but the scuffed folding chairs and plastic tables were beneath this exotic specimen who spent her evenings discussing finances in a designer pantsuit. I'm sure my face betrayed me again, but I kept my comments to myself.

"Probably smart, though the guajillo pico de gallo there is worth the cab fare, even on a night like this."

Really, Lizzie? This is the best you can do? Salsa talk?

"I'm partial to their mole, but this is hardly the weather for this chat."

I shook my head, glad for her intuition. "Very true. I was just surprised to see you out in the wild. I won't keep you any longer."

"I'll see you Monday at muster, Serena. You can borrow this in the meantime." From her shoulder bag, she swept out a bundle of plush fabric. After a quick handoff and a smile that should've been illegal, she turned her back and lifted her hood. She was gone, over the crosswalk and out of sight in the direction of AH's headquarters, before I managed to glance down at the trundle she'd left behind.

The cloth unrolled in my hands, revealing a waist-length cape of cashmere lined with panels of breathable vinyl in a matching shade of cobalt blue. The hood, also reversable, was trimmed with braided cord, as was the hem, beautifully holding the two layers together. I didn't see a maker's tag or any sign of its origin, but it was impeccably made and runway ready.

I pulled it on, the vinyl side out to reflect the sleet that had begun in the flakes' wake. The softness helped me forget the savage wind as a familiar scent enveloped me. It threw me backward through time.

Lilies.

Mom.

I closed my eyes, finding a meditative moment amidst the sounds of traffic and the hurried chatter of scurrying pedestrians. Transported back to her gravesite, I could feel the soft earth at my feet, the summer sun warming my skin, and the smooth finish of her headstone. The stethoscope etching above her name materialized in my mind's eye. Regret, sorrow, and guilt swept through me as bitter thoughts propelled me back to the present.

Whatcha gonna do, Lizzie? Cry about it? She's dead. She's been dead for decades. Everyone else has moved on. Penance isn't gonna come from her.

Tucking myself inside Su's cape, I wandered home mindlessly, forgetting every step of the journey when I found myself at the building's front stoop. As I touched the pull handle to the front door, I glanced upward.

"I'm sorry, Mom. I'll come see you. I promise."

Philadelphia, PA, 2015

February began on a balmy note, tempting the city dwellers with a taste of spring. The walk into work was a pleasant one, though I'd had to dig out a lightweight suit jacket from my warmer weather wear. The delay cost me ten minutes of valuable time, making my routine trip to the micro-roaster on 16th and Market impossible. I already felt the pull of caffeine withdrawal as I descended to The Red Room. Relief would have to wait until lunch. Tim Darren's idea of office coffee was simply unacceptable.

The elevator doors cracked open, revealing the dimly lit cylinder of our shared workspace. Finding my spoke of the wheel, I settled in among those who'd already arrived. We were all expected to be seated and working by eight. I was number fourteen this morning, though I was usually last. The fifteenth, yet unaccounted for, was Avery.

I analyzed his abandoned station. The monitors and CPU were powered down. I'd never seen him arrive late, and missing a day was out of the question for the overzealous programmer. I logged in, tucked in an earbud, and pulled up our in-house messaging app. I then doubled-clicked Vera's avatar.

For a reason beyond my comprehension, the two of them got along gangbusters. I, on the other hand, still hadn't forgotten her slight back in December and had no intention of forgiving it. Serena was habitually cordial, but no salutation preceded my question. That was the best I could manage.

Where's Avery?

I peeked across the ring to her desk and watched her eyes narrow on her monitor. Within seconds, a chime erupted in my ear.

`Upstairs. Ms. Saracco deigned to join us, then pulled him away ten minutes ago.`

I considered the motives of an HR intervention first thing in the morning. Only one made sense to me. I wasn't privy to all the details, but I imagined it had something to do with his suspicions and paranoia. Evidenced by his powered-down computer, he'd started his morning just as apprehensive as he ended them. The rest of us were content to lock our systems and change passwords when we stepped away from our workspaces. Avery was extra fearful, even compared to us wary folk.

I replied with quick fingers.

`More conspiracy theories?`

Vera's response took a little longer.

`Ad nauseum. He messaged all senior leadership. He's positive his space isn't safe. I almost pity Ms. Saracco. His deposition is going to be exhausting.`

I wondered if Vera's studiousness or pride was responsible for her being such a stickler about full names. Our CEO was "Drew" by preference, but if you asked the junior know-it-all, she'd tell you he was born Mr. Hightower and calling him anything else was "uncivilized." No one corrected her, not even top brass, so I simply rolled my eyes and typed out a reply.

`Deposition? Is he on trial?`

Her response was quick.

`Not yet.`

I'd reached the end of my patience with her evasive nonsense. I closed the conversation and pulled up the in-house email address book. The Philly office of AH consisted of only twenty. Fifteen of us were holed up in The Red Room. Our supervisor's office was adjoined to the circular space, though Blake rarely occupied it. He split his precious time between our Center City Red Room and the one at the Tucson office, strategically planning his trips during Philly's bitterest weeks. The only other names displayed were the biggies, namely Tsumugi Iruma, Joy Saracco, Drew Hightower, and Tim Darren.

Who would bother messing with his desk? The big wigs have access to our systems and network. I doubt he said anything to Blake. He's so freaked out that he went straight to the top. I mean, I would, but still.

As baffled as ever, I made a mental note to tap into his personal email and social media accounts when I got home. With every keystroke captured in this stronghold, my nefarious efforts waited until the workday was over.

The orb positioned in the center of our work circle began to glow, slowly increasing in brightness as it always did when a message was incoming. Gradually, every eye flicked from computer monitor to the globe until we all were focused on the spectacle. I fought the urge to call it indoctrination, but it certainly felt like it as my behaviors became increasingly compulsory.

Drew Hightower, in a suit of blue pinstripes, appeared with a jovial expression. His voice emerged in my earbud, a dulcet tone with a touch of New England accent clouding the edges. "Good morning and welcome to

Thursday morning. Today's muster is cancelled as senior leadership is occupied by unforeseen circumstances."

The boss's voice continued though I was no longer interested in the presentation. Every programmer was glancing around the circle, mystified and awestruck. Never in the history of the company had muster been cancelled, not even when a blizzard descended on the city the month before. On that blustery morning, I'd been one of only six to show up. So many absences meant the meeting took three minutes, but it was still held despite the lackluster attendance.

This was unprecedented and inexplicable. Foreseeing unforeseen circumstances, safeguarding against them, and reinforcing the company's outer walls were The Red Room's most important efforts. I tuned back in just in time to hear Drew's closing comments.

"Your leaders are investigating the circumstances. Rest assured that you will be informed at the first possible opportunity. Enjoy the unseasonable warmth and conquer the day!"

The globe dimmed as my earpiece fell silent. A second later, a new message displayed on my monitor, a pop-up from Blake. The Tucson office had the pleasure of his company this morning. As everyone else's eyes also flashed back to their screens, I realized Blake had summoned us all.

`Heads down. Find it.`

I snickered. Our manager was as awestruck, suspicious, and unconcerned about the CEO's commands to stand idle as we were. We all would've started digging even without permission being given. His orders removed culpability and set us free.

I speculated whether AH's venture clients knew anything or could've been the cause of the potential breach. While the others around me hunted through internal systems and online sources, I scoured the contracts, contacts, and correspondence between our investment recipients and our internal support staff. AH's Tucson office was the headquarters most of the world knew about, where these business ventures and their owners solicited AH's financial support. Wires went out of those corporate accounts, and the bulk of the business's marketing originated there. All I could do was tap into the repository and browse. My penchant for analyzing contracts and disclosures set me apart from my peers. I was equally capable of critiquing binary readouts, but those around me avoided the legalese I craved.

The best clues were almost always tucked away in the fine print. I'd survived my probationary period by proving that. A half-dozen venture relationships with AH had ended due to their exploitation of loopholes in their contracts. I'd been responsible for reviewing the behavior, then revealing it online, steering the public into believing our former clients were in the wrong. They'd been deceitful and manipulative, desecrating the best intentions of a company that only sought to help them. Sometimes they were guilty of exactly that, and sometimes the line between intent and action grew foggy. Either way, once I was done, the company had a much tougher time finding funding elsewhere.

Two hours passed before I heard the familiar bleep of an elevator's arrival. Fourteen sets of eyes glanced up as the doors slid open and Avery appeared, his pallor as incriminating as his pensive demeanor. He took his seat, placed his earbuds, and powered on his system. No speech was allowed. The room was monitored for sound by Blake ten states away. There were dozens of questions on our lips, but no one dared ask aloud.

As soon as he appeared online and active, his status was set to "do not disturb," barring any possibility of text correspondence with the most recent arrival. I chanced a glance in his direction, donning as sympathetic an expression as I could. He avoided my eyes, focused squarely on his central monitor.

By lunchtime, caffeine withdrawal caused a lightning storm between my temples. Reading fine print for hours hadn't helped. When I sat back and rubbed my face, I could still see endless lines of ten-point Courier New font behind my eyelids. I normally took a protein bar and a bottle of green tea to the park across the street during lunch, but today, I prayed that Supremo Caffe's line wouldn't be wrapped around the block. If I lucked out, I could make it there and back in the half-hour I was allotted.

These day-to-day restrictions on my freedom were only troublesome on days like this one. I could've made more money as a private contractor, accepting surreptitious tasks in exchange for cash and making my own schedule, but I'd learned more about white-collar crime and shady business dealings in the past two years than I'd ever imagined. I'd also been afforded clearance to AH's inner workings, plus those of every client they contracted. I was endlessly stunned at the truths revealed to me, at how nefarious some of these online businesses and transactions were, and how dark the corners of the web could be. I tiptoed down the line of ethics and made a handsome living doing it, all the while monitoring and watching for my idol's taps at the backdoor.

Serena pretended it was just a day job. Lizzie knew it was much more than that.

No wonder esTre11aN3gra *loves this. The corporate world's rife with greedy bastards. It's a veritable goldmine out there.*

I locked my computer down, left my meal bar and tea behind, and made for the elevator as soon as the globe projector's clock kicked off our lunchbreak. Two other nerds joined me, their frozen lunches in hand as their elevator ascended to street level. I buttoned my sage suit jacket and made for the front doors without pause, already tasting the smooth brew waiting patiently for me.

"Serena?"

I winced imperceptibly at the female voice over my shoulder. I knew the tone. We'd crossed paths and shared words a few times since that fateful night in December, but I still wasn't sure how to bridge the gap with her. Trying seemed too risky an endeavor.

I turned back with a resigned smile. "Su, what can I do for you?"

As she slid over to join me, wrapped in a pale blue crepe pantsuit, I couldn't help envying her grace and elegance. Tall and lean with a quiet smile and patient eyes, I could understand her proclivity in calming clients and human capital alike. Even her choice of perfume spoke of quiet confidence. I wasn't close enough to catch the scent of her skin, but I'd never forget it. The sweet floral aroma had lingered on the cape I'd regrettably returned the morning after we'd parted ways in the squall.

Her tone was light, but concern drew creases between her fine, charcoal brows. "You seem hurried. Is there an emergency?"

I tried my best to focus on her rather than the expeditious drumline playing between my ears. "It's nothing, really. I've got a massive caffeine headache."

"Then you're hoping to hit Supremo before the big boss calls you back to work. Only the best beans for you, am I correct?"

"Wow, I'm impressed you remembered," I managed, glancing at my smartwatch. "I'm down to twenty-four minutes, so if you'll excuse me."

"Of course, unless you'd like company on the journey?"

... Huh?

Barren of intelligent thought, I forced back the stammer. "I mean, you're more than welcome to. I'm just on a tight timetable. I'd hate to rush you."

A late model iPhone in a crystalline case was swept from her suit jacket's pocket. With swift thumbs, she tapped on the screen, then touched the lower corner with her index finger. I watched as the phone was deftly returned to its satin-lined home. Her tone took on a matter-of-fact quality, on par with my ritziest private clients back in Whitehall. "That's no problem. Once those messages are marked as read, you're officially on company business. Shall we?"

"Oh. Well, then, sure. And here, let me get that for you." I managed, sweeping the massive glass door of Anderson-Hilliance inward, letting in a warm blast of air and the sounds of bustling commotion from the street. "After you, Su."

"Thank you, Serena. Since we're on business, I finally get to use my new platinum corporate card." She leaned in ever so slightly as she passed by. "No solo espressos for us today."

The brush of her frame so close to mine instantly transported me back to Biddle's Buds, on the corner of Jackson and Everly, picking up an overpriced trundle of lilies destined to wilt alongside a desolate grave. My coffee cohort was a few strides away, down the front entries' stone stairs, before I regained my senses and followed behind like a dutiful schoolboy.

* * * * *

"When was that?" I asked, a caffe Americano in an upcycled paper cup cradled in my palms. We'd commandeered a simple iron table just outside Supremo's door, wiped clean and placed on the sidewalk a good three months before the store normally did. Though we'd arrived at peak lunch hour, the city streets were practically vacated now. Most office-dwellers were back to work while I fixated on my coffee break conspirator.

"Four years ago," Su replied. "Did you know he wears sleeve garters?"

My gaze narrowed. "Sleeve garters? Is it eighteen-ninety?"

Su's expression brightened instantly, a peal of sweet laughter ringing out. "He claims that his tailor purposefully stitches his sleeves too long to ensure he'll go back more often. As a show of defiance, he bought three sets of Italian sleeve garters in navy, black and white. He wears them so that his shirt cuffs show just enough when he shakes the dozens of hands he's presented daily."

I mused over the scuttlebutt about Tim Darren, breaking off a piece of the pistachio biscotti I'd chosen. "It makes sense, but only because Tim's such a character. Drew doesn't seem like the type to be so fussy."

"Tim's trying to sell Drew on them. I'm subjected to Tim's hem conspiracies and fashion advice at every meeting. It's grueling. I'm considering buying a set myself, writing Tim's name on the gift tag, and leaving it on Drew's desk. Drew has offered his own tailor's services, but Tim's relentless. It's quite sad, really."

"We all have our crosses to bear," I remarked, chancing a grin. I was relieved to see Su return it. I'd been carefully soliciting input on a variety of subjects over the last hour, searching out a safe median between Serena's naivete and Lizzie's sarcasm. Fortunately, Su was a natural conversationalist. Silence had only settled between us when sips or bites were taken from our company-paid lunch.

"Speaking of fashion," Su replied, dabbing a hunk of lemon poppy biscotti into her cup of Kenyan Reserve, then onto a napkin to avoid drips on her immaculate suit. "Has Joy exploited your talents yet?"

I shook my head. "No, though we did email a few months back. Our schedules haven't lined up. I thought I was busy, but she trumps me. If I may say so, you're very stylish. Perhaps you'd be better at assisting anyway."

"She's so monopolized because she's my sole HR business partner now. Leslie, the Arizona HR partner, moved on to greener pastures six months ago. Joy's holding down the fort while I seek out an honorable ally for her."

"Joy's responsible for you coming to AH, but she works for you?"

Su nodded primly, tossing her right knee over her left. "Indeed. Any more talk of former employment will violate my NDAs, so I'll instead ask about your employment. Your reviews and attendance are stellar, and your in-depth knowledge of contractual obligation is top-notch. Blake reports positively to senior leadership often. In truth, though, I'm more concerned with your work-life balance, your acclimation to Philadelphia, and your relations with your peers. Care to provide some feedback for the good of the organization?"

Sure, butter me up, then get me to dish. Now, how would goody-two-shoes Serena play this?

"Philly's fine. The work keeps us siloed, but it's part of the job. Programmers spend more time in cyberspace than outside in the real world, after all."

"You missed your calling in public relations for the government," she told me before sipping her coffee with the subtlest lift of a crescent brow. "Maybe Father would hire you to write his press releases. He's always looking for aseptic, guarded, and nebulous responses to genuine questions."

Um. Damn.

I leaned forward, a tiny, appreciative grin on display. "Wow, no wonder AH only recruits the finest. You don't take it from anyone, do you?"

"I have a reputation to uphold. Will knowing a bit more about me make this easier? I like artisan coffee, quality clothing, high-dollar cosmetics, and plush bedding. Otherwise, I'm just an unattached workaholic. I like simple things. I can't deny an obsession with Tex-Mex and sourdough bread. I've attended a few concerts with Drew. And here we are, enjoying fair trade coffee, biscotti, and discussion about nothing. I'd hoped you'd be more open about your employment and experiences, but if it will take time to grow accustomed to the business world's demeanor, you coming straight from college and a quieter existence, I understand."

Oh, I already know plenty about you, Tsumugi, and about the business world's demeanor, as you put it. You're getting sexier by the second.

I slapped on a shy smile. "I appreciate your asking, don't get me wrong. You're the CXO. I just wasn't sure you cared about a minion's day-to-day doings, and an uninteresting minion at that."

Her face shifted into contemplation for a split second, then back to its neutral, welcoming expression. "I wouldn't consider you uninteresting. That jacket is last-season McQueen, and fierce, by the way. You listen to nothing but hard rock, Joy has all her chips piled on you, and your online dating profile's impressive and apparently very popular. All those things are interesting."

I've been "researched." Curious.

My own hypervigilance in investigating AH was woefully outdone by the company's effort to hide its transgressions. I'd found very few strings to pull in my two-plus years under their roof. It wasn't farfetched to imagine the seniors of the company were more talented in online reconnaissance than entire government organizations. They'd known enough to find and recruit us. They knew enough to draw up those employment contracts. They knew enough to take retina scans and fingerprints surreptitiously. I'd put in more time with AH than I'd anticipated, but the operation captivated me. I didn't mind the delay, especially if it meant sharing an hour with Su.

I finished off my Americano and replaced the lid. "I'm glad you find me so fascinating. I'm not breaking any rules being on dating sites, as far as my employment contracts go. I did make it through the Online Presence document before going completely cross-eyed."

"I'm sure you read every word of every document. Your team is unparalleled, but you are stellar among them, Serena. I surmise you were meeting a potential suitor on that blustery December night?"

I nodded. "I was. A few drinks, mindless chatter about his family business, and a split check. At least I didn't have to pay for every drink that night. Avery was kind enough to pick up one for me. I guess my blind date was traumatic to onlookers as well."

"Avery," Su repeated, lifting her squat cup. "Three seats down from you, yes?"

I nodded again. "He's arguably the most social of us all. I can't remember a Friday afternoon when he hasn't solicited everyone for after-work drinks. Only a few ever take him up on it, and those who go know he's a check-grabber."

"You're self-sufficient, so you must've met there by happenstance."

"I have no desire to spend a lot of time with Avery. He loves drama, but his brand of it irritates me a little more with each passing minute."

Su's lips turned up at the corners. "There's one in every office. That drama tends to flourish in workspaces."

I released a breath, leaning over the table and lowering my tone a bit. "No worries there. The drama is illogical obsession. No one downstairs believes in his conspiracies. Our office is more secure than the Pentagon. If anyone tampered with anything, they'd either trigger the perimeter sensors during off-hours or the noise detection systems, or both. Spending too much time absorbed in computer work can warp your mind. I'm sure you know a few who've lost themselves in the web. It happens all the time."

Su sighed with a nod of her own. "I've had to terminate a few. That's why I take time to discuss work-life balance and to prioritize our human capital. I'd hate to see concerns like his create an office of suspicion when a simple conversation and logical thought can absolve the entire situation. It seems we agree on that approach."

"Why did he end up in HR this morning? Did he bring his concerns upstairs?"

"Oh, that I can't say," she replied after tipping back her coffee cup to drain it. "We all signed contracts and there's HR law to take into consideration."

That's a yes, then.

"Oh, well, I doubt his concerns will amount to anything. His desk chair being moved or his computer being tampered with just isn't possible. A few of us have told him so. I hope, whatever's wrong with him, he gets it sorted out. He's the best Java engineer I've ever met. I know it probably doesn't mean much to you, but he skipped right over Python and went straight into Java, too. That's no easy feat."

"I'm not familiar with the finer points of your work, but I will follow up with Joy. Thanks for your transparency." Su rose slowly. "Now, let's get back to the office. Should anyone ask about your extended lunch, feel free to give them as much or as little information as you see fit."

"I won't be telling them anything," I confirmed, standing, and pushing in both our chairs. "I'd rather them guess how I got away with it. Just because I don't water the grapevine doesn't mean I don't enjoy watching it grow."

"Of course," Su replied, donning a smile as we began the trek back to AH headquarters under the mid-afternoon sun.

Undisclosed, 2022

My forearm throbbed. It rested on the desk beside my wireless keyboard. The white letters on the silicone were faded out of existence, proof that the past months had been a ceaseless maelstrom for my clients and myself. I was receiving press releases, social media posts, and website updates from them all now, sometimes multiple per day, as their popularity and their families grew exponentially. A few golden trophies and glossy photos of their baby bassinettes made them household institutions.

Aren't I the hipster, being a true fan and loyal listener years before all these newbs?

With a scathing chuckle, I took a long pull from the room temperature coffee to my right. I kept typing, my fingers knowing the keys though their labels were long gone. I'd learned complex coding over the past year, a product of necessity, not enthusiasm. So many websites were easily commandeered and overwritten despite their reputed safety measures. Java was now the fifth language in my repertoire. Behind the scenes, I was privy to the kinds of knowledge of which online advertisers dreamed.

The biggest scuttlebutt sites used simple underwriting. A surreptitious program delivering a four-oh-four error to some hapless user for five seconds bought me enough time to load in my tampered content and make a clean getaway before the internet noticed a thing. Blissfully unaware and riddled with non-existent attention spans, consumers had no patience to file issues with webmasters for errors that came and went in mere moments. On their next attempt, they were accessing the page, and I was escaping out the back door, complete with a robber's sack, the kind emblazoned with dollar signs, slung over my shoulder and a grin on my lips.

Accessing private sites and accounts required a bit of artistry. The world had access to VPNs, encryption software, and multi-level authentication everywhere they did business. Underhanded tactics were called for when nameless monsters, hiding behind their computer screens, insulted or threatened my clients. My time in the private sector taught me that no one plays fair, especially not those who stay relevant in the tech industry for long. It was an unfortunate side effect of capitalism. The top dog gets the kibble while the lowly mutt starves to death. Cracking evened the playing field.

Encryption wasn't just for emails anymore. Cell phone text validation was an unforgiving bitch to circumnavigate. It took me almost a year to sort it out. After much trial and error, I was now capable of manipulation with the major cell carriers. Hardware, the physical phone in the customer's hand, was impossible to hijack. Software and apps were another story. If I could duplicate and reroute a text message by tapping into their account remotely, my capabilities remained intact.

Who would know their one-time code was sent to more than one person?

Obliviousness and misplaced trust continued to sideline logic, making my day job easy enough to perform on autopilot when sleep took a back seat to obligation. I'd managed less than twelve hours of meaningful rest in four days. The painkillers wore off before I could get comfortable in bed.

Persistent heartbeats just under the makeshift bandages kept my mind preoccupied, even when I was too exhausted to get up for more pills.

I'd rewrapped the war wound earlier in the day, frustrated to see the laceration refusing to bind together. The gouge was a dry but deep, angry crimson chasm, so I stayed the course, applying the recommended cream, wrapping it tight, and dosing myself with ibuprofen to dull the ache. I'd momentarily considered revealing my delivery pilot's identity in exchange for a few narcotics. Whether it was persistence or stubbornness to blame, I'd dismissed that idea in short order.

I was elbow deep in a news outlet's programming now, scrubbing potentially damning articles and replacing them with advertisements for weight loss supplements. A struggle with post-partum depression meant one of my clients was spending a few nights in a mental health facility. The world was captivated by her silent battle. Speculation on her mental state swirled like a category five hurricane. The bags under my eyes detailed the effort it had taken to remove any trace of truth and supposition from the public eye. Her husband, a comedy writer and actor, had also assigned his social media accounts and online presence responsibilities to me so I could coordinate the attack. Managing the workload despite the sudden influx convinced me that I'd oversee their accounts long after she was released from treatment.

I bet the others are devastated for her. She's fortunate to have support like theirs.

I sat back and rubbed my eyes. If work ever slowed down, I might find the time to feel lonely again. For now, a second of misplaced focus meant my livelihood was in danger, as was theirs.

An incoming call thrusted me out of autopilot. On the screen, my client's name flashed. The brilliant Middle Eastern bassist and the big boss's second-in-command was waiting for a video chat. Over the past five years, I'd allowed my customers to see my face on the rarest of occasions. She must've had good reason to reach out. She was a habitual emailer.

I lifted the phone, debated answering the summons, but then considered how easy she made my life. Perennially cordial and admirably patient, she was the best of the five. Channeling what little Serena was left inside me, I swiped a finger across the screen and centered the camera on my face.

"Good morning, Boss Number Two."

"Good evening," she corrected sweetly, her effervescent smile on full display. She was seated in front of a picture window I recognized immediately. I'd secretly lived in that home's basement for a short time and had managed to sneak upstairs for a quick, private tour during my stint as their resident shut in. "I'm checking on the patient. Your primary care physician is occupied."

"Oh, I know," I replied with disdain. "I've got six work orders with her name on them. Is she trying to work me to death since I refused medical care?"

"I can see how you'd think so, but no. She's just a workaholic. Simon's en route to Haven. I'll ask him to intervene. You need a little reprieve."

"You're telling me," I grumbled, lifting my wounded arm into view. "Is this why you called?"

She nodded pertly. "I need to see the damage. Is there any tingling, heat, or pus in the area?"

"No, not really, and ick, in that order," I replied, unfurling the bandage to reveal the two-inch slit in my skin. "I'm following orders, keeping it clean and all, but it's distracting. The overtime is no problem. This damn thing keeps me up when I lay down, though."

Her lips curved downward slightly. "Rate the pain from one to ten for me."

"Right now, with ibuprofen in my system, it's a four. When the meds wear off, it jumps to a six or seven. I can feel my heartbeat in it all the time."

"How much ibuprofen are you taking?"

"Twelve, sometimes sixteen a day. I think they're the two hundreds."

"Jesus," she murmured. "That needs to stop. You're already a quick bleeder. Your liver is weeping for mercy."

"So's my waking mind. Stopping pain meds is out of the question."

My impromptu physician sighed in frustration, the exact same derisive tone her boss had tossed my way days before. "And you won't acquiesce to proper medical care?"

"If and when all other options are ineffective, I might consider it. It's a two-day hike to the nearest medical facility, and it's a remote care station for outdoorsy types, not a proper hospital."

"When's your next drop shipment?"

"Ten days from today."

"Have you used a saline wash on it yet?"

"No, just gentle soap and water, per the doc."

"When we're done here, boil a gallon of water for no less than five minutes. While it's warm, add two cups of salt to it. Once it's cooled to body temperature, dip a clean cotton cloth in it. Wrap your arm. Let it sit for twenty minutes. Remove it carefully and let your arm air-dry. Repeat that process three times a day for the next three days. In between treatments, keep the bandage lightly wrapped and don't use ointment."

"I assume I have to boil the water again between treatments."

"That's not necessary. Keep it in a sealed, sanitized container. We'll try this first. Plan B is much less pleasant."

"What's Plan B involve?"

"Pineapple. A lot of it."

"I'm sorry, what?"

She chuckled, tossing back her mane of chocolate hair. "We're too late for stitches. The wound may need debriding. A waystation's medical facility won't have the surgical equipment. It'll be on you. Enzymatic debridement isn't ideal. It's a last resort if this saline treatment doesn't work."

"Pineapple, huh? Are you hoping the bromelain in it will eat away the scabby parts?"

The doctor nodded again. "I'd send you silver sulfadiazine cream, but you won't let me. We'll try saline first. Managing the healing is priority one."

"Thanks," I replied meekly. "I really hate being such a burden."

A loving smile brightened her amber eyes. "You're important to us all. We can't have you suffering in no man's land."

"You know, for the record, you're the best client I've ever had."

Her smile shifted into a polite laugh. "I imagine that's true. I see a need for work-life balance. The boss doesn't care about asinine things like that."

"The word 'pedantic' comes to mind."

"She's been called worse," the caller told me. "But thank you. What do you need from us?"

Huh?

"Um, well," I stammered, reclining in my office chair. "Other than a day to rest, which I'll never get, nothing. I'm good."

Her camera angle shifted as she lowered her phone to her lap. "I'm messaging Simon now. You've got one more day to suffer through. Will you make it?"

I sighed pathetically. "I guess."

"Good girl," she told me, lifting the phone again to center her face in frame. "Next week, I'll have releases for you. We're visiting family first. I'm telling you now so you can watch the web before it's officially announced. I'm expecting. I'm only nine weeks along, but it'll get out eventually."

My stomach clenched instinctively. Good news for her meant more work for me. "I'll monitor the usual suspects. Give me precise timelines for revealing the intimate details."

"You know I will. I do have one question for you, though, before I sign off."

"And that is?"

"Are you okay?"

Wow, she is one hell of a diagnostician. No wonder she kills it in pediatrics.

Genuine concern haunted her expression, the kind an overworked mother would show for their latchkey tween. I recognized the delivery and the intention. It'd been years since I'd seen that kind of consideration. Lying felt petty, so I gave the most truthful answer I could manage.

"I can't complain."

"Sure, you can," she told me. "Your best client is asking, after all."

It was my turn to laugh. "Damn, that came around to bite me, didn't it?"

"It always does. Now, are you okay?"

"I mean, sure. I'm happy here. I've got the life I always wanted. I manage myself and only answer to those I respect. Loads of people are way worse off."

"Understood, but I'm asking you. I'm not asking loads of people. I'm asking you, our brilliant social media manager and online recovery specialist. I'm asking the one who happens to be on our minds constantly."

"'Our' minds?"

"I speak for all of us. I'm better at the 'mushy stuff,' apparently. I just need you to know one thing."

"And that is?"

She exhaled slowly, fixing that intense gaze on the camera once again. "We're not your bosses. We're more like your team. You're more of a manager than you may realize. You carry a bigger burden than we do in lots of ways. We report to you. You run the show in ways we never will. You're our ringer, our ninth-inning closer, and our entire cyber security system. You work miracles so we can sleep soundly. Do you get that?"

I felt the edges of my eyelids burn as I fought back a flood of surging emotions. I wanted to argue, to say I'd be trapped in a tiny cell and wishing for death if not for their largesse. Instead, I landed squarely on a single word reply.

"Yes."

"Good," she replied, her eyes softening from insistence to sweetness again. "I'm signing off. One of us will call you in three days. Make sure you answer. If you scare the boss, there'll be hell to pay."

"Don't I know it."

"Take care of yourself," she told me before the connection cut.

I sat forward, laying my elbows on the desk and rubbing my stinging eyes. This melancholy should've been drummed out of me by now. Despair was so passé. Besides, I had work to do. Their sweet dreams were my responsibility.

You wanted this. You worked for it. Handle it.

Philadelphia, PA, 2015

The first week of March ushered in yet another nor'easter, the fourth of the year. The radical shifts from sixty-degree Mondays to five-degree Fridays had my immune system in a stranglehold. Working endless overtime in The Red Room didn't help. We'd been inundated for weeks. AH's client list burgeoned with online personalities and eCommerce entities. Zinc supplements were a food group in my diet. I wasn't shocked when the metal detector at the train station beeped as I passed through.

"Your bag, ma'am," the jaded security drone uttered to my right.

Ma'am? Ugh.

I swept off my charcoal Coach backpack and whirred the zipper back. The ogre in the wrinkled uniform spared a two-second glance inside, then waved me through. Masses of waiting commuters huddled on metal benches in parkas and knit caps. Breath escaped their lips in gray wisps as a line of sleek silver cars swept down the tunnel and disappeared into the dark cavern beyond. The squeal of metal wheel on rail lingered even after the train was gone from sight.

I tugged my hood back to read the overhead sign. The blue grid's text read, "Arrived, Back Bay Station, Track Two."

Shit. How are the Boston trains are on time today?

Jefferson Station's lower level was a tangled web of overlapping train tracks and bustling travelers ferrying bags and toddlers in their arms. I hustled down an escalator, brushing past two middle-aged women in far less of a hurry. I rounded the bottom of the revolving staircase and came face to face with my college friend. His long arms crossed over his chest, bundled snugly under a heavy black wool peacoat with pearlized buttons. He was obnoxiously and flamboyantly perturbed, a scowl tugging up the corner of his lip, but I saw through it. With perennially ruddy cheeks and eyes like moss, I found him jolly no matter how grumpy he tried to look.

"Thanks for showing up," he scoffed. "I wouldn't have been worried if *someone* answered her damn text messages, ever."

I puffed out a breath and tossed my arms over his shoulders. "For God's sake, you were due in ten minutes ago and I was running the whole way. Cut me a break."

"Never," he murmured, hugging me back. "That's not my style, darling."

"Don't I know it. You look good. Is that coat Armani?"

He smirked with an impudent shrug. "Of course. I am a senior VP now, I'll have you know."

I'd been guiding him upstairs, but turned back on the escalator step, my mouth agape. "The a-hole finally promoted you! When were you planning on telling me that?"

"Just now," he replied easily. "I figured we could celebrate Philly-style, maybe with a cheesesteak and a brew someplace. Nothing special."

"Oh, give it a rest. *Nothing special.*" I rolled my eyes, stepping off the escalator and taking his arm. "Nonsense. We're going all out tonight. Unless this little promotion is because you finally put out, in which case, I'll need all the details before we go anywhere."

He chuckled, planting a peck on my cheek. "Anything for you, dearest. Good thing I packed my new Givenchy smoking jacket. Wait until you see this beauty. Crimson. Silk. Lapels."

"God, you're fabulous," I told him as we strolled to the baggage pick-up.

* * * * *

The three-thousand-dollar onyx jacket was every bit as incredible as Bryan promised. Whether he'd meant to draw every onlooker's jealous gaze or not, he certainly did as we strolled into Fouquet's grand chamber. The illustrious French eatery was a two-story square. A balcony trimmed in golden fencing overlooked the main dining room below. In the very center of the opulent space was a rectangular bar made of French oak, shined to a gleam, and bordered with tufted cobalt stools. Above the Saturday night jubilance, oil paintings in gilded frames hung from invisible wire, many of them replicas of the fifteenth-century portrait paintings that made the restaurant's namesake famous.

I'd chosen an ensemble from my I-wish-I-was-Emmi-Vendetta collection, a silk brocade bustier trimmed with Belgian lace, under a trim black pencil skirt suit. I'd opted for a pocket square of crimson silk, matching Bryan's lapels and my stiletto pumps flawlessly. I'd nearly broken my ankle walking from our rented Range Rover's valet spot to the restaurant's maître d', but the peanut gallery's fascination with our arrival more than made up for the momentarily slip and subsequent embarrassed giggle.

If not for his flamboyance, we may have passed for a power couple. Instead, we looked every bit the affluent chums we were.

Seated along the balcony's west edge, Bryan and I settled in for a seven-course tasting menu, one I'd heard was a bucket list item for elite gourmands. My buddy's achievement was worth the effort it had taken to finagle the Saturday evening table. The eatery was booked out twelve months in advance, but that was no reason to dine elsewhere. I outmaneuvered the restaurant's reservation system, supplanting a state representative and his wife's names with our own. I hoped he'd remember his station and his reputation when he arrived at the front desk to find himself suddenly and inexplicably without the reserved space he'd called to confirm the day before.

Our evening began with a bottle of champagne. Before long, I was beginning to see familiar faces in the ancient paintings. I no longer had a college kid's tolerance, and I hadn't been on a bender since the move to Philly. I blinked back the dots of fuzz that haunted my peripheral vision and shrugged my heavy shoulders.

"This is incredible. The Back Bay crowd's gonna weep with envy," Bryan uttered from his side of the table. He was busy scanning and memorizing the eatery's every detail. "You are a miracle worker, *Serena.*"

The inflection on the last word made me snort. "I try. Tell me about this new role. Are you still reporting to the dickhead?"

"Oh, he's all but done running the show. He finally decided to delegate since we're taking finance houses as clients. Three SVPs now run the whole place. This buttoned-up bore, Lynette, runs the personnel side, Boston

College grad and unfortunate dalliance of mine, Peter, runs the operations side, and I'm heading up the cyber security and access departments. Remember my former intern, the one from years ago? He's my lead. And before you get your pretty little panties in a bunch, he's married. To a woman. And he's not queer."

"Give him time," I retorted, lifting my water glass of Arctic spring water.

"Hah. So, yes, Midas is still a shitshow, but I have a company car, a housing stipend so I can live closer to work, and a handsome travel allowance. I'm finally in your leagues, sweet stuff. Oh, and if anyone asks, we're 'consulting' right now."

"Got it. And you'll lap me in no time. I haven't gotten a penny more in the past two years. My rent's up three hundred bucks and I'm wearing, gasp, last season off-the-rack to the office."

Bryan lifted a dramatic palm to his forehead and tipped back in his seat. "Oh, no. That hurts my little heart. What are you learning in exchange for this incredible sacrifice?"

"So much."

The server, dressed in an immaculate burgundy tailcoat, delivered two round plates trimmed in silver. "And for the pair, Chef Henri presents *canard à la rouennaise.*"

Grateful for the opportunity to flex my French muscle, I smiled to the server. "*Merci bien, et je voudrais plus d'eau, s'il vous plaît.*"

The server's brows drew together.

With a sigh, I gestured to the etched carafe on the table. "The same brand, please."

The server bowed curtly and retreated. Bryan rolled his eyes at me. "You're in Philadelphia, *Mademoiselle.* Calm your tits."

"This is the classiest and priciest French restaurant east of the Mississippi, and the servers can't speak the language?"

"You just can't help being a hoity twat, can you?"

I snickered and lifted my fork. The petite portion of duck on my plate was crowned in a golden sauce that smelled faintly of warm liquor and brass. Sometimes it was better to not know what a French chef considered a delicacy. With a shrug, I used the heaviest table knife I'd ever held to cut the three-inch filet in half.

"So, back to business," Bryan interjected, segmenting his meal into bites. "What have you managed to find? For example, is there anything about a certain black star in their books?"

"Less than I'd hoped, but the company is more vigilant than any others are or would even think to be. There must be a reason for that."

Bryan considered my words and the flavor of his food, his curled lip portraying hesitance on both accounts. "With the millions in payroll they're pumping into The Red Room, there's gotta be something they're hiding."

Bryan was the only soul outside AH's network that knew my office's moniker. Any eavesdropping ears would assume such a place was a brothel based on the context. Overpaid hookers in a velvet-wrapped lounge made more sense than the truth, anyway.

"We're protecting the place at every turn. The hatches are tightened a little more every day. Last month, the big boss called us to arms. Well, not exactly, but we can't sit by when there's an undisclosed threat. Every hired eye was scouring. No muster means big trouble. There were no breaches. There were no weak spots to exploit, let alone any cause to think there was. The explanation from Drew was some bullshit about ransomware."

"I remember that. You called me that night. He seriously thought you'd all believe it was ransomware?"

I shook my head, lifting a bite to my lips. "The black star was silent that day. I just know there's shit to find. I'm not lucking out. Maybe they're striking out with AH, too."

"You said you made a little progress with some internal drives."

"I got into the email server and saw some back-and-forth between the execs, but nothing damning. Our muse hasn't been mentioned once, by anyone, anywhere I've been able to look."

"There's no way this is a dead end," Bryan insisted, poking at the remnants on his plate. "*N3gra* is hard at work. I'd bet this jacket on it. If you're seriously not finding anything sketchy in their network, is something else going on?"

"What, like the company paid them off?"

"Either that, or our little star had a change of heart and just isn't interested in big business shenanigans anymore."

We both fell silent before erupting into laughter. The table beside us glanced over with contempt, but the server ferried over our water refill before I could return their scathing glare.

We sat idly, talking shop and feeling rich for two hours. Each course presented was as illustriously intricate as the last. Cheese cask-aged longer than I'd been alive, crackers made from Andalusian wheat, and berries topped with a pale green glaze reminiscent of Christmas trees made appearances. Bryan had also been a shade of green when the server explained the duck course's origin. It had been slaughtered in-house, then braised in its own blood. Perhaps he'd have enjoyed a greasy sandwich more, but I was determined to celebrate his success and burn through his expendable income while we were young enough to enjoy it.

I foisted the bill on Bryan. His trust fund and new pay rate dwarfed my income. He scoffed at me but wordlessly tucked his corporate card plus four twenties for gratuity into the leather bifold. I lifted a squat porcelain cup filled with pitch black magic while he handled the pleasantries. A single sip told me the espresso was a South Pacific varietal, its bitterness exquisitely roasted and brewed out of existence.

Bryan had spent the downtime in our conversation peering over the rail. He'd already called my attention to a blonde gold digger and her geriatric bedfellow, a server catching his coattails on a table's edge and nearly pulling the cloth from under the dishes, and a peculiar stain left on the marble flooring after a passionate couple departed. I was proud to give him an evening of unabashed people-watching, a hobby he'd fostered for decades. I observed him affectionately, a potent dose of caffeine nestled in my fingers, as he critiqued the clientele along the illustrious bar's edge. This was the closest thing to heaven that I'd ever find.

"What's her deal?"

I followed his gaze to the bar's far corner. On the stool perched a lean female frame, clad in a long sheath dress, pure white and with a slit to the knee. Her back was to me, but the towering slingback heels, silver cashmere pashmina tossed over one shoulder, and the fluted highball of brown liquor in her manicured hand spoke volumes. A mane of black silk flowed down over the shawl, twisting and creping as she tipped her head toward the gent seated to her left.

"Hmm," I replied in a murmur. "Classy, and honestly so. There's no flash there. It's pure confidence."

"Daring, but subtle," he added, sipping the pristine vodka-laden tonic water he'd ordered. "I imagine she's a lawyer's wife, or a wealthy hotelier's side piece. A white dress in weather like this is a show of prowess. What practical woman wears cashmere in a squall?"

I smiled at his passive judgement. The words weren't spiked with malice but were far from breezy. I was glad for such a magnificent cup of coffee. All the bitterness I could tolerate was ebbing off Bryan. Faced with any more resentment, I'd succumb to jealousy, too.

"Oh, sweetie," I cooed. "You'll find some rich, terminally ill sugar daddy someday. I have faith."

"I have credit debt and misplaced youth. You're the 'hot one,' remember?"

Vera's snipe from the year before came tumbling back to me. I snorted derisively. "I'm not interested. I went on enough pointless and demeaning dates to show sincere effort in finding a mate. Being done with dating is an appropriate reaction. No red flags here."

"But what about Lizzie?"

"She's fine. A crush is enough to sustain her for a long time. That, and a toy or two, of course."

"Of course," he mimicked, turning back to the crowd below.

The server returned, ushering us from our observation spot as the crowd in the restaurant's atrium burgeoned. We vacated the table, making our way downstairs on protracted steps. A few heads turned in our direction and Bryan winked at a few, a brazen move befitting his newfound success. I giggled as we rounded the base of the grand staircase, strolling past the bar toward the exit.

"Serena?"

I froze on the spot. That same voice, the one that haunted my dreams, was again sneaking its way into my ear. It shook me as I turned to its origin. There, at the corner of the bar, in that white sheath dress and plush wrap, was Anderson-Hilliance's crown jewel.

"Su," I responded, wandering in her direction and tugging Bryan unwittingly along with me. "What a pleasant surprise. You look incredible."

"You as well. Who is this stunning gentleman?"

Bryan stepped up alongside and offered his source of envy a curved palm. "Bryan, my love. I'm her fashionista friend from Back Bay. That shawl is fantastic. Is it designer?"

Su shook his palm gently, as she'd done with mine years before. "It's artisan. An acquaintance visited Kashmir in December and brought it back for me. I've been searching for an excuse to display it. That jacket makes quite a statement, you know. You two are a stunning pair."

Bryan, oblivious to her compliment, wilted just a touch, imperceptibly to outsiders but unmistakable to his closest ally. I knew the sting of envying handcrafted items, the ones that couldn't be reproduced, no matter how hard the drive. I also knew the cost of such an import and the value of it as a gift.

I accepted the compliment for him and glanced at the gent to her left. "Thank you, and this is?"

The ordinary business crony with a mop of ashy hair turned at the sound of my voice. He smiled, but Su spoke before he could. "Oh, we just met. This is Stuart. I snuck in beside him, and he was kind enough to hold my seat while I took a call."

Stuart nodded once and turned back to his drink, his cheeks like a glowing ruby in the restaurant's ambient lighting.

"Are you celebrating this evening?" Su asked jovially. "It certainly seems so."

I turned to my friend, taking his bicep in my hands. "This one was just promoted after years of tireless service. I figured he could afford a meal like this to celebrate."

When she smiled, I felt Bryan's arm tighten. His words were kind but curt. "It was all her idea. I would've been happy with a cheesesteak."

"You loved every minute, even the duck bathed in its own juices." I argued sweetly.

He winced a little and touched his belly. "Don't remind me. I'm sneaking off to the little girls' room. Be back in a jiff."

Once I released his arm, he dashed toward the shadowed hallway by the kitchen door. I turned back to Su once he disappeared. "That's a shame. I figured he'd appreciate French cuisine."

"*Oui, c'est dommage.*"

I smiled in appreciation. "It is indeed a shame, and I didn't know you spoke French."

"I know you do," Su replied easily after setting her glass on the bar. "French, Spanish and American Sign, if I'm not mistaken."

"Did you memorize my resumé?"

Her grin could've melted an iceberg. "I have my mother's memory and my father's business acumen. It's quite fortuitous. How have you been since we last spoke?"

You're as eloquent and stunning as ever, Su.

"A bit stymied and overworked, but I'm glad to have Bryan here. Blake assured me I won't be called back to the salt mines until Monday morning. I was ready to turn off my phone a few days ago."

Su soured. "I was concerned about this very thing. When I ask others, I'm told all's well and their workload is manageable. I, again, appreciate your transparency."

"I'll always be honest," I told Su with a straight face.

Watch lightning strike me dead right here.

"I am grateful for that. I'll take measures Monday to ensure some normalcy returns. We're bound to lose even more of you should this continue."

Her fears were well-founded. In the past month, we'd lost six of the fourteen souls seated around me in The Red Room. Replacing them at all, let alone quickly, was nigh impossible. With only nine of us left, we felt like Atlas, schlepping the Earth around on our backs. I wasn't all that shocked to hear I was the only one willing to say so to the CXO.

"That would be helpful, but we know how important our roles are and that any inconvenience is temporary. Besides, Blake's considering letting us work from home when we're on call. I'll believe it when I see it."

"It seems he and I have some discussions ahead of us. This is work talk, though, and we're both off the clock. Perhaps you'd be willing to discuss this further on Monday morning? I can meet you at Supremo at seven-fifteen. It's become a morning requirement for me as well."

It's not a date. She's your boss. Breathe.

"Absolutely," I managed, tucking my hands behind my back. "I'll be there."

"Excellent. I hope you won't mind the company on the walk to work. I'd hate to intrude on what little private time you manage these days."

I was unable to avoid the baited hook. Hell, I wanted it. "I'd be honored."

Her gaze lifted over my shoulder. "Ah, your gentleman returns," she told me, eyeing Bryan as he returned to my side. "I hope you two enjoy your evening and your time together tomorrow."

"Thank you, Su," I replied, taking Bryan's elbow. "Get home safe."

"Be careful," she told me, then spun on her stool. For the briefest moment, the scent of blooming lilies permeated my soul as her hair whipped over her shoulder.

I stood silently, my eyes on the back of her head for what felt like hours before Bryan tugged me toward the door. "Off we go, kiddo. Where to next?"

Snapping back to reality, I plastered on a smile. "There's a queer club on Chancellor that's right up your alley. You want to go hit on some twenty-somethings, buy them a bunch of drinks, watch them hook up with someone else, and then go home together?"

"You know me so well."

*****

Midnight was a memory as we stumbled through my apartment's door. My houseguest had insisted on a hotel, but I'd insisted he save his cash for our shopping spree Sunday. If I had my way, he'd triumphantly return to Back Bay with thousands of dollars in designer duds.

Starting the night with champagne and ending it with whiskey was a rookie move. A haunting headache plagued me already, wrapping twisted fingers to the back of my skull and squeezing mercilessly. I wanted a shower, but ended up taking more of a bath, perched on the ledge of the tub while Bryan threw up every ounce he'd imbibed into the adjacent toilet.

An hour later, I'd made it to my twin bed, jammed alongside my computer setup in my quasi-office, but not before crushing my toe against the metal leg of the frame. That jolt sobered me up just enough to tuck myself in. Once the throbbing stopped, the rest of the night passed in a blink.

When I regained consciousness, I smelled coffee. Faint beams of sunshine illuminated the backside of my blinds. The day had begun without my say-so in the matter.

I managed to swing my feet to the floor and stand without descending face first onto the trampled carpeting. With a wince and a sway, I wandered out into the living room. Bryan was gripping the kitchen counter, arched like a question mark, fading in and out while the percolator bubbled three feet from his face. Laying a palm on his shoulder jerked him to life with a squeal.

"Oh, Lord, don't take me now!"

I chortled. "Good morning, precious. Go have a seat. I got this."

With an undead groan, he wobbled down the hall. I heard the bathroom door close and the familiar sounds of heaving as the coffee pot fell silent. I found a second mug tucked in the back of the cabinet, poured us both some limited-edition Sulawesi, and wandered in his direction.

The ungodly gurgles through the wooden door gave me pause. Rather than interrupt the abstract artist painting the inside of a porcelain bowl, I set the coffees down on my desk, dampened a dish towel with cold water, and returned to my office chair. I'd be ready for a forehead mop job whenever he managed to swallow again.

Sipping on the dark roast, I wiggled the mouse. I was astonished to see I was logged in, a watchdog website on display. Detailed was the destructive path of righteousness *esTre11aN3gra* had left behind the day before. An investment firm's dirty laundry was on full display, their CEO and CIO on blast for insider trading. The vigilante had also managed to corner and then expose a Massachusetts-based in-home nursing care company's misdeeds. Elder abuse, specifically financial exploitation, joined reports of neglect, false licensing, and labor law violations.

Yikes. They were on a tangent while I was up to my elbows in pretention, flirting with my boss and eating out of her hand like a parakeet.

Bryan joined me a few minutes later. I initiated a software security scan and swiveled my chair to watch him stagger to my side, collapse to the floor in a heap, and rest his chin on my knee. As sympathetically as I could, nursing a massive hangover myself, I swept the cool cloth over the nape of his neck. "You gonna make it, trooper?"

His response registered between a listless groan and a lowkey whine. He turned his face into my palm, puffed out a breath that lifted his wispy bangs, and made me giggle. Tugging his chin up gently with both hands, I placed a gentle smacker on his forehead. His tone was threadbare when words finally emerged. "If there's a burger and designer shops in my future, I'm already on the mend, darling."

"That's my boy," I told him amicably. "How'd you manage to get logged in?"

"Keystroke monitoring and multi-factor authentication are my bread and butter. How do you think I proved my worth to Midas's asshat owner?"

My brows lifted. "Impressive. If you're so good at it, Mr. Big Stuff, maybe you can give AH's firewall a shot."

"Not a chance, precious," he replied quickly, moving to the foot of my bed. "I'll supply pointers, yes, but I'm *not* doing your dirty work for you. No way."

"If that's the case," I answered, turning my chair to refocus on the monitors. "Share your wisdom with me, Gateway Guru. I'm all ears."

"Don't sell yourself short, lovey."

Bryan's acumen surpassed mine by a country mile. Envy enraptured me when his tactics permitted me access to AH's Java build, tucked behind a firewall built by the socially inept and utterly cruel Cal Tech grad seated a few desks down from me in The Red Room. Though my major wasn't in coding or development, I knew Vera's programming was flawless. Avery's mastery of the computing language was evident, too, and that brought another wave of ineptitude sweeping through my soul like a kamikaze pilot.

"Wow, this is some next-level shit," Bryan murmured by my ear. He'd shifted over my shoulder, watching as I scrolled through endless lines of code. Fortunately for me, he'd brushed his teeth twice since we'd returned home. "You said Avery's a fellow MIT grad?"

I nodded. "*Magna cum laude*, dual major, and Palantir Grant recipient. He writes half the guides on GitHub. He's a fucking pro. What's this applet?"

I pointed at the screen and Bryan's eyes narrowed on the spot. "It's an interactive web browser function. It runs automatically. The SQL's buried here."

He pointed to a string of commands nestled between greater-than and less-than symbols. It was indented in weird places. "I see it, but what am I looking at?"

"It's capturing search patterns on browsers. Let's see what this little spyglass reveals." Bryan snagged a sheet of paper from my printer's drawer, immediately scribbling a mess of symbols on it with my black felt pen. "Enter these parameters and let's see what we come up with."

I did as instructed with quick fingers, using the app designer's query functions to pull any data captured by the applet. Sure enough, a massive list of character strings generated in a plain, white pop-up box. After exporting the data to a spreadsheet, I was rewarded with thousands of caret-delimited rows of search terms used by those in The Red Room.

"Interesting," Bryan mused. "There's a lot here, but it looks like your cronies are checking the same sites over and over for new data. What have we learned from our star-monikered vigilante?"

"You never tap the same keg twice," I answered automatically, adjusting the search criteria in Avery's applet to narrow down the results. "This is gonna help me big time. Now I know what corners of the web my fellow hackers aren't searching. Maybe there's something in AH's cookie jar after all."

Bryan sipped his tepid coffee, circling back to the foot of the bed and sitting cross-legged on the duvet. "Pop quiz, darling. You've got something to hide and a bunch of tech-savvy, habitually lazy drones on your tail. Where would you hide your dirty secrets, hmm?"

I couldn't hide my grin. "Say no more."

He mimicked my smirk, releasing a slow sigh. "You're a step behind, but you're a quick learner. What would you do without me?"

"I'd live a lackluster, off-the-rack life filled with monotony and agoraphobia. Or, perhaps, I'd be an upstanding thirty-something with a ranch house and a few rug rats nipping at my heels."

We both shared a haughty laugh as I returned to the query screen and reverse-engineered the script to show me the least commonly searched terms. I sat back while the computer buzzed through millions of lines of code. The last of my caffeine dose was on its way to my nervous system by the time the pop-up window appeared once again.

"Well, lookie here. Someone researched *N3gra* eight weeks ago, then again five weeks ago. They haven't tried again since. Let's see who our culprit is."

"I know you're too smart to show your hand on the office network. Which of your cult brothers is tapping at our little star's backdoor on company time?"

"Someone with a death wish," I mumbled, scrolling through the returned data to locate a user ID. The result floored me.

Avery? Why?

"Wow. It's none other than our resident Java expert. I'm flabbergasted. He has to know AH's capabilities. Foolhardy doesn't begin to cover it, and that's me saying that."

Bryan's lips pursed. "He's the paranoid one, right? Maybe he figured that, if our muse couldn't get in surreptitiously, they'd make it through the physical barriers. He's convinced his station's being tampered with. You said the guards are dimwitted. Just how thick are they?"

I released a deep breath. "I mean, there's not the brightest, believe me, but it's not just goons guarding the gates. There's a retina scan and fingerprint readers. They'd also have to know about the security systems, as least well enough to bypass them. We're talking motion cameras, sound alarms, and proximity sensors. If an EMP was activated, maybe they could sneak past that stuff, but it'd wipe out all the computers, too."

"You watch too many cat burglar movies," Bryan told me from my bedroom threshold as he retreated for more coffee. "Give me your mug and use your brain, ya sexy dolt."

He snuck off with both vessels, a bit steadier on his feet. After a self-scathing chuckle, I rubbed my eyes, my dehydrated brain on overdrive. A lightbulb buzzed to life above my head as I pondered Bryan's cryptic encouragement.

Maybe his searches don't mean anything. Maybe what he found does.

With newfound zeal, I used the keystroke capture and Avery's user ID to access his desktop. I'd have to be careful from here out. The most suspicious Red Room associate was already on high alert. Now I was giving him reason to be. Even an innocuous error would spell my doom and curse my occupational future.

Unsurprisingly, there was little to find in the conventional hidey-holes. His web history was scrubbed. He'd deftly avoided the most common pratfalls, the ones I habitually checked first when researching the dregs of society. A holistic search resulted in nothing more than false leads and wasted time. Bryan was handing my mug back before realization dawned on me like a verdant meadow.

He's a programmer, not a criminal. I'm going about this the wrong way.

Rather than diving deep, I floated back to the surface. File folders chock full of process notes, walkthrough analyses, and coding symbols blurred into endless wingdings before my eyes. With a fresh dose of Indonesian bliss warming me from the inside out, I set the keystroke investigation app to work. Results gradually populated in the form of an itemized list. Hundreds of hours were spent building, testing, and protecting his coding. Unique keys for firewall adaptation included Vera's user ID while encryption capabilities were signed off on by Kavish. His projects were more collaborative than I'd known, potentially exposing him to infiltration from peers he most likely considered his friends.

Oh, Avery. There can be no trust between hackers. Just because we're on the same payroll doesn't mean we're all altruistic.

"What's the verdict?" Bryan asked, perching on my bed again after handing my mug back.

I sat back in my office chair, nestling the steaming brew in my palms. "Nothing about *N3gra.* He spends most of his time doing actual work. His search histories are scrubbed automatically every three hours, same as mine, and if the last time he checked up on the vigilante was indeed weeks ago, there's nothing here to find."

"You're right," Bryan told me. "But why? Why's there nothing to find, my love?"

"I'm already sick of your insufferable riddles. Do you manage your staff like this, too?"

He beamed a saccharine smile I recognized as pure contempt. "Don't make me call you Lizzie, *Serena.* Get with it. You're better than this. I swear, becoming a corporate stooge has ruined you."

"Insults and disapproval before breakfast? Jesus, maybe I should've left you on the bathroom floor last night."

"I'd be in smarter company if you had."

I shot him both middle fingers as I returned focus on the monitors. My brain churned, contemplating his implied lesson while loathing my life decisions. The whiskey hangover wasn't to blame for my rusty skill set. I'd spent too many hours in the past two years twiddling my manicured thumbs in AH's basement. I was spinning my wheels and losing my edge. As I'd feared, and as Bryan so deftly pointed out, Serena was taking over every aspect of my life.

If it's not here, where is it?

Once again, consciousness peeked out from behind the storm clouds, tempting me with a view forward. No wonder Bryan had been so short with me.

It's not here because he knows better than to leave it here. It's bad enough he searched on his work computer. I'm seriously slipping.

"Fuck me," I muttered, pulling up his PC's hard drive. He'd likely used a proximity transfer. RFID wouldn't make it through AH's firewall, so he'd need a more covert peripheral, something innocent enough to be considered mundane.

Dude, you didn't, did you? Well, maybe I'm not the only one that's slipping nowadays.

With a Christmas-sabotaging Grinch grin, I downed a generous gulp of South Pacific glory. Bryan reclined on the bed with his hands tucked behind his neck, humming a sweet ditty. He always sung like a songbird when the proverbial noose tightened around an evildoer's collar. It was one of his most endearing quirks.

I found Avery's cell phone number, cellular carrier, and his closest transmission tower seconds later. Basic knowledge in binary and in bypassing forgotten password underwriting got me into his online account. He only had half a gig of mobile data left for the month, and he'd sent seventy-eight text messages to his mother in the past nine days.

"Momma's boy," I murmured, elbow-deep in his personal business. "She sends him pics of the church bulletin every week. No wonder he's so pushy to befriend us at work. He's socially stunted."

"Fascinating," Bryan commented dryly. "You're dancing around paydirt. Quit dawdling."

"You're insufferable and your feet smell like a French cheese shop."

"Cavalli can design delicious shoes, but the bastard hates aerated linings."

"Take a shower, or is that below your station now, you haughty prick?"

"God, I love you," he told me, rising to his feet with an exaggerated, groaning stretch. "The clock's ticking. When I'm done, you better be, too."

He disappeared into the hallway. I could only shake my head derisively.

Before the showerhead kicked on, I was sifting through Avery's cloud account. Searching for the vigilante's handle generated no results. I knew the timeline of his searches, narrowing down the data to a dozen or so pages of endless letters and numbers with no spaces or delimiters between them. The drawback of raw data was the crude presentation. The benefits were far greater. The fewer filters and processes running in the background, the more furtive my research.

Pearls of wisdom brought a shifty smile to my face. Avery had spent hours eliminating likely suspects of the supposed Red Room infiltration. Among them were the most well-known watchdogs and hackers, including *esTre11aN3gra*. Astonishingly, he'd unearthed some identifying information. Without pause, I copied the data on my muse and pasted it into my own records. Carefully and methodically, I logged out and bricked up the passage behind me. The last thing I needed was Avery's paranoia amplified by what he believed to be a targeted attack on his personal accounts as well as his work ones.

I mean, that's exactly what this is, but I'm not lining up to hear his babbling dissertation on the subject.

When Bryan emerged from the bathroom, wet headed and ruddy cheeked, I was casually slung in my office chair with a twisted smile. He paused in the doorway. Silence persisted between us until I rolled my chair backward, waving my open palm toward the monitor. He strode up, leaned toward the display, and reviewed my findings.

"No way," he gushed, scrolling through the data I'd collected. "There's a physical ping to an IP address here. We're sure it's not a VPN?"

I hummed in assurance behind him. "There's no encryption signature. It's certifiable, my friend. The star's within three hundred miles of Albuquerque, New Mexico. With a Hispanic-sounding handle, that's not surprising."

"A central American dark web champion," he murmured to no one in particular. "And it's a single entity. You were right all along, darling."

"*N3gra* flies solo. It's safer that way."

He released a slow breath. "Damn. Avery sniffed out more than we ever could. If his chair was moved and his desk was fuddled with, I can see why he moved on to other possibilities. Who'd fly from New Mexico to Philly to break into a corporate office?"

"Operatives closer to Center City would make more sense," I added, finishing off the last sips of tepid brew. "The most interesting thing's this, though. Look."

I scrolled down the very bottom of the document. Avery's applets had captured an interesting set of data points. It was unmistakable that AH's firewall had been compromised, their outermost defenses tapped upon by the object of my adoration. *N3gra* had made several attempts to hack into the company's repository, evidently unsuccessfully but persistently enough to generate results on the Java expert's analysis.

"Anderson-Hilliance is on their radar," Bryan realized aloud. "Holy shit. The Red Room has stymied the efforts of the most illustrious hacker of the twenty-first century. I bet it burns *N3gra's* ass."

"Undoubtedly, but I'm more convinced than ever. There's dirty laundry in the washer."

"Skeletons in the broom closet?"

"Something stinky swept under the plush carpeting."

"Tracks are being covered, Boo," Bryan told me. "Whatever you need from here, just say the word."

"Oh, I will," I told him. I felt rekindled passion burning a hole in my soul. It was a fire that could only be quenched by the truth.

Granogue, DE, 2016

My watch buzzed to life as another text flashed on the screen.

`This is awesome. Welcome on board!`

Despite being completely alone in the basement of a potentially haunted eighteenth-century manor house, the welcome felt genuine. I was hoping this wasn't another ill-fated adventure. It certainly didn't feel like one.

The frozen January morning had been a cacophonous mess of group chatter centered around my acquisition and skillset. Replies were rarely needed. My new boss was handling the bulk of the introductions and inquiries. The henhouse was occupying itself while I watched quietly by the barn door.

Another text vibrated my wrist. The boss's name appeared above it.

`We have a call with her in an hour. No one misses it.`

That final command brought the grand total to forty-four texts in just under an hour. Five minutes passed without another word. Enamored and impressed by the boss's prowess, I got to work setting up my new CPU and peripherals.

I'd been blessed with an opportunity to redeem myself. The VPN access and security measures afforded me were proof of my newfound fortune with this career move. This subterranean hideout was another.

This locale was a temporary stop, a convenient but dangerous option that wouldn't last any longer than strictly necessary. Just being here put my saviors-slash-employers at risk. There were fewer and fewer safe corners left on Earth. The unfinished yet private square of cold stone, the ramshackle cot topped with simple cotton, and the folding table with my totes of belongings stashed underneath were a boon. Being stuck in a ten-by-ten with a cellmate was a far worse, yet readily available, option.

This is my last chance. I can't botch this.

Once my accommodations were as well-appointed as possible, I readied myself for the web meeting with the new supervisors. Breathing deeply through butterflies, I logged into the app and switched off the webcam. Per my boss's legal counsel, I was to remain a sight unseen to those I was assigned to serve. Ideally, they'd hear my voice on the rarest of occasions, but only one among them would ever know my identity, see my face, or share liability in this operation.

It should have a moniker, this new labor of mine. Operation Second Chance?

I shook my head to clear the lousy proposal. A stock image took the place of my webcam's capture, a portrait of a sketched woman with hash marks over each eye and a black mask covering the bottom half of her face. I hoped it portrayed a sense of impending doom for those who sought to wrong my new clients, though I felt like a fifteen-year-old trying to scare their grandparents on social media.

The boss logged in five minutes early, her blonde hair ironed straight and burgundy-hued lips turned up at the corners. Silence continued between us as her eyes panned right to left. I'd only been in her company twice, but I knew more about her than most. Every moment of her life was monetized. Every brain cell bouncing between her ears worked tirelessly during her waking hours. Envy and pity resonated within me.

A minute later, a dazzling and exotic Middle Eastern brunette logged in, her face a meter away from the webcam's capture. I recognized her immediately. With a white lab coat's collar showing above an ivory silk blouse and her amber mane tied back, she was clearly on duty. Moments later, another blonde's visage appeared. A pair of noise-cancelling headphones hugged her head as she exhaled a deep breath. The room around her was dim, her porcelain complexion gleaming in the computer's glow.

As the meeting's begin time flashed on my monitor, two more faces appeared. A spritely Asian female was occupied with a massive bread roll, donning more crumbs than a toddler making a similar attempt. Below her square on my monitor, the sexiest redhead I'd ever seen was applying mascara with deft fingers. Her face was already a contoured canvas of dusty rose with amethyst-lined eyes of lively green. I found myself short of breath gazing upon these five women in all their glory.

Pull it together. You get one shot at this, and they're more at risk than you've ever been. They just don't know it yet.

The first arrival's voice rung out as the makeup artist stashed her stock and the Korean goddess licked her fingers clean. "All right. I'm going to outline the rules for our newest hire's services, then you can ask your questions after she speaks. We have ten minutes. I'll make it quick."

Damn. Every minute is accounted for, and she's an uber-professional with her friends, too.

Avoiding any kind of personal connection or interest at work suited me just fine. I'd had enough of pseudo-relationships and enough emotional upheaval to keep a therapist busy for years.

The boss continued, filling the silence as the other four faces focused on their screens. Without tipping her hand, she deftly discussed my qualifications and backstory. Ambiguous enough to keep my location and identity safe, but thorough enough to demonstrate my aptitude, her audience listened with narrowed eyes and tipped heads. No one questioned her explanations, her reasons for the cloak-and-dagger approach to our arrangement, nor her insistence on keeping our working contract on a need-to-know basis. The media and public wouldn't be privy to my existence, let alone my work.

The boss was hiding me in plain sight. To the public, the girls managed their own accounts, created their own content, and issued their own press releases. In truth, they'd never be saddled with those mundane responsibilities again.

Three minutes passed before the mic was turned over to me. I released a slow breath before unmuting my burner phone. I'd opened an audio modification app, giving my voice a muddy, baritone hum. "Ladies, it's a pleasure to be among you and to offer my services. From this moment forward, all digital, online and print communications must be sent to me for distribution. This includes social media posts, website content, tour information, typed interviews, magazine articles, selfies, and memoranda meant for viewing by the public. The comprehensive list of affected communications is in my contract. Allow me to make this clear. These requirements are non-negotiable, and any posts made or content shared outside my scope places your organization at elevated risk."

"Um, wait," the redhead chimed in, her pencil-textured eyebrow arched. "I understand the benefit of coordinating public statements and managing the website, but you can't have my social media accounts."

The boss sat forward, but I stepped in before she could admonish. "Are you alone in that sentiment?"

The Asian female, reclining comfortably with her pastry long gone, replied first. "I mean, I'm fine with it. It's one less thing to deal with."

"I understand. It's critical to have an experienced hand managing it," the Armenian brunette added.

"You guys are less active online," the redhead argued. "I post multiple times a day. I have ten million followers. Engagement is everything. Now I'm supposed to clear every word through someone else?"

Hold your tongue. You were ready for the backlash. Here it is.

"It's for your protection," the big boss responded, her jewel tone eyes fixed on her screen.

The redhead's voice grew insistent. "I've never been hacked. I change passwords monthly at least. I do multi-factor authentication. I don't use public Wi-Fi. I know the rules."

You sweet thing. Let me show you something.

I spoke up, slowing my words for emphasis. "Those are good precautions. You're to be commended for your awareness. I can provide a counterargument, however. Are you aware of the term 'ever-presence?'"

"That just means there's always evidence of something, right?" She replied quickly.

"Correct, though it's not always a physical presence. Ever-presence is the internet's most valuable attribute. The world wide web spins minute by minute. It never sleeps. It never forgets. It never disappears. Your footprint is eternally etched into its mobius strip. Allow me to show its wicked capabilities to you now."

I launched the lurker software program I'd designed the day before. Within seconds, four in my audience froze in fear. Flickers of light illuminated their troubled faces as they began scrolling through dozens of pop-up notifications. Their panic amplified as they surveyed the damage done. Freshly published posts revealed their passwords, cell phone contacts, and personal photo galleries across Instagram. Some photos were racy enough to merit censor bars, but I left them unedited for emphasis.

A deluge of user comments flooded in instantly. Two of the ladies' accounts were disabled due to inappropriate content. I waited patiently as they descended into madness, attempting to log into their accounts and to change their cell phone passcodes, only to find themselves locked out. Their multi-factor authentication phone numbers had been changed to the burner phone resting on the desk beside me. I turned on my camera for five seconds, keeping my face and location concealed, but going live just long enough to elevate my phone into view. On the messages screen, their requests for one-time passcodes popped up one after another. The intimidating profile pic I'd chosen flashed twice across their screens before affixing itself above my meeting dial-in number once again.

"You are ever-present, ladies. You are immortal online, and at the mercy of those with skillsets that rival mine. This little coup is child's play, I assure you."

The boss closed her eyes. She'd been the only silent party during our little demonstration. She'd also been the only one privy to the sabotage. I'd asked for a lot of patience and trust on her part, challenging her coworkers this way, but I needed to prove a point. Based on their hysterical, tearful, and awestruck reactions, I'd done so immaculately.

"Bring it in," the boss commanded, ending the mayhem.

"You've been spoofed." I told the ladies. "The posts aren't real. I am responsible for this entirely. Dummy accounts were set up to auto-comment. Those aren't real, either. No one's access has been revoked. This demonstration is fakery, though the potential outcome isn't. This is the reality of lackluster communication management. One post, one misquoted phrase, or one easy-to-guess password can end it all."

"This," the petite, platinum blonde in headphones interjected. "This was terrifying. I still can't get into my account, though."

"And you don't need to ever again," the boss responded. "We're in more capable hands now."

I wiped the records of the spoof before closing the lurker program. "I can keep you safer than you knew you needed to be. I can make this very simple for you. Send me your content, allow me to post it per your instructions, and to boobytrap the way in for anyone stupid enough to approach. That's my role, one I'm trained to do, and one I take seriously."

"We're in different time zones all the time," the stunning brunette told me. "When can we expect service once we're in touch?"

The boss answered before I could. "She's on twelve-hour shifts, seven-to-seven Eastern, until further notice. Posts can be scheduled or will be released as soon as possible after they're received. And I assume we can schedule future posts to any news outlet or social media site through you as well?"

"Absolutely," I replied. "If they don't allow it now, they will once I'm through with them."

The Korean vixen smirked. "I'm a big fan of this. And what happens when someone slanders us? If we can't answer for ourselves, what then?"

My chuckle sounded sick and twisted when manipulated by the vocal mod software. "First, the post will be deleted thoroughly, not just on the surface where it lays. Then, one of three things will happen to the perpetrator and in very short order. They'll be blacklisted from every internet site I can access, they'll be subject to litigation at the hands of your legal counsel, or they'll be defamed in kind. That's only if the comment makes it through my forcefield. I'm already scrubbing, peering into the darkest corners, and sniffing out the slander before it goes live. Spyware gets a bad name. I intend to utilize it, plus a half-dozen other advances in monitoring software, to keep your antics quiet and your reputations clean, before or after a malicious attack. You will be protected and avenged. This I swear."

"This is the genius of online presence and recovery management," the boss told the participants. "We're at ten minutes. Any questions?"

The eerie silence, laden with amazement and humility, reassured me to my core.

* * * * *

I was lying in my cot hours later while an early January dawn warmed the stone structure above me. I had no view of its arrival. I relied on a webcam positioned along the state's shoreline for weather updates. That was the closest thing to a window I was afforded until my isolated home was move-in ready.

Good morning. Day two of Operation Second Chance begins in earnest.

Once the golden ball crested the horizon, I used a burner smartphone to search the web for updates. The online vigilante I'd once idolized had all but disappeared from the public eye. No new discoveries or exposés were found on the normal sites. It was the end of an era. I'd spent years in their shadow, trying to surpass their might, only to be left in their dust.

The only messages in my inbox were from my new employers. I'd delighted in astonishing them, in proving just how vulnerable anyone could be at the hands of a cracker or self-interested paparazzi. No one understood this better than my new boss, and together, we'd make it perilous and unwise to tamper with their good name. Yesterday's demonstration, though faux in its execution, was flawless in its result. They now understood just how many would suffer should the enemy storm their gates.

I released a deep breath, knowing I'd be sequestered at least another week in this makeshift bunker. Tucked below the front entry of the manor, I observed dozens of footfalls the day before, those belonging to three of the very souls I'd scared with my display. I was tasked with avoiding them at all costs. While the hours and days ticked by, I was to expect deliveries outside the basement bulkhead's metal doors after nightfall, and to do my magic online without alerting those on the level above me.

The delivery the night before was a godsend. The four-cubic-foot stainless steel fridge had been a pain to heft downstairs, but the coffeepot and rations in the box beside it made the labor worthwhile. I now had a stash of chilled drinks, artisan macadamia milk, fair trade beans, and fresh produce to live on. The coffeepot was a mass-market, pour-over model worth fifty bucks tops, but it beat the hell out of caffeine headaches. My mother's spoon, shined to a gleam, was tucked inside a long, white box meant for bracelets. I fell to my knees, overcome by emotion at the sight of it. Nothing could keep me from enjoying my spoils in the late-night hours.

At six-thirty, I grew tired of scrolling. I rose and returned to my computer setup. The first order of business was scrubbing their cloud accounts, then saving all data externally until it could be archived. This project would take hours. Two-and-a-half decades of info needed meticulous analysis.

My phone chimed with an incoming text message. The unlisted number began with an area code I didn't recognize. A quick search revealed it to be central Oregon.

Does your small business need funding? Get 500k in minutes with no credit check. More details here!

I held back a belly laugh. Even holed up in a basement, on a burner phone and surrounded by foot-thick ancient stone, I was still getting smished. It never failed to amaze me how quickly a human could be sniffed out if they carried a tracking device in their pocket.

A quick smack with a heavy boot destroyed the burner's SD card. The plastic casing, now devoid of any identifying systems within, would be disposed of at my first opportunity. I dug out another burner from the stash, activating it and starting over, as I'd done sixteen times in the past month alone.

With five celebrities to protect and millions of ne'er-do-wells lurking at the gate, I began my first full day of service. I intended to use ill-gotten talents for the good of my clients for the rest of my life.

It's about time.

Philadelphia, PA, 2015

"The songs come first, then the lyrics are backfilled."

"That seems unnecessarily challenging. Syllabic timing is flawless in their catalog. It's even more astounding to think it's reverse engineered."

"It's hard to argue its efficacy."

"Most certainly," Su agreed as we rounded the city street corner. Our office building was on the next block, gleaming in the sun's rays. This Thursday in early May was almost as beautiful as my escort. "Five studio albums, all relatively well received, plus music videos that defy description. I'm glad to know a fellow fan. Drew doesn't "get" them."

"We can talk Tool anytime," I told her. "And I have a few CDs you really should borrow. It's older stuff mainly, but it was revolutionary for me. I have fond memories of sitting on a roof, drinking fruity wine, and wasting hours between dusk and dawn."

Her gentle smile made my heart backflip as we crossed the street, headed for Anderson-Hilliance's headquarters. It stretched toward the azure sky like a beacon. We'd followed this same path every weekday morning for months. She was an unparalleled listener, and I found myself willing to admit truths I'd sequestered away since arriving in Philly. I was mindful of Serena's proclivities, but Lizzie kept peeking out, unabashedly attracted to the Asian charisma and eloquent charm of my coffee accomplice.

I fought back inappropriate thoughts constantly, struggling against my regrown virginity's stranglehold. As the weather warmed and Su's business attire shifted to clingy fabrics in brilliant pastels, all I wanted was a taste of the spice hidden below the sophistication.

"Oh, did you read the flyer in Supremo's window?"

Deftly dodging a pair of commuters, we stepped onto the pavement just outside our office's door. I turned to face her once the fear of being bowled over passed. "No. Was it a special?"

"An event, actually," she told me. "They collaborated with a local distillery. Tomorrow night, a ticket-only event is being hosted to celebrate their combined efforts."

"I wish I'd been more observant," I mused aloud. "Is it liqueur-infused beans or bean-infused liqueur?"

Her shrug and smirk were so playful, I almost forgot the pedigree behind them. "I haven't a clue, but I think it might be worth a taste."

"I'll get us tickets. Will you meet me there tomorrow?"

She nodded once. "I'll be there at seven precisely."

"I have no doubt."

As was customary, I held open the massive glass door after Su scanned her access card. She passed by me and into the lobby, close enough to flood my senses with lily. Just like always, it mesmerized me as the door closed gently behind our backs. She'd stay two steps ahead and turn back before ascending the escalator to her office. I'd remain calm with my palms folded over my lap, waiting until she initiated the farewell. I refused to deviate from the norm, knowing one false move could result in the dissolution of this thrilling arrangement.

"Conquer the day," Su told me as she approached the foot of the escalator. "I'll see you at muster."

I edged around her, headed for the clandestine elevator. "Thank you. Bye, Su."

She lifted her coffee in my direction, a mock toast of sorts, as a metal stair carried her toward The Third Circle. I always snuck a glance when she faced forward, watching as she sipped her espresso with gently closed eyes, and wishing I could trade places with the recycled plastic lid. I'd gained her favor and garnered a bit of her courtesy. I hated that I needed more. Anything short of her passion felt insufficient.

I'm patient, but this is torture.

In the safety of the elevator, I tucked my coffee in my elbow and wrung my hands. I was lying at every turn now. I'd clearly spent too much time in this stage play, pretending to be a perfect angel while Lizzie wasted away in the wings. I was so blissfully close, though. I'd made so many strides since Bryan's visit months before. Giving up now simply wasn't an option. The revelation was right around the corner, the dossier of AH's dirtiest secrets within my grasp. I just needed to keep my eyes on the prize.

But which prize am I eyeing, exactly?

With a self-deprecating snort, I emerged from the elevator, striding into The Red Room, and returning to my spoke in the wheel of menial labor. Though I was punctual, I was the last to arrive yet again. Avery lifted his gaze to me as I set my bag down and slipped out of my suit jacket. Feeling lighter than I had in months, riding high on the adrenaline of yet another successful stroll with Su, I shot him a wink before taking my seat. His oval glasses twinkled as his head tipped, his curious expression illuminated by his computer screen.

Within seconds of opening our office chat software, a pop-up message grabbed my attention.

`Someone's having a good morning.`

Avery. Of course, he'd take the bait. I'd been foolish in thinking a harmless gesture would go unnoticed. He did purposefully follow me to the elevator every day at lunch. His leering, masquerading as a shy guy's attempt at game, was pitiful. I responded after making him wait a full, excruciating minute.

`Another day in paradise.`

Once my earbuds were comfortably nudged in place, they chimed with another incoming message.

`How about a drink after work, on me?`

I perused a few emails, letting him stew while the notification icon blinked away. His palms were probably damp already. Little did he know, I was about to accept. I'd reached a stalemate with the company's firewall and knew exploiting Vera was a waste of time. He was my next inadvertent ally. An entire metal song played in my ear before I sent a reply.

`Sure. Sake?`

I chanced a peek in his direction, enamored to see his brow crest above the rim of his black frames. I refocused on my screen as his reply appeared.

Yeah. I'll book two bar spots at *Taki*. We can head there from here if that's cool.

I reread the text twice. Two seats for the two of us. He was playing right into my hands.

You got it.

I hid my smirk. I had a few hours to plan. I'd need every minute of it.

* * * * *

Playing it cool and keeping appropriate distance between us while avoiding direct eye contact, Avery courted me from Anderson-Hilliance's front door to the Japanese eatery four blocks away. He'd chosen well. It was two doors' down from Supremo, my daily coffee stop, but I'd never bothered to try *Taki's* wares. The minimalist décor, squat tables surrounded by ruby velvet-covered mats, and muted conversation around us stole my breath, as did the bar along the far back wall. Styled like a waterfall below thin layers of acetate, flowing water channeled under the serving counter and down into the floor behind the legs of the bar's patrons. Occasionally, faux koi of brilliant crimson crested and descended with the water, disappearing below the floor only to reappear elsewhere along the bar's twenty-foot length.

Avery checked us in. A squat host in a pristine black kimono guided us to the bar's corner, sweeping the "Reserved" placard from the bar top and pulling out my tufted stool. Avery stood at my elbow until I was safely onboard the cushion, then sat a few inches to my left. Before us, a narrow wooden bifold menu waited alongside two sets of silk-wrapped, carved ebony chopsticks.

"I'm very impressed," I told Avery. "Let's see if I can remember Japanese etiquette. A transfer student in my high school invited me over and taught me the ropes, but that was years ago."

And it's a total lie. Bryan loves this stuff and drug me to so many all-night sushi joints over the years. It'll come back to me.

He swapped his sunglasses for his indoor specs, then tucked the shaded pair into his jacket's breast pocket. "The key's to not touch anything until it's needed, or so I understand. I'm not the biggest sake snob, so I'm winging this. I hope you appreciate honesty over showmanship."

I glanced over before snagging the menu. "Honesty is always best."

"Good to know, but I gotta ask. Why did you finally say yes?"

"To drinks, you mean?"

"Yeah. I saw you at that bar months ago, but I haven't seen you there since, and you never say yes to anything social. Why's today different?"

Of course, he's suspicious. He couldn't just go with it. I guess that was asking too much.

"Well, to be honest, I wanted to talk shop. I hope you're all right with that."

"I'm not sure I have a choice. Besides, you're here."

That pure smile, so full of hope and optimism, burned like acid rain on my soul. Tinkering with his boy had to be a cardinal sin. Fortunately, I didn't believe in Hell, or at least the version that haunted the wicked after death. Life was hellish enough to doubt the existence of something worse.

"I sure am," I told him, slapping Serena's smile on before perusing the sake selections. Most offerings were three hundred milliliters or less, reminding me of how pungent the good stuff could be. A *Junmai* aged five years was tagged at the same cost as a month's rent. Its appeal launched into the stratosphere when I considered its implied quality. I'd be back for that one before long. "If you're not a connoisseur, how about we take the bartender's recommendations?"

"Sounds like a plan. I drink IPA, so it's all going to taste like lighter fluid to me."

"Then why'd you agree to this? We could've gone anywhere."

"Simple. You wanted sake."

God help me.

"And you figured the swankiest spot, with the most impressive atmosphere, would sweep me off my feet?"

"Did it?"

"Kind of," I told him with a snicker. "Thanks for making the arrangements. I don't expect you to pick up the tab in a place this fancy."

"I'm going to. That was our deal. Considering how much I've spent on Kavish and Vera, only to be insulted endlessly, this evening already has great ROI."

I shook my head sympathetically. "You could just stop hanging out with them."

He put on a pathetic pout. "What choice did I have? You always said no, we work around the clock, and my last date ended when she took an emergency call and never came back."

"Okay, that's too sad. I'll need hard liquor if you're going to keep playing the Pitiful Loser card."

"I play the hand I'm dealt."

Conversation paused while we questioned the bartender and ordered more than we should have. Shallow vessels soon surrounded us, filled with black salt dusted edamame, golden seared gyoza, paper thin pickles, and daikon shreds in soup so clear, the hand-painted cherry blossoms on the bottom of the bowl glistened. We shared a *tokkuri* of chilled *Ginjyo*, one with a fruity burn that dried my mouth after swallowing. Avery suffered through the cuisine like a trooper, trying his best to hide his disdain behind his silken napkin while I reminisced with every bite. On his next trip down, Bryan and I were coming here straight from the train station.

"You wanted to talk about work," he began after peeling open a pod to extract the soybeans inside. "While I'm glad for the time with you, we could've texted."

"Not a chance," I replied, finishing off the pickles before fetching my cell phone from my purse. "You should know why."

"I'm as careful as anyone, but we could've texted on our personal phones."

I figured you for a true conspiracy theorist. You think AH can't tap into anyone's phone records? We do worse. Hell, they pay us to.

While he finished the last ounce of his sake, I covertly activated the voice recorder, setting the phone face down on the bar. The simple act didn't seem to raise any red flags for my dinner companion. He simply set his cup down and turned on his stool to face me.

"What are we discussing then? You get the same news I get."

I released a breath. I was on a thin rail, but I loved the thrill of the ride. "Has there been any progress with your suspicions? It's been a while since you met with HR. Did anything come of it?"

He shifted uncomfortably, glancing over his shoulder for a split second before lowering his gaze to the floor. "I was dismissed. Joy was understanding but disinterested. She'd already decided I was crazy before I set foot in the office. I never spoke to anyone else, and I got a form email the next day, saying they found no proof of a perimeter breach."

"That meeting was the same day that they cancelled muster. Do you know why?"

He shrugged. "You know as much as I do about that. It was a cyberattack. They didn't get in. Vera spent fifty-two straight hours looking for evidence. They were willing to pay her premium pay for a phantom threat, but my real one resulted in nothing. It's incredibly frustrating."

"It's still frustrating?"

"Sure. It's still happening. I swear, my chair's moved just a little sometimes. My pen's pointed at four o'clock rather than three o'clock. I don't know. This all must seem so weird, but I swear it's true. Someone's breaking into the office. I just don't know why it's only my desk."

"I'm not sure the others would notice such tiny changes. I've been careful since you mentioned it before, but I don't see anything obvious. I figured this nonsense stopped after you went to HR."

He shook his head. "I feel like I'm losing it. Maybe it really is all in my head. How could anyone get in anyway? Anyone with permission to get in has their own computer elsewhere in the building. Why risk getting caught just to sneak downstairs? Plus, they'd have to know how to bypass the alarms. How many people outside AH know they even exist, let alone how to get around them?"

I'd stewed over the same questions a million times already. Bryan and I had no answers, either. What I was hoping for was permission to do what I'd already begun doing. I couldn't finish without his help. I needed to see his system from the inside, to investigate the looming threat he'd dismissed too quickly.

"Hmm," I murmured, feigning concern. "Is there a way to see if it's another person on our team?"

His face sunk instantly. "You think it's an inside job?"

"How can it not be? You said it yourself. The perpetrator knows our systems as well as we do. They know our working hours. They know how important your work is specifically. What other explanation could there be?"

His quizzical expression turned dour. "My work? You think that's why they chose my computer?"

I leaned in just a little, letting my oceanic perfume infiltrate his senses. His breath caught. He was hooked. "Yes, Avery. *Your* work is important. It's the basis of our programming, isn't it? You can't build a firewall, create a repository, or write systems without the program foundation to put it on. Am I wrong?"

His dark eyes twinkled behind his lenses. "You're…"

"Yes, I know your work. Vera, Kavish, all of us; we'd be fighting a losing battle without your expertise. Is there any way you'd consider a backup plan to make sure your work doesn't get wiped when this thief's jealousy turns to malice?"

"Malice," he repeated. "You think they'll wipe my work?"

"Or worse," I insisted dramatically. "If they can access and understand it, they can tamper with it. They can corrupt it, then put your name on the malware and call it yours. There could be a mole among us. You can't underestimate the potential fallout."

His jaw dropped. "You want me to back up my work externally? You know that could get me fired or worse."

"I'm just worried about you, Avery."

Just a little more. He's almost there.

He lowered his head as his eyes gently closed. "Damn it. I can't believe you believe me. I guess I couldn't believe anyone would. I can transfer on a personal cloud account if-"

"Oh, no," I interrupted. "You think you're the only one who knows how the cloud works?"

You've already done digital transfers. That's how I know about your research into vigilantes, you dolt. Get a clue.

He narrowed his gaze on my face. "You're more suspicious than I thought."

"I've learned a lot since college," I admitted. "The world's more selfish than I hoped."

"I've got three years of data on my PC. Every code I've written is there for the taking."

"How many gigs, do you think?"

"Two terabytes. Maybe a little less. It's a lot."

Two terabytes! That's three times what I could see from home.

"That *is* a lot. It's so much liability, especially if this terrorist knows your login already. I'm so sorry, Avery."

"So, what do I need to do?"

I lowered my voice slightly. "All I know is that AH expects your stuff to be kept safe. If you think it's not, what can you do?"

He sat back, considering his options while my subconscious screamed for him to realize the obvious move here. I was a chess grandmaster, watching a two-hundred-level amateur struggle across the table and tapping my fingernails while the seconds ticked by.

His voice finally emerged as a threadbare whisper. "I can wrap a hard drive in a cell phone skin and get it into the office. I'd need to destroy my USB drive once the transfer's complete, but it'd be safer than a cloud transfer. There'd be no digital trace left behind."

I sighed, assuming a visage of disappointment at his unscrupulous idea. Hidden in my pointed-toe pumps, though, my toes tingled with excitement.

Of course, it is. A USB sniffer and CPU skimmer will get me a copy of those delicious records. Hell, I've got a backup thumb drive in my purse for causes just like this.

He continued with his eyes trained on his lap. "I'll get a good one and bring it Monday. If I'm there first, it'll be done before anyone sees anything."

"Oh, Avery," I sighed wistfully. "I'm so sorry this is happening. Are you sure this is a good idea?"

"What choice do I have? I have to protect myself. My career and my employer's reputation are on the line."

"I just wish there was another way."

"Me, too," he told me listlessly, pouring more sake into his porcelain cup.

I turned on my stool to face forward, pinning a gyoza between chopsticks and popping it into my mouth. While chewing, I switched off the voice recorder, saving his plan to my phone's hard drive. All I'd done, per this recording, was try to talk him out of this cockamamie plan.

"Serena?"

I clicked the phone's side button to blacken the screen before setting it down. "Yeah?"

"Thanks for tonight."

His smile was so pure. All I could do was mimic it like the method actor I'd become.

My God, this is like taking candy from a baby.

* * * * *

A little after ten the following evening, I was staggering out of Supremo on strappy heels. I'd chosen a cobalt blue sheath with an abbreviated hem, perhaps too light an ensemble for the lingering chill that settled after dusk, but it'd been perfect in the crowded café. The elegant Japanese executive, wrapped in a thin cashmere sweater dress and Dior booties, kept pace with me as we sampled cocktail after cocktail amongst the erudite aficionados. Premium coffees infused with brandy, cognac, and bourbon from the city's top distillery, mixed with imported, top-shelf booze and artisan garnishes, formed ethereal creations I'd never dreamed of. The aroma of my two favorite drugs mingling in the clear plastic sampling cups, along with the flowery scent of her skin, slowed my pulse and relaxed every muscle.

The hip spot, trimmed in dark wood, was even more celebratory than usual, with a DJ's jazzy selections playing over the store's speaker system and mingling yuppies clamoring for the limited-edition offerings. I'd ordered an exclusive box set for delivery, a pound of each of their brown liquor-infused beans, before succumbing to the booze's influence. There was no telling how much damage I'd have done if I'd waited any longer to order, or if there would've been anything left for me to buy.

Su gripped my right arm, hustling alongside me as we snuck away from the café. Her cheeks were glowing as she dragged us to a stop near the corner. Cadres of socializing twenty-somethings passed us by as we paused. Her voice was half murmur and half exclamation when it finally emerged.

"I haven't had this much to drink in years. I'm not sure if I'm exhausted or exhilarated."

I felt the same chaotic existence surging through me. Caffeine spurred me forward, but alcohol weighed me down like an anvil. Rather than the forces counteracting, they confounded each other, their joint effect seemingly overwhelming us both. My response was a slurred, contented hum. "I'm so happy you told me about this. I would've had serious regrets Monday morning. Those beans are going to sell out."

"I snatched the last bottle of espresso liqueur out from under some witless girl's nose. She was too busy gloating on social media." To prove her point, she tucked a hand into her shoulder bag and lifted a frosted glass bottle into view between the zipper's lips. "I seem to recall paying for it. I certainly hope I did."

"Me too. That's our hot spot. If we got blackballed, where would we go for six-dollar Americanos and imported biscotti?"

"We can go to Italy," she replied dreamily, leading me down the sidewalk. "We'd arrive in time for daybreak *ristretto* alongside the *Darsena di Milano*. Two dishes of *stracciatella* and a tour of the local basilicas would be a beautiful way to round out the afternoon, wouldn't you say?"

I released a slow breath, inches from her side and thousands of miles away in my mind. Her daydreaming was pure delirium, but it involved me, by some miracle. "That's bliss in its truest form. A tour of the designer shops might also be in order."

Her tinkling giggle rung out in the narrow alley. "No need to pack luggage, then. I have thousands of frequent flyer miles. La Guardia to Osaka International racks them up, I assure you. We could leave now."

The erudite pride in her stature and demeanor at the office had me convinced she was above everyone's pay rate. Even pretentious Lizzie and goody-two-shoes Serena were ten steps down on her illustrious staircase. I couldn't help facilitating her fantasy a little longer. I was just drunk enough to push the limits of our intimacy.

"My passport's in my safe. I'm a few blocks past the office. This way."

I tugged her gently, but she was frozen on the spot, a thin smartphone nestled in her fingers. Her gaze narrowed as a white screen with six empty blocks appeared below AH's corporate logo. I watched her drag a finger across the digital keyboard, filling in the six digits deftly before laying her pointer finger on the screen above the one-inch circle that appeared. The display flashed green for an instant. With a deft wrist flick, the phone was slipped into her bag once again.

She'd checked that AH app periodically throughout the evening, never too far from its siren call. Even now, with her rosy cheeks and staggering gait, it tempted and distracted her. Fortunately for me, she'd been careless enough, perhaps due to trust or intoxication, to grant me a fleeting glance at our employer's security passcode.

J58H62. That code and her fingerprint are the golden ticket to AH.

"I'm sorry, Serena," she murmured, finally allowing me to tug her along through the frigid wind. "It's nice to dream, but as soon as I doze, reality resets the alarm. I need to stop by the office."

Oh, we're not done yet.

I turned puppy dog eyes to her, a gaze laden with childish hope and fear of disappointment. "Su, we've both had too much. It's probably not the best idea to show up at work like this."

"I don't have the option to decline."

"Let me go in first, to make sure there's no security there. If anyone catches me, you'd be the one they'd report it to, right? If you get caught, it'll be Sleeve-Garters-Tim lowering the boom on you."

She snorted, the first time I heard such a philistine sound from the exotic elite. "You don't need to worry. Security's on call after nine p.m. I really shouldn't take you up to The Third Circle, though." She glanced at me, a finely penciled brow cresting intriguingly. "Eh. Screw it."

I grinned at her. "So, you know about that little nickname, huh?"

She nodded and winked conspiratorially at me. "I listen to whispers for a living."

We swayed slightly on the walk, finally ascending the pale stone steps ten minutes later. Su's keycard blipped against the sensor near the entry. A heavy click sounded as the lock sprung on the right door. Bitter wind transformed to dry, forced air as we crossed the high-rise's threshold. Su stayed a step ahead of me. The stark lobby was hauntingly still, only illuminated by the streetlights beyond the lofty windows. The door shut behind us, its dull thud echoing around the deserted space.

Ahead, the escalator was still and silent. She approached it nonetheless, ascending the metal-slatted stairs carefully on stilettos. I followed silently, goosebumps prickling my skin as I watched her toned legs carry her upward.

We stood shoulder to shoulder at her office door. The thick, opalescent glass hid the treasures beyond. I quaked at the idea of catching a glimpse of the life I so envied. She didn't seem concerned about the cameras, the fingerprint scanners, or the proximity alarms now.

Did that code shut everything off?

She twisted a key in the brass lock before pushing the heavy door open halfway. She took my forearm and ushered me through, staying behind to allow the door to close against her back. I heard the lock engage while I lingered in the dim space. A subtle mechanical hum and our breaths were the only sounds in the vast, plush office.

"Lights are staying off," she told me. "Higher-up's rules. Want a drink?"

My eyes slowly adjusted, bringing subtle details into focus. Her desk was similar stylistically to Joy's; solid wood and vast, stretching along the east wall with a leg protruding toward the center of the space. On the west wall was a plush sofa in pale yellow. An armchair of simple lines and muted linen fabric waited alongside. On the squat, lacquered coffee table rested two books, one of modern art and the other of seventeenth-century Japanese netsuke figurines.

I wandered instinctively toward the origin of the hum, a bespoke chestnut, twin-doored cabinet, on which a pristinely cut crystal decanter of amber liquid and a half-dozen matching glasses rested patiently. On a shelf below the display was a stainless-steel mini fridge, its engine whirring. What was inside and what hid behind the finely carved doors to its left was anyone's guess, but I knew it was top-notch sight unseen.

"My head's already spinning from the infused bourbon, so why not? Is this decanter more bourbon?"

I turned in time to see her wiggle her computer mouse, both monitors on her desktop jolting to life and casting her fine features in a sky-blue glow. "My father would stone me in the town square if it was. It's a *Yamazaki*, twelve-year. Give me a minute."

I watched, pretending to only be taking subtle interest in her movements, as I paced a slow line near her immaculate liquor cabinet. "No worries. I'm so glad you decided to not end the evening prematurely. It's been so perfect."

She smiled at my words, glancing up at me for a split second before returning to the task at hand. The screen flashed red, then yellow, and I knew she was accessing the company's security monitoring software. I'd logged in and followed the multi-stage verification a million times before. She stood, leaning down to show me a little décolletage as she typed a few quick bursts of characters, waited a few seconds, then closed the software program. The screens remained aglow.

She entered a key, granted permission, and logged out. Hmm, interesting.

She was at my side a moment later, her flowery perfume infiltrating my senses yet again. It clung to the snug cashmere wrapped around her, sending wisps to my nose as she reached for the glass vessel. With smoothness like a lazy river, she dosed a few ounces into two glasses. "This is for real wins, for when life works out just right. It sure seems that way right now."

"The feeling's mutual," I replied, taking the proffered pour from her fingers. "To class, sophistication, and paying over the odds for them both."

Her gentle laughter bewitched me as she clinked her glass against mine. "And to finding what you're looking for, no matter how deeply it's buried."

I kept my gaze locked on hers as I lifted the rim to my lips. The scent of blistered firewood, bubbling caramel, and tangy citrus greeted me as the first ounce passed down my throat. Essences of toasted wheat and malt danced over my tongue, lingering like a fading melody as we lowered our glasses in tandem. A little of the liquid gold was left behind, but I was too distracted by her gaze to bother. I could only manage a single word as the potion warmed me from throat to navel.

"Stunning."

"It is exquisite, isn't it?" She set her glass alongside the decanter.

"Yes, but I wasn't talking about the liquor."

Her gaze returned to me in an instant, her expression one of sincere surprise and admiration. "Did I not read your dating profile closely enough?"

"Well," I began, closing the foot of distance between us gingerly. "I assume you only needed a cursory glance to satisfy the HR provisions. I'd be surprised if you really 'read' it."

"Then you should be surprised," she told me, a lilt in her voice showing off the Asian accent I'd regrettably overlooked lately. "I'm guilty of doing a little private research, Serena."

It'd been too long since I'd been so tempted. I was inches from her now. I could feel the heat of intoxication and allure ebbing off her lithe frame. I just needed a little more of her, of her time and of her attention, to call the night a true success.

"No harm in that. And speaking of knowledge, I know a little something about this twelve-year *Yamazaki*."

"And that would be?"

With as much restraint as I could manage, I tipped my head a little to the right, lifting my gaze to hers. "It tastes better warmed up just a little."

"Does it?" She murmured, her eyes lowering to my lips as they parted. "Shall I take your word for it, or is there a little lingering on that refined palate of yours?"

Sweet Jesus. Serena's over her head. This is on you, Lizzie.

With the steering wheel handed over after years of repression, I took another sip, my pulse racing like a greyhound after a coursing hare. She tugged the glass from my fingers, setting it next to hers without tearing her eyes away. Her face edged to mine as I watched, fascinated by her grace and astonished at her brazenness. I'd simply dangled a carrot. Incredibly, she'd stretched out for a bite.

I was face to face with her now. Memories of our ongoing flirtation-tinged friendship faded into the ether as my mind tripped forward into the glorious potential before me. A civil war broke out in my mind. Warring factions on both sides pointed muskets at each other. General Lizzie's internal voice screamed, "Fire!" All hell broke loose.

Our lips just barely touched. The bullets' explosive blast rung out between my ears, my chest tight and my patience stretched to its limit. The lilies on her skin intoxicated me, dizzying me more than the liquor ever could. Like a Spartan warrior, I held fast, keeping my lips soft but docile as she captured them with her own. I'd forgotten to breathe. I'd forgotten to think. I'd forgotten sense, logic, or reason. Gravitation pulled me relentlessly into her orbit, and I loved every moment of it.

Five innocent seconds passed before her face pulled back a few inches. "Serena."

There was promise in that word, in that name I'd adopted so casually and so mindlessly hid behind. Inexplicably, she was interested in Serena, the goody-two-shoes from Western Pennsylvania. Or was she seeing my illicit tendencies, eking through Serena's mesh visage?

There's one way to find out.

I consciously opened my eyes as slowly as I could, observing her pupils as they dilated just a touch more in the dim of her silent office. "Su."

"It is better," she told me in a silken voice. "But this is a mistake. You know that."

She wants to talk? Ugh. Fine.

"Sure. You're wasting an exquisite twelve-year on a peon. I'm a basement-dweller who idolizes the ground you walk on. That's a mistake in the truest sense."

The timbre of my voice, as silken as I could manage, kept her eyes gentle, but shifted her expression into an impressed grin. "Getting close to you risks my entire livelihood, as well as yours. I'm putting you in terrible danger."

"Oh, Ms. Iruma," I murmured and reached up slowly, letting the sight of my palm enter her peripheral vision before running disciplined fingertips through the satin mane draped over her shoulder. "I hate to break it to you. I'm the danger."

That delicious grin touched the corners of her eyes, crinkling them as her face edged closer to mine again. The need for words receded as her taut frame collided with mine, the amber warmth on her breath merging with my own. Before I made sense of the moment, or of the incredulous serendipity I'd been graced, we were a tumble of limbs on her office's couch.

* * * * *

I managed to slide, stiff and tingly, to the floor below the cushions. She remained on the plush settee, her dress bunched around her middle, bare above and below the ivory cashmere ring. We'd managed two lust-soaked sessions, with six ounces of whiskey between them, and she'd finally collapsed onto my chest twenty minutes before. Panting turned to docile breaths as fatigue overcame her. On the other hand, I was as wired as a house festooned with Christmas lights, my cheeks and libido aglow.

Her office was a mélange of shadows originating from her monitor's sapphire display. I found my dress on the floor by Su's overhanging feet, though my heels were tossed farther away. She'd giggled immensely at the recklessness, attacking me with curious palms as soon as the shoes were aloft. I'd forgotten about my now-wrinkled sheath and scuffed heels as soon as they were out of sight.

Dressed and set to rights, I turned to eye the vixen I'd undone. It'd been too long since I'd so thoroughly enjoyed someone's company. Visions of a certain strawberry blonde in a lace-trimmed camisole, toting garden goods alongside me and offering me a taste of vinaigrette from her fingertip flashed to mind, sending me hurdling backward through time. She'd smelled of sweet blossoms, too. I shook loose the sentiment, refocusing on her computer and the forbidden opportunity I'd been granted.

Ensuring the speakers were turned off and that a gossamer facial tissue remained wrapped around my forefingers, I attached a USB cable from my cell to her desktop. I then restarted her computer. The initial processes were monitored constantly by the keystroke app I had opened and waiting. Before the background image of a burnt sienna butte in the American Southwest was fully generated, the app picked up dozens of repeated keystrokes, many of which were used in the last eight hours.

It took three minutes to determine her desktop password. With a flash, the background image changed to a centered photo of a dapper Japanese couple, perhaps my age or younger, dressed in traditional kimono between two blossoming cherry trees. The female wore royal red, mimicking the under layer on the proud gentleman's chest. His face was staunch in expression and aura. In a frilly dress more Western in appearance, a girl of maybe six stood between them, clutching a basket brimming with silvery blooms. Blunt bangs skimmed her forehead, and the ebony eyes below them were fixed forward. She favored her mother strongly, but there was a wideness to her cheeks, a plumpness to her meek smile, that bore resemblance to neither parent. I analyzed the image as briefly as I could before opening the intranet and accessing the company's internal software program.

She's got some serious security clearance. What can she help me get away with?

The keystroke analyzer gave me seven lines of binary. Translating in the dim glow of her monitors, I found sixteen possible sets of characters. The password requirements were complex but predictable, narrowing the potential suspects to twelve. With gentle, tissue-shrouded taps, I tried them in order. I had nine tries before the system locked me out. The eighth set worked, by some miracle.

Accessing her account allowed me to review her permissions. Unsurprisingly, she had *carte blanche*. Her cell phone, also company-issued, was outfitted with the same impressive security capabilities. Past activity showed she'd disabled the proximity sensors, the sound recording software, and the cameras across the lobby, the elevator corridor behind it, within the elevator itself, and inside The Red Room in the minutes before we arrived. Even now, the systems were disarmed. My reign of tyranny was nearly at an end, though. I was on a tight timetable, with twenty-four minutes of freedom remaining before the systems turned back on.

I peeked left, catching sight of her recumbent frame, passed out face down with one arm tossed off the side of the sofa. While I had the opportunity and while she slumbered so sweetly, I checked her personnel file in the HR system. A pop-up modal slowed me up for a second, prompting me to access new notifications in her inbox, but without marking them as read, I was able to circumvent the screen.

Hmm, let's see. Tsumugi Iruma, age thirty-eight. Native language is Japanese. Her height is five-nine, her weight is undefined, and the phone number and mailing address are the office's.

I kept digging, uncovering previous employers, education, and contact info from her saved CV. She'd graduated with honors from the universities I'd seen online. Her previous addresses all showed condo or apartment numbers. She'd completed an internship at a government agency outside Boston before taking her first major position, an HR director role at Gideon International.

Gideon? No shit. It looks like they canned her last, right before they sold the desks and chairs to the highest bidder.

With a derisive scowl, I read on. I found documentation of her immigration and her family status next. She'd achieved citizenship during college. Two attached files were loaded to her profile, one from the courts of California detailing her American status, and the other from Interpol. With a narrowed gaze, I placed the cursor over the Interpol file, poised to click as I heard her frame shift on the cushions to my left.

I froze on the spot, stealing a glance as she tossed onto her back, her palm moving to her forehead as she groaned listlessly. A few tenuous seconds later, her figure relaxed and she returned to sleep without another sound, her face turned to me with lips parted as if she awaited another kiss.

I waited until her chest rose and fell in a rhythmic cadence before returning to work. I didn't have much time left. I still wanted to venture downstairs before the security systems went back to work.

I clicked the Interpol file only to find it encrypted. The scramble of wingdings and system symbols required more time and experience than I had. The four-terabyte thumb drive in my purse was the perfect size for retrieving Avery's stashed files, with room left over for this little doozy of a cryptogram. I plugged the drive into the USB port and downloaded a copy of the file in less than thirty seconds. I'd page through Avery's programming files over my morning Kenyan blend, and send this unreadable mess to an expert I just happened to know well. With the USB tucked into my right bra cup, I was back on the hunt.

Before I could call my investigation comprehensive, I also pulled the files of the top brass, perusing for any suspicious data. There were no surprises in Drew's profile, not even his exorbitant salary nor the location of his Society Hill manor house. Likewise, Tim's data was incredible yet expected, his resume adorned with the best-known and most illustrious venture capital and start-up tech companies in the country. He'd given his money, his support, and his assistance to the blue chips before assuredly joining AH to do the same.

HR's only business partner, Joy, also had an extensive resume, including education from Su's alma mater, UCLA. Her first real job post-graduation was an entry-level data management position. The employer's name left me agape.

Gideon? Her, too?

She'd left their employment a month before Su, the reason for termination related to the company's financial demise. Su fired her, and yet they worked together here. It was a complicated and risky arrangement, one that felt devious at its core.

Her email address was listed below her corporate cell number and a Fishtown address.

`J.Hernandez@zmail.com.`

My eyes widened at the screen before my past crashed through the wall and into my present. Emerald eyes fixed lustily on me. I was again engaged in an illicit interlude with the window open enough for eavesdropping. A night that created quite the reputation for me at MIT came rushing back, along with the cracking I'd done just before. Doubt swirled with awe as I snickered silently at the screen.

I've come full circle. Joy Saracco is J. Hernandez? Damn, I wish there was more here.

With an incredulous headshake, I logged out completely, ensuring nothing looked untoward. The security software showed another eighteen minutes of freedom before the lockdown was scheduled to resume. That was enough time to make my way downstairs, nag the contents of Avery's hard drive, and be gone before the sound sensors picked up a single footfall.

The elevator posed a slight problem. Once I used my keycard, I'd be traceable. The fire escape plan on Su's wall gave me an idea. Six flights of descending stairs would get me to The Red Room. A firmly locked metal door formed the barrier between our work area and that clandestine staircase. A surreptitious operation was clearly more important than obeying fire codes.

I snuck out of the office, leaving behind only a dirty whiskey glass as proof I'd ever been there. A little of her lily essence stuck to my skin as I snuck down the escalator, careful to avoid any prying eyes from beyond the building's plate glass windows. On muted steps, I made my way to the staircase's door, tucked behind the security guard's station in the unoccupied lobby. Using the barrier tissue from Su's office, I grasped the door handle, relieved to see it acquiesce to a gentle twist and push. Within the dark, ten-foot-square cavern of descending steps, I used my cell phone's glow to cast a pale halo on the path. The metal grids on them rung out as I descended on narrow heels.

After passing five unmarked doors with two dozen steps between them, I arrived at the bottom of the alcove. The metal door looked the same on this side as the other. With tissue between my palm and the doorknob, I gripped it, only to find it unforgivingly stuck.

Fuck.

I checked my watch. I had twelve minutes remaining before the world clamped tight around me.

I'd picked locks in less time, but not without my toolkit. Inside my evening purse, I found tweezers and a hairpin, enough to get the job done, though not elegantly. Four minutes later, I was delving into my repertoire of colorful curses, my fingers tense and my irritation growing by the second. I needed six minutes to log in, transfer the data and get out. That gave me another ninety seconds of screwing around with this thing before I had to give up and trudge home a loser.

A minute later, the hairpin flipped the last tumbler and the knob mechanism jiggled encouragingly. With a shoulder nudge and a grunt, I pushed the heavy door in, awash in amber light originating from the projection globe at the center of the ring of power. With no time to spare, I emerged from the stairwell, astonished to catch movement in my peripheral vision.

Avery's chair spun, coming to a lazy stop, facing away from his computer as I stopped dead in my tracks.

* * * * *

"Any idea who it was?" He asked as I strolled down the dark and deserted city street.

"Not a clue. I took the extra minute I had and did a lap. Manager's door was locked. Nothing else was touched. Elevator was lobby level, so they must've used it to get out. All security systems were down. They knew exactly when to hit The Red Room."

"How curious," Bryan hummed in my ear, enjoying the mystery as much as I did. "Was the boy's computer unlocked?"

"Nope. Whoever it was managed to lock it up before I got the damn door open. If I'd been a little quieter, I'd have caught them red-handed. Hell, if I'd gone down there before I hacked the boss's computer, I'd have been golden."

"If only you'd prioritized the task at hand over finding your Valentino's in the boss's dark office."

"They're Blahnik's, you swine," I scolded without venom, turning the corner onto my street. "Not only did I snag the deets from the overly social nerd, but I also have a pretty little treasure I wasn't expecting to find. Keep insulting me and I won't share."

"It's probably more work for me anyway."

"Got it in one," I told him, tugging open the apartment building's entrance and heading to the elevator. "It's a beaut, too, but way above my pay grade. Would an SVP at the Northeast's most successful cyber security firm like a challenge?"

"You're assuming it'll be one," he scoffed snootily, like he'd been offered rail vodka. "I'll give it a shot. No digital transfers allowed. Put a code-locked thumb drive in the mail to my office, no tracking or delivery confirmation, and use your mom's birthday as the eight-digit code. Got it?"

My eyelids quivered instinctively. Her birthday passed the week before. She'd been a Taurus through and through, from her steadfast honor to her hardworking determination. The positive memories swept in first, followed immediately by saw-toothed guilt over missing dozens of graveside visits. I'd also been a wretchedly misbehaved daughter, especially after her diagnosis saddled the Daly household. That sat heavy on my soul, too.

You absolute bastard, bringing her up after such a perfect evening.

I swallowed back bile, erring on the side of caution by holding my tongue. I needed his neck on the line with this Interpol file, and I needed an ally in this delicate work. I'd regret snapping back. Silence lingered a little too long, a few extra blinks, before he interrupted my self-loathing.

"Earth to whatever-you're-calling-yourself. Thumb drive. Code locked. Overnight it. Got it?"

"I heard ya," I replied curtly, kicking off my heels. "It'll be out by nine. Anything else?"

"Yeah, quit stewing. You're killing the game in Philly. She'd be proud. Besides, misery doesn't suit you. Those heels with that sheath dress, on the other hand, must've been an absolute showstopper in that shithole town."

A warm wave washed over my heart at his quip. "It certainly got Su's attention. Thanks for your help with this."

"Anytime. Oh, and don't let up on Avery. Keep him in your back pocket, and for God's sake, girl, don't get ahead of yourself. This is unfolding like a Dickens novel."

I was too busy reminiscing to hear the rest of his sign off. I hung up and collapsed onto my office chair, my mind cemented twenty years in the past.

Whitehall, SC, 1993

The only thing she loved more than lilies was a cookies and cream chocolate bar, the ones wrapped in gray foil from the shop on the corner of Abington and Commerce. I snuck out early, hopping from my windowsill to the sturdy branch of the oak tree four feet away. It was my favorite means of escape from the house I'd grown to hate. Mike and Phil's putrid feet and hollering at sports turned my quiet house into a rowdy pigpen. Mom smiled through it all, offering snacks to Mike's legion of drunk buddies, but I knew better.

She's being nice. She misses peace. She just won't admit it.

I dashed to the shed. My bike, a simple three-speed with chipped yellow paint and worn padding on the handlebars, waited next to Phil's obnoxious charcoal ten-speed. I flicked up the kickstand and was gone in a flash. The sage green farmhouse disappeared from my rear-view mirror.

This was my favorite time of day, when dew weighed down the tall grasses, birds sung because they could, and the world didn't bother with me. Once everyone was awake and dressed, riding in their cars and pickup trucks to their boring nine-to-five grinds, the town turned cruel.

I hate the way they look at me.

I shook off the pity and rode like the wind. I'd forgotten a jacket. I didn't dare go back for it. I was grounded at home and on the radar at school. Detention the afternoon before meant I'd been trapped in my room all night. My Walkman and TV were taken away. That fate was to continue the entire following week.

All I did was use the library's computers outside school hours. Sheesh. Big deal.

I'd need to be back in less than a half-hour to escape unnoticed. I was cutting it close, but I had a lie ready in case Mom asked how I got the candy bar in the first place.

Clyde's opened at six a.m. sharp. It was the only place in town that offered coffee in paper cups. The place was crazy when I got there. A dozen people pushed their way in and out of the single door, ready to climb back into their cars and get to work. I edged inside, tucking between two old ladies bickering over the last ring of cardboard they called a "sleeve."

The shop owner's son eyed me carefully from the checkout, his mouth pulled down just a little as I made my way to the candy shelf. I was used to it, though. Everyone felt bad for me. They all spoke too quietly and stared at me for a little too long. No one thought I noticed. I noticed it all. How could I not?

Poor little Lizzie with the dead dad. Maybe if she hadn't been so terrible, he'd still be alive.

I grabbed the candy bar, keeping my eyes down on the way to the register. Alongside, the shop owner traded empty coffeepots for full ones. Adults with their hands jammed in their pockets fidgeted as they waited. I brushed by them without a word.

Dewey, Clyde's son and head cashier, was a high school junior. It was cruel of his dad to make him work before the bus made it to Commerce, but

Clyde was too busy brewing and dosing coffee to worry about his kid's feelings. The yawning teenager was a nice-looking guy, though, with brown hair hanging below his ears, pure grunge style, and a totally chill attitude.

"'What's up, Lizzie," Dewey asked casually, keying in my purchase. "Is that it?"

"Yeah, that's it."

He held out his hand without telling me the price. I knew it already. This was an almost weekly purchase. I had to suck up to Mom a whole lot nowadays, maybe too often, but this always did the trick. I handed over two quarters and a nickel and waved off the receipt. I was counting the seconds until I needed to be home.

"See ya," Dewey told me, stepping back once I had the bar tucked into my pocket.

I ran through the mass at the door, jumping back on my bike and picking up speed as the town gave way to cornfields. Early spring meant the tall stalks were missing. The road home was a straight shot, flat and narrow, all the way to my driveway. Across the street, the Goodings were propping open the massive doors of their farm's barn. On the walk from parking my bike to the towering tree outside my window, I watched their twin collies run circles around the couple as they led two horses out to pasture.

I climbed back up, glad to see my room exactly as I left it. The walls were covered with music posters bought on mall trips with Dad. I refused to take them down, even though most of the groups were either gone from radio play or had put out lousy singles lately. I also refused to take down the picture of us together at the state fair three years before, alongside the stage and waiting for the main act to go on. He looked so happy in that photo. The years since made no sense to me.

As quietly as I could manage, I snuck downstairs to the kitchen table. It was six-fifteen. Phil was probably already inhaling breakfast. We were normally at the table and elbow-deep in arguments before the parents made appearances. Mike was usually downstairs by six-thirty and gone within five minutes, his crusty coffee mug in hand as he hobbled to his pickup with as few words as possible. Mom took another ten minutes after him most mornings. She'd appear with her navy scrubs on. Her brown hair was always tied up in a loose bun. She was a burst of energy in the morning. That was yet another thing that made her marriage to Mike feel so weird. They were total opposites, just like Phil was to me.

Sure enough, Phil was at the table, a mixing bowl of sugary mess on the table in front of him. Like the neighbor's pigs eating from their trough, he inhaled the soggy slop. He was a little too focused on the back of the cereal box. I stood in the doorway watching him struggle with the circular maze until I couldn't hold back pitying laughter any longer.

"Left to the first bend, then right," I told him over his shoulder. "Three more lefts and you're there. And if you ever have trouble getting your shoes tied, I can ask Mike to pick you up some Velcro ones."

He snorted and kept eating wordlessly as I poured myself some juice and sat opposite him. Without my headphones, I was forced to listen to him slurp and chomp. I made it three minutes before launching to my feet. I lifted the phone hanging on the wall and used the rotary wheel to dial

Chey's number. She'd be up by now. I couldn't handle one more second of Phil.

It rang twice before she answered. "What's up, Lizzie?"

"Second time I heard that this morning," I replied, leaning against the wall. I couldn't go far. The coiled cord stretched five feet from wall to receiver. "Dewey's working again this morning, if you wanna stop in before the bus gets to you."

"Why would I wanna do that?" She asked, the sounds of water running in the background. Her parents had a cordless phone on the second floor, which made me jealous. She could hide her conversations easier than I could, and she knew who was calling before picking up. "He's a dope."

"He's a cute dope, or so your diary told me."

"Dude, seriously? When did you read my diary?"

I snickered automatically. "You fell asleep first and left it out. You should hide it better if you're embarrassed by it. Besides, Dewey's already said he's running that shop once his pop's gone. He's told the entire school. You'd get free stuff all the time."

"I don't need free stuff. I get an allowance every week because I never get detention for doing stupid crap."

I grumbled. "Goody two shoes. What are you doing after school?"

"It's Friday. Swim's until four-thirty, then homework before Mom drags me to her friend's house to babysit their kids while she has too much wine and complains about how worthless Dad is for three hours."

"Bummer," I remarked dryly. "See ya in first period."

"Yep, later."

She hung up first. I knew the rest of her morning consisted of slapping on the department store makeup I was apparently "too young for," saying good morning prayers with her father, and sliding on the high-top sneakers she'd gotten for Christmas. Not only was her family religious in a way I didn't understand, they were also loaded. Her daddy was a business lawyer, the type that couldn't talk about work when he got home, and her mother didn't have to work at all. I resented her family and their perfect household. The aging farmhouse I lived in was hardly worth bragging about.

I hung up just in time to see Mike walk into the kitchen. He was dressed in the normal, dingy flannel, worn jeans, and heavy boots he lived in. He eyed me impatiently as he passed on his way to the coffeepot. His tone was as unimpressive as his clothing. "No phone, either, kid."

I rolled my eyes. "You can't tell me what to do."

"He can tell you what *not* to do," Phil replied instantly, still fixated on his cereal.

"He can try."

With his cup filled and an irritated scowl on his dumb face, Mike approached me. "Watch it. Your mother's having a tough morning, and your escapades aren't helping. You want her dealing with your nonsense, too?"

I exhaled, crossing my arms. "Don't pretend like you know what I want."

In a voice lowered against his son's ears, he murmured to me as he brushed past. "You want your dad back, and he's gone. I'm here now. Deal with it."

The front door slammed as I gritted my teeth. This morning was just awesome, just like so many others had been lately. The only difference was

Mom wouldn't be working today. She'd gotten sick weeks before, and she'd been distant and not hungry ever since. She worked for two weeks despite the low fevers and constant aches, but as of Monday, she'd been calling out.

She and Mike whispered a lot behind closed doors, and she hadn't gone anywhere socially in a while. Her eyes looked more tired than usual. Basic chores had been handed over to Phil and me. Mike tried to grocery shop for her, but always forgot things and never brought me along to help. I knew what she liked best. No one asked me. I'd have been better at that than cleaning anyway.

I lingered in the doorway another minute, torn between biking to school early just to escape this place and waiting for Mom to finally appear from the upstairs bedroom. I'd gone to the trouble of getting the candy bar and didn't want to wait until after dinner to give it to her. Besides, the longer it sat in my pocket, the more tempting it was. I'd shied away from food since Mom's illness started. It was all I could do to show support and let her know she wasn't alone.

A loud honk startled me. I jumped, slamming my shoulder into the phone. The handset dropped to the floor with a clatter. I rubbed the sore spot, pins and needles extending down my arm as Phil tossed his plastic bowl and spoon into the sink. He'd slung his backpack over his shoulder and was headed for the front door before I could replace the handset.

I screamed from the doorway as he brushed past. "It goes in the dishwasher, dill hole!"

"Buzz off," he called back as he escaped. He left the door wide open.

I followed him to the stoop. With fists on hips, I scowled at his back. His friend, the captain of the high school football team, leaned across the bench seat to toss open the passenger door of his pickup. Before he hopped aboard, Phil turned back to me with a provoking grin. I turned my back and slammed the door as hard as I could. Every framed photo of my new "family" jittered on the walls as the house fell slowly back into the silence I missed so much.

Chiding rung out from the top of the staircase a few seconds later. "Elizabeth Cushing, you know better. He's your brother. You gotta pick your battles a little better."

"Whatever," I mumbled. "He's not my brother. I don't have a brother."

Mom was wrapped in a plush robe and her eyes were more tired than I'd ever seen. She descended slower than usual. "Stop being so shortsighted, honey. Right now, he's a stinky lug that eats us out of house and home, but he's a lot bigger than you, he's got loads of buddies, and he's family."

"I didn't ask for that. I don't want more family."

Once she'd reached the bottom of the staircase, she cupped my cheek with her hand, dragging my attention up from my ankles. "You're right, you didn't. *I* wanted more family. You're my family, so you're along for the ride. And we're done arguing about this. Go get your bookbag before the bus gets here. You just gotta get through today, then you've got two whole days to do nothing."

With a grunt, I walked back into the kitchen. I was ready for some more juice. The scolding left my mouth dry. My bag was hanging on the kitchen table's far chair, exactly where I'd left it the afternoon before. I slung it over my back while Mom poured herself a cup of coffee with a shaky hand. I watched her struggle getting the pot back onto the burner. She sighed. It was a hollow sound. I'd never heard her make a sound like that before. I made my way to the counter and hopped up, sitting alongside the steaming mug before reaching for her spoon.

"Lizzie, my love," she told me, handing it over with a little smile. "You've been stirring my coffee for, what, eleven years now?"

"Since my second birthday," I told her before dumping in some sugar and counting to ten aloud as I swirled the spoon in the inky black. I handed it back so it could make its way into the dishwasher's rack. "And I'll keep doing it. Oh, I almost forgot." I reached into my pocket and pulled out the candy bar, handing it over. "Look what I found."

She smiled again but shook her head judgingly as her palm closed around it. "Should I ask where this came from?"

I shook my head no and she laughed. She snuck the chocolate into her robe pocket before laying her arms around my middle. Our heights were even, so I could finally read the struggle in her eyes. They were brown like mine, but way more tired.

"Mom, what's going on? I hear you and Mike talking and I hear you crying. Why are you sick?"

She exhaled. "Lizzie, it's a lot. Are you sure you want to know?"

I gaped. "Of course! Come on. I'm not a kid anymore. I already lost Dad. That was a lot. Just tell me."

My mother wilted even more at the mention of my father. She released another deep breath. "I am sick, Lizzie, as you know. It's not something I'm going to recover from. The doctors know what it is, but that doesn't mean there's a cure for it."

I was instantly confused. The world felt smaller in that moment, like all I'd known had been a lie. "What are you talking about? You work at a hospital. No one knows how to make this better?"

"Oh, honey," she continued listlessly. "All I can say is that I'm glad you and Mike don't have it, too. It's contagious, but only in certain ways. Your dad had it, too."

"But," I began, tripping back through memories. "Dad didn't die of a disease. He–"

"Yes, I know," she interrupted. "He knew he was sick. He didn't want to lose control. He made a choice. I'm not going to do that, but that doesn't mean I'm going to get better. It's time to come to terms with it. It's something that can't be cured right now, and I have it."

"I wish Mike had it," I muttered. "I'd rather him be sick than you."

Her expression soured. "Come on. You don't have to love him. Just be nice. He's doing his best. Have a heart."

"Why do I have to be nice to someone who hates me?"

"He doesn't hate you. He just doesn't understand you. There are going to be a lot of people in this world who don't understand you. They won't get why you make the decisions you make, or why you say what you say, but that doesn't mean they're not worth your time."

"Why would I waste my time with people like that?"

"Because there's something to be learned from everyone on this planet, my dear. Sometimes they tell you what you need to know, and sometimes you gotta read between the lines and figure them out on your own. Either way, that's why we're here on Earth, to learn from each other. You'll see."

* * * * *

I learned a tough lesson from a stranger four days later. The doctor in the emergency room came out from behind the swinging doors to tell us she'd died. Mike sat down without a word and Phil turned his back on the doc. That Tuesday came and went, followed by a Wednesday, Thursday and Friday filled with delivered flowers, Mike's short temper, and Phil's awkward silence. I camped in my bedroom, staring at photos of Mom, Dad, and me. I refused to eat, to shower, or to do anything asked of me. I knew I'd be gone, too, before long.

Saturday morning was humid and overcast. I was restless, same as I'd been all week. Twin knocks on the door made me sigh. Two more knocks rung out in the wake of my silence.

I finally shouted, knowing they'd never leave. "What?"

The door edged open. Phil's dopey face appeared. He looked sorry. The sympathy couldn't have been legit. "Hey, we're leaving in a half-hour. We gotta be there early."

"I'm not going."

He huffed. "I don't want to go, either, but we gotta." He pulled the door open a bit more before tossing a black bundle of fabric onto my bed. It landed on my bare legs. "You're supposed to wear this."

"I'm not going."

He shook his head and closed the door, leaving me alone again.

Once I heard his footsteps on the stairs, I grabbed for the delivery. It was a long black dress, a straight shaft of cotton from shoulder to ankle, without any decorations or trimmings at all. I'd worn simple black to Dad's funeral, too. This was just a few sizes bigger.

I jumped up, tugged open the window, and tossed the dress outside. It landed in a heap on the dead grass around the giant oak. I hoped Mike was sitting on the couch in the living room so he could see it fall.

Now that Mike's the only one left, he won't let me stay here. I might as well pack my bag now.

I retrieved my small suitcase, tucking a few outfits into it. Once I'd added a few books, photos, and dollar bills to the stash, I realized I couldn't leave without Mom's spoon. It was all I had left of her. Her other possessions had been cleared in the days before, including anything I would've liked to keep, but I knew the simple spoon was still in the drawer beside the bent forks and dull knives.

I snuck from my room and made my way to the bottom of the stairs, relieved to find no one there and her spoon where it always was. I fetched it, tucked it into my pocket, and was halfway back to the stairs before Mike appeared. His expression was half angry and half pitiful as he pitched the dirty funeral dress at me.

"Put it on. Let's go."

I dropped the dress again, letting it pool around my feet. "No. I'm not wearing this. I'm not going."

I watched tears crest his eyelid before his hands moved up to hide them. "Lizzie, dear God, please. Just put the dress on and come on. I'm asking nicely. Please, just do this for me, Hell, do it for your mother. Do it for your dad. I don't care. Just stop being difficult today and put the damn dress on before…"

He stopped there, his words trailing off as he disappeared out the front door, letting it slam behind. I stood still for a few seconds, knowing how his sentence would've ended if he'd finished it. I'd been dead on. I was headed for an orphanage. He'd take over the house with Phil, and I'd be trashed like a moldy onion.

Like Hell, I will. I'm gone.

* * * * *

When the preacher finally stopped talking and all the adults I knew from Mom's work left two at a time, I started looking for Chey. I knew she was there. This was her church. She spent every Sunday here.

I found my friend on the steps up to the altar, tucked between her parents. All three were on their knees with closed eyes, in the shadow of the life-sized bronze figure on the cross hanging above us. My stride slowed to a stop as I watched them pray so passionately in words I couldn't hear. A few seconds passed before I felt a tap on my shoulder. I spun on my heels, astounded to find Dewey standing there. He fidgeted a bit in a navy suit jacket with a band tee beneath. He was clearly as uncomfortable as I was.

"Hey there," he said in a weak voice. "I know you've heard this a million times, but I'm really sorry."

I looked away, nodding a little. "Yeah, it's all right."

"It's really not," he told me. "I see how everyone looks at you. It's not cool."

"It's just pity. I'm used to it."

"You wanna get out of here?"

I did, more than anything. I met his gaze and took his hand without thinking. "Yes. Now."

He nodded once and led me outside. My eyes were on our feet as I kept in step with him. As we made our way down the center aisle and out the front doors, I heard conversations stop in my wake. I wasn't free yet, though Dewey was doing what he could.

He paused at the far end of the parking lot, turning back to me as he pulled open a blue car's passenger door. "Hop in."

I did, settling in the cloth seat as he closed the door behind me. I could hear wandering funeral attendants making their way to cars around me. I turned my back to the darkly tinted window, watching as Dewey slid in behind the wheel and tugged his own door shut. He turned to me across the center console and gazed around his car's windows. "In ten minutes, everyone'll be gone. Can you make it that long?"

I wasn't sure why he was being so kind or so patient with me. He was just a junior that sold me candy bars sometimes. I was a thirteen-year-old freshman. He wasn't a jock like Phil or a popular kid as far as I knew. The Seattle soundtrack playing around us meant he spent a lot of time in his head, much like I did. Maybe that's why he cared. I wasn't sure.

"I have to," I told him. "I've got a bag packed at home. I'm running once they're asleep."

His voice lifted and sharpened. "What? Why?"

"I'm the only Cushing left, that's why." I told him, mimicking his tone. "Mike's got the house now. Phil's the favorite. I'm just a reminder of who's dead and gone." I huffed, holding my tears. "It's easier for everyone if I just disappear. I've got the cash Dad left me. That's good enough."

"No, Lizzie," he told me, his voice quieting again. "Mike's not like that. He's not gonna toss you out."

"He already threatened to. I'm a thorn in his side. You don't know the shit I've dealt with since he's come around. And now I don't have Mom on my side anymore."

"So, find a better way out. You're smart. Shit, you're smarter than half the assholes in this town. I know. I hear them bickering and acting like idiots every morning at the shop. Didn't you get suspended for hacking into the school's grades?"

I snickered. Word got around fast, but the gossip wasn't exactly true. "That's hearsay. I got detention for being in the library computer lab before the school opened. I'd deleted the history and cookies before I got caught, but that's just between you and me."

"See?" His amber eyes twinkled just a little, excited for me in a way I'd never seen before. "How'd you learn that shit?"

I just shrugged. I had no intention of telling him anything.

This is just him being nice. He doesn't care. No one does.

He reclined back on his seat, his eyes on the roof of the car. "Man, I wish I could tinker with grades. Did you change yours?"

"I don't need to," I replied. "I just wanted to see if this uppity bitch in my class really did ace a geography test. She told everyone she did, but she's an idiot and the test was hard. She got a C. Liar."

He snorted, looking over at me with a smile. In that moment, I understood why Chey thought he was cute. There was something fascinating about his casual pose and his dark brows. He had the income and freedom I envied. He was old enough to be cool and young enough to be a friend at the same time.

I guess I gazed a little too long because he sat up again, edging across the console and into my personal bubble. He said my name softly, a little too sweetly, and my stomach flipped.

There, in the church parking lot behind tinted windows, Dewey reached for me. He cupped my cheek the way my mother once had, laid his lips on mine, and gave me an escape from reality. I'd studied how to use computers, how to solve complicated algebra, and the ins and outs of my history textbooks, but I'd never bothered with this. No one had ever bothered with me. Here, in Dewey's front seat, with his warm breath on my face, I forgot all about everyone and everything else.

I even forgot Chey and her interest in him as his hands slipped down to my shoulders and his face tipped right to kiss me harder. I was just as excited as he was. Before long, his fingers were exploring under my clothes. The whole encounter was over so quickly, I barely remembered it happening at all.

In the passenger seat, winded with my underwear in my right hand, I panted and closed my eyes. Silence filled the space for a few seconds before he screamed, "Oh, my God! What the fuck!"

I jumped in the seat, my eyes instantly fixating on the same spot as his. Between my legs, below the hem of the dress he's rucked up, blood flowed from me. It saturated his seat and dripped to the floorboards as my vision narrowed. A long gray tunnel followed by blackness swallowed me whole.

* * * * *

The sun set over the sage farmhouse hours later. I pushed the front door open and ran upstairs in my formal flats. Mike gave chase with Phil close behind, shouting unanswered questions at his father's back. I managed to get my bedroom door closed and locked with a second to spare. Mike slammed into it, but thankfully, it didn't budge.

"Lizzie! Open this door right now!"

I panted, winded and scared, with my back pressed to the door. I felt his heavy thuds against my spine as I slid to the floor, tears pouring from my eyes. The funeral scared me. Dewey scared me. Mike scared me. Now, I was scaring myself most of all.

While Mike's pounding continued, I tugged off my dirty dress. The blood had dried, disappearing onto the black fabric, though the smell of old pennies remained. All I could think about was the horror on Dewey's face, then quickly throwing open his car door and sprinting across the lot to get away from it. After what we'd done, seeing the panic and the anger in his eyes was terrifying. I needed to get away. With nowhere else to go, I ran to

Chey's house, blood dripping down my thighs onto her doormat while I waited for someone, anyone, to answer the door. Her mother watched in horror as Chey led me to a bathroom, wiped me clean, brought me some juice to stop my dizziness, and talked me down. Unfortunately, Mike was waiting with her mother outside the bathroom door when I emerged, puffy-eyed and exhausted.

After a silent ride home with Mike and Phil in their suit jackets and me in my blood-stiffened dress, I'd made it this far. Sitting on the floor in my bra and shoes, I cried as quietly as I could.

The pounding on the door stopped after a few minutes. I didn't hear any footsteps down the hall beyond, but I didn't risk moving. I just needed to wait another hour or two, then make my way down the oak tree's branches and to freedom. I didn't owe anyone any explanations. I just needed to be gone.

"Lizzie?"

My eyes snapped open, tears drying on my cheeks as I slipped away from the door. "Go away, Phil."

"I can't," he told me, his voice barely audible through the wood. "Just let me in, would you?"

"Is Mike gone?"

"Yeah, he's gone. Let me in."

I didn't trust Phil's word and expected to see Mike's vicious face again. I slid on a red shirt and shorts before opening the door warily. "What do you want?"

Phil was alone, dressed in a white tee and his dress pants. He eyed me with sorrow. I was getting tired of the pity and wished I'd kept the door closed. "Can I come in?"

With a huff, I moved aside. "Make it quick."

He stepped inside before turning back to me. "I'm sorry, Lizzie. Today's sucked for us all, but it's been way worse for you."

I watched him carefully, trying to decide if his words were sincere, or if Mike had put him up to this. It wouldn't have surprised me to know I was being played with. "What do you care?"

"What do I care?" He repeated heatedly, flopping onto my bed without an invitation. "Do you think I don't? Susan was as much my mother as yours. You don't get it, do you?"

I couldn't help raising my voice as I squared off with him. "*Get* what? And what the hell are you talking about?"

He lowered his face into his palms. "Jesus, Lizzie. My mom's gone, too, in case you didn't notice. Did it ever occur to you that I've lost two parents, too, you absolute bitch? If you pulled your head out of your ass for two fucking seconds..."

His voice trailed off as he descended into tears. I watched as the varsity fullback wept on my lavender bedspread like a baby. For the first time in three years, I saw him in a new light. Right now, he wasn't just an obnoxious jock, vying for my mother's attention. Unfortunately, though, I had no patience for his outrageous outburst.

"Don't you *dare*," I warned, turning my back on him before the pathetic routine worked on me. "Your mom died a hero. My dad died as a laughingstock. It's a little different."

"They both died by bullets," he told me. "They both died without saying goodbye. And I don't care what you think or what you say. Susan was a mom to me, too."

"You still have your dad," I contested as I lifted the state fair photo from my suitcase, still waiting on the floor by the window. "You've got someone. I'm alone. And now I'm a laughingstock, too. Dewey's gonna tell his friends everything."

"No, he's not."

The tone of his voice, the heat in it, made me turn around to face him. "What? How are you so sure?"

He leaned forward, his soggy eyes suddenly determined. "I told him to keep his mouth shut about whatever happened. I told him I'd beat the shit out of him, then turn him over to the entire offensive line for their turns, if he opens his damn mouth. And I will. I'll destroy him myself. You're my sister, even if you don't see it that way. What he did wasn't cool."

I released a slow breath. Word was already out. I figured it would be once Chey's Christian mother saw me bleeding like that. "Truth is, I didn't stop him. He was kind enough. He didn't force me. I just bled a lot after. I guess that happens. Chey told me it's normal to bleed a little, but not like that."

"Dad said that Susan told him years ago that you bleed a lot when you get hurt. Is that true?"

I nodded a little. "Yeah, and I bruise a lot, too."

Phil nodded. "You'll bruise from this, too. The first time I had sex, she bled and bruised, too, but not that much. A little bit of red came out. I wouldn't have noticed if she hadn't said something. She said her inner thighs bruised up a little the next day. It freaked me out when she told me, like I'd really hurt her. She said it was okay. I believed her. And she was fine a day or two later."

I slowly made my way across the room, settling beside him with a few inches between our knees. "When was that? How old were you?"

"Younger than you. I was at a party in eighth grade. We got dared to kiss. It went farther than that. She said it was okay to, and I had a condom on me. It wasn't as big a deal as some people say it is. I just worried that she'd regret it. She didn't seem to. I didn't, either. We never did anything else, and she moved away that summer."

I nodded but stayed silent. I'd forgotten about condoms. Worry now crept its way up my throat along with the shame I already felt.

He turned to face me, sliding his knee up onto the blanket. "Did Dewey use protection?"

I didn't answer. I didn't even look at him.

"Shit," he murmured, turning back to place both feet on the floor. "You're not going to like this question, but that's tough nuts for you. Have you had a period yet?"

Mom and I had "the talk" the year before. I'd been unexcitedly waiting for it ever since. I managed to shake my head with my eyes locked on my feet.

"Okay," he replied after releasing a deep breath. "You're probably fine, then. I'll ask Sonya to grab you a test just in case. You gotta wait a week or two before you use it, though. Tony's embarrassed buying condoms, but the dope thinks it's less embarrassing to make his girlfriend buy pregnancy tests. What a moron."

I knew those names peripherally. Tony had brought Sonya by to watch a game with Phil and Mike before. They'd seemed nice, normal, and kind. I never thought about them having sex, nor pictured it until that moment. I never wanted to imagine it in the first place, but now I'd never unsee it.

"I'm just letting you know," Phil continued with a patient tone. "There's nothing wrong with what you did, no matter what anyone else says. You didn't 'lose' anything. You didn't make a 'mistake.' It was just a choice. Try not to worry about it too much. People are going to talk, whether Dewey does or not. People saw you run almost a mile with blood on your legs. People might assume they know what happened and who started it, but I'll be damned if I'll let Dewey badmouth you. Just keep your head up until everyone finds the next piece of shit to talk about."

I glanced over at Phil, astonished to find him so put-together. He'd wept for his Marine mother minutes before, and now he was acting like the big brother I never asked for. "You don't know what it's like to be a girl, to be the daughter of two dead parents, to get pitied like I do. I can't go anywhere or say anything without people thinking I'm just some damaged kid. I'm sick of it. I'm leaving. I hate it here."

"And where are you going?" He gestured to my packed bag. "If that's all you're taking, you'll be back by morning."

I huffed, crossing my arms.

"Look, Lizzie, neither of us wants this to be how it is, but it is. You can keep hating me and giving me shit if you want, if it makes you feel better. You can be a bitch to Dad, but it'll only make things worse. We're in this shit together. He's not such a bad guy. He's just never been around girls much. I play football. I like burgers. I'm the boy he raised. You're not."

"Thank God," I murmured. "I'd be a tougher dude than you."

Phil chuckled. "You'd be a bigger pain in the ass, that's for sure. Dad's gotta work to keep bills paid. I'm gonna work to help pay for stuff, too, but you're too young. He's not gonna have time for you, so don't worry about him being all over you all the time. Just try not to be so fucking difficult, would you? I have a feeling I'll be the one chasing you all over town like I did today."

"You," I looked over, shocked. "You followed me?"

"Get a clue, Lizzie. It's a good thing the coach runs us so hard. You're quick. Did you think I'd let you run off by yourself when you were clearly hurt? Once you got to Chey's, I doubled back on Dewey, but not before I knew you were okay."

I released a shaky breath, my eyes blurring with tears. "I… I had no idea."

"I know," Phil replied quietly. "I got you, Lizzie. I've always got you. Just try not to screw me too much, all right?"

Philadelphia, PA, 2013

"It's absolutely the truth," I told my happy hour companion. "Half the town blamed him, and half the town blamed me. It was both our faults, but no matter what we told people, they had their opinions."

The full-time security guard from Anderson-Hilliance was fascinated by my tales of past dalliances, though I'd dialed them way down and changed the parties' names to protect the innocents of Whitehall. Serena had never been to South Carolina and wouldn't have had her first encounter at thirteen outside a church after her mother's funeral. She'd been sixteen and in the backseat of her high school crush's SUV at a district championship basketball game in Cranberry Township.

"I wouldn't have taken you for the type," the chocolate-skinned hulk told me, sitting forward at the bar just a bit. His eyes narrowed, darting from my gaze to my cleavage and back. "I guess the middle-class polish hides a wild child, huh?"

His tortured metaphor and incorrect turn of phrase made Lizzie cringe, but Serena displayed a courteous smile. I continued to garner Julian's undivided attention. It'd all begun the moment I pushed open the towering glass door of the Philly headquarters in that tailored interview suit months before. Getting him to agree to a drink at the Fishtown pub had been no problem at all. I'd chosen a place far enough from work to not raise coworker's suspicion. No one from The Red Room would come into a pool hall like this on a weeknight.

His heavy watch clanged on the bar top as he gestured for another drink. This was number three. I was nursing a second glass of red, navigating the tangle of flirtation and covert reconnaissance while he imbibed doubles of top-shelf gin diluted with store-brand tonic. He'd offered me the limes from the previous two doses, hoping I'd take the bait and bite them with our eyes locked, but I'd simply eaten them whole, astonishing him into an impressed smirk. He still watched me chew, and his gaze followed the lump down my throat to my collarbone, his imagination no doubt going wild.

His third round arrived. I repeated the show yet again when the wedge of citrus was passed to me on a square napkin. He snickered aloud this time, lifting his glass in my direction before downing half in a single swallow. I sipped, waiting for his gulp before bothering to ask my next inquiry.

"How long have you worked with Greg at AH?"

His onyx brows narrowed ever so slightly. "It's been about a year. He's a nice enough guy, but he's all business. I've invited him out on nights with my boys a dozen times. He's always got other shit going on. The bosses like how straight he plays it. I think he's boring as hell."

Exactly as I figured. Good to know I'm sniffing at the right hydrant.

"Shame," I murmured. "I only ever see the two of you working. It'd be nice if he'd be more social, since you're already together so much. I guess you can't make someone do anything, though, right?"

He nodded, feigning wisdom, before lazily laying an arm over the back of his barstool, turning on it to face me with a glazy look. Reclined like this, with his muscled arms and chest outlined by snug cotton, plus a cleanly-trimmed beard, he would've been a real treat for a genuinely interested party. He clearly knew the routine and what vapid women expected. He had no idea what I was after, though. That much was clear when another boujie drink arrived at his elbow.

Time to up the ante. He's a high roller.

I deigned to cross my leg a little slower than strictly necessary, my linen-blend skirt shifting up on my thigh. A stiletto sandal strapped over my pedicured foot arched up into his field of vision as my right knee nestled atop my left. I tapped the underside of the bar with my right foot before tossing my hair back over my shoulder. With wine glass delicately resting in my palm and my head tipped to the right, I mimicked his confident smirk, taking a slow sip while he tucked his lips between his teeth.

"I'm glad I get to see you every day, Serena," he told me in a honeyed voice. "I'd do a whole lot for you if you asked."

Mm hmm. And?

"Oh?" I hummed sweetly, finishing off the last of my Shiraz. "It's a good thing I'd only ask for your time and attention, Julian. No harm in either of those things, is there?"

"Nah," he replied casually with a grin that would've melted a sweeter girl's heart. "You've got both, whenever you want 'em."

I nodded appreciatively, setting my empty balloon glass on the bar, and waving off a refill when the bartender whisked it away. I'd suffered a long enough delay and was rounding the clubhouse turn with this guy. He clearly hadn't read his employment contracts as closely as I had. Either that, or he played wilder and looser than I dared.

"I guess I'd just want to know one thing."

"And that is?"

I leaned forward on my barstool, close enough to recapture the pungent musk of his cologne over the smell of lager and fried food around us. "Sometimes, when I'm working," I let my voice trail off, lifting a brow for emphasis before continuing in a hushed tone. "I need a little release, so to speak. I hope you know a place we can sneak away to, if the mood strikes."

He sat forward, mere inches between us as his expression turned to pure sin. "There are only five spots I know of in that whole place, and only one I've got access to."

"Oh?" I repeated in that same damsel tone. "Where are we meeting, then?"

His chuckle was audacious and appreciative. He clearly was more than a little flattered at my open invitation. "You gotta get past Greg, Boo. The stairs down to your office is the only place I know of, and the door's behind where he sits. Lobby's watched twenty-four-seven. It won't be easy."

So, the other four spots are the exec's offices, then. Gotcha.

"Greg's Joy's go-to. I'm sure he's called away often enough. I'll tell you what." I parted my lips slowly, touching the tip of my tongue to my left incisor with a playful expression. "I'll let you know when it's on. You get rid of him. We're golden, and you, well," I paused to bite my bottom lip. "You'll be so satisfied that you might just forgive my little interruption."

His glassy eyes twinkled just a little as he reclined again, downing the rest of his fourth dose. "Damn, girl. If that's what you want, you got it."

Sigh. This wasn't even a challenge.

With my prey ensnared, all I needed was an out. While he was distracted by yet another refill, I shot off a clandestine text. Five seconds later, my phone rang. Bryan's number displayed broadly as I slid off my stool.

"Shit, I was worried about this," I told him, feigning irritation. "I gotta run. Thanks for the drinks, Julian, and don't you worry." I winked at him as he wilted with disappointment. "I'll be in touch."

I sauntered away, out onto the street and out of sight before lifting my phone to my ear. "You're a lifesaver."

"How did our little operation go?" Bryan asked slyly.

"Like taking candy from a man-baby," I told him, slipping on a pair of designer shades and merging into the pedestrian flow of traffic.

* * * * *

Julian was missing from the guard station when I arrived two mornings later. It wasn't a huge surprise. After waving flirtatiously the following morning on my way downstairs, I anonymously reported him for fraternization. While I waited to muster alongside my peers, I knew he was detained in Joy's office, cologne-tinged sweat pouring off him while regretting his decision to meet me that night. If he was anything like my dopey stepbrother's deputy, though, he'd protect my honor and not say a word. Even if he did throw me under the bus to save his own skin, I'd simply deny the whole thing. There'd been no witnesses. His word against mine meant I'd be chosen, as hourly security was a whole lot easier to replace than Red Room specialists.

Sure enough, muster progressed as usual with only Greg at the security desk. I waited a few minutes afterward, but Julian hadn't reappeared. With any luck, he'd be dismissed for the clear breach of his contract, and I'd be done with that loose end.

I stepped away from the lobby, on my way to the descending elevator shaft, when a voice over my shoulder stopped me. "Serena, a moment, if you would?"

I turned back, slapping on a smile as Joy approached on swift steps. Her blonde hair had been trimmed into a modest bob, her bright eyes appraising me in the hall's dimmed lights. My response was light and jovial. "Of course, Joy. What can I help with?"

"I have a document to go over with you. I tried to catch you last night before you left, but I guess you got held up?"

I nodded once. I'd stayed late to get our newest client's contracts reviewed before they went live. "Sorry, I didn't know you needed me. I'd have come up to your office."

"Oh, it's okay. You're here now. Come with me, please."

I nodded pertly and followed her as she ascended the escalator to the corporate wing. Whatever document she had to show me was important enough to pull me away from cementing this new client. I just prayed it didn't have Julian's name on it.

Inside her expansive office, with the door firmly closed, she turned to me with that same incandescent smile. "Pull up a chair, would you?"

She gestured to the long side of her desk, then to the rolling armchairs positioned around the interview table I recognized. Following commands, I maneuvered one alongside her desk while she positioned her office chair on the opposite side, facing me with the eighteen inches of polished wood between us. From her top desk drawer appeared a white document, covered in black text with headers and footers, plus yesterday's date on display. I perused the cover page, relieved to see the words "Performance Review - Probationary" emblazoned on it.

Wow, it's been three months already?

"The bulk of this document is formulary. It's based on your job description," Joy began, turning the document around so it faced me. "The last two pages are customized."

I nodded once and leaned over the review of my position's expectations, bullet pointed as they'd been on my employment contract. There were no surprises.

"Job performance is here," she told me, flipping to the second to last page. "It's broken out into three grading criteria, on a scale from one to five. Your supervisor rates you on overall performance, then collaborates with upper management to rate your intrinsic value to the organization. The third criteria is based on peer review."

"I wasn't asked to review anyone for their evaluations," I spoke aloud, though I hadn't meant to.

Joy managed a cordial smile. "Based on your performance so far, I have every confidence you'll be tapped for feedback before long."

The page detailing my job performance was as expected, too. There were no negative comments to find, and I was praised for my thorough analysis and punctuality in both attendance and task completion. The word "satisfactory" was written in alongside signatures belonging to each of the three bigwigs in the adjacent offices.

Joy flipped to the last page. "This is the behavioral and engagement page. Just like the page before, it's made up of feedback from your supervisor, the top brass, and your peers. The evaluation survey asks about things like overall attitude toward your coworkers, willingness to be a team player, and showing effort to learn from each other. I was a little surprised at the findings here."

She wasn't the only one. I gazed down the page, astonished to see more twos and threes than I wanted to. The page before was studded with fours and fives.

Am I the office prig?

"I..." I exhaled, sitting back with crossed arms. "It's only been three months and I'm still acclimating to working alongside others like this. I'm not happy with this and a little put-off by it."

This is a disgrace. I've been nothing but tolerant of those dopey nerds.

"Fortunately, this doesn't account for much of your final rating, and as you can see, you're satisfactory overall. Try not to worry too much. Like you said, you're new and most of your peers graduated together from the same school. Many of them knew each other before."

They're MIT grads, just like me. I'm just a few years ahead, and it's a boys' club down there.

I released a slow breath. "I understand. I'd hate to see this continue, as it's something I'm not sure how to fix. Job performance and diligence, those I can adjust. How others perceive me isn't in my control."

Truth unspoken; I didn't want to be "perceived" that closely. Evidently my peers had picked up on that simple fact. Being standoffish at work suddenly meant I was at risk of losing this job and my only shot at finding my idol. I was existing in the gray area and being scolded for it. I hated that reality more than how kindly Joy was treating me, despite the criticism on display between us.

"You have more influence on that than you think," she replied, laying her palms on her lap. "I know Philly is new to you and maybe you're not used to being here quite yet but trying to fit in a little better might alleviate some of this. I'd love to see you make some connections here, to get to know your peers as more than just coworkers, and to let them see who Serena really is. You're the only quiet one at muster, standing off by yourself. It's probably not who you really are, but it comes off the wrong way. You're a valuable member of this team. I'd hate to see you walk away from this thinking no one wants you here."

That's not it, you twit. The truth is much worse. I don't want to be here. I'm here because I have to be. Maybe I'm not hiding that fact well.

I mimicked her posture, lowering my eyes to the document again. "You're suggesting I get out more? This is a workplace. I've never been asked to be social as part of work requirements."

"And that makes us a weird place to work, I know," she confirmed, tucking a blonde lock behind her ear. "Su designed it to be different, to be more inclusive and to better suit a modern workforce. It's bad enough that we lock you all in a silent basement. She and I couldn't see denying you all from making connections on your own time. Of course, not dating connections, but anything up to that."

I hid the snicker, knowing the boom had dropped on Julian in this very office not long before I sauntered in. The idea was clearly fresh in her mind.

"Oh, I'd never dally with a coworker," I confirmed confidently. "I guess I'm struggling with finding a compromise between keeping my private life private and not seeming too distant. I've never had to balance them before, and certainly not for a grade."

Joy handed me a blue pen. "Write that at the bottom of this last page. It's the truth and I know it. I'd love to see you find a middle ground. There are so many personalities here, and there's so much potential. Reach out and be yourself. It'll all work out in the end."

Her lips tugged up at the corners. I was out of practice, but I was sure I caught a glimpse of something nefarious in the spark of her eyes.

Her voice cut through my thoughts. "All I need's a signature, then you're cut loose."

After adding my pseudonym below my handwritten comments, I turned the document back around to face her. She slid a paperclip onto the corner before standing.

I rose with her, following her to her office door. Her voice rung out into the atrium beyond as she stepped through. "Thanks for your time, Serena. Let me know if you have any other concerns."

"I will," I told her before stepping to the escalator, my palms obnoxiously sweating. I needed to get away and rethink my strategy before this whole operation went tits up.

"Oh, and Serena?"

I turned back with a quizzical expression just as the top step began to carry me downward.

"Conquer the day," she told me, her expression blithe and neutral as it disappeared from view.

Philadelphia, PA, 2015

As if nothing had happened between us, I met Su outside Supremo bright and early on Monday morning. She'd texted asking if we were still on for our usual stop. I, without reason to deny the pleasure, responded affirmatively. No mention was made of our liaison, and I hadn't reached out since fleeing her office.

The flash drive was on its way to Bryan, estimated to arrive tomorrow by lunch, and I hadn't heard a word from anyone at AH since leaving Friday afternoon. If a data breach or security alert had triggered, my work cell would've rung instantly. I felt home free. All seemed right with the world, and I was loving every moment of it.

Su's expression also eased my mind as she came into view, a beautiful shift dress of immaculate white on her towering frame. Her black hair was braided modestly, a bit of sheen radiating from her forehead as the summer sun crested the horizon beyond the high-rises. The week promised brutally hot and humid temperatures. I thought moving to Philadelphia would mean escaping the oppression. I'd been wrong every summer day since.

"Hey there," she greeted as I tossed open the café's door for her. "It feels like we were just here."

"I spent all weekend recovering, yet here I am, back for more."

"They're the illness and the antidote, I suppose," she commiserated, stepping to my side as we waited in line. The counter was cleared of the booze bottles and celebratory advertising, the dining room set to rights, and the employees better rested than I felt. Though I'd foisted the Interpol document off on Bryan, I'd still spent hours the night before pouring over it, trying desperately to unearth its secrets. I'd come up empty.

Once our precise coffee orders were in hand, our trek to the office began. The air was heavy, stagnant, and laced with the scent of ozone as we traversed the gray concrete sidewalks with dozens of other commuters. Conversation continued between us, though I scarcely heard a word. I was still in awe of her, especially now that I'd seen her naked and vulnerable. This magnificent creature condescended to not only befriend me, but also acquiesce to my illicit demands. To what godly entity I owed this honor, I had no idea, but I intended to worship it for eternity.

"Serena," Su murmured as we approached AH's front steps. "What's on your agenda tonight?"

I shook my head. "Nothing important. Most Mondays, I hit the market on the way home to stock up. That's about all I feel like doing after sifting through all the emails I missed over the weekend."

"Do you mind some company?"

Are you kidding?

I waited to awaken from this sweet dream, but the noise of traffic and passing chatter continued around us. As far as I could tell, this was reality. "You want to come along?"

She laughed adorably, her exotic eyes twinkling. "Yes. I assume you mean Reading Terminal. I haven't been there in a while. I assume it still closes at six?"

I nodded, still awestruck. "Yeah, but after five is when you get the best deals. I picked up some fair-trade Chiapas for five bucks a pound and perfect satsumas for a buck a piece two weeks ago. If you're willing to deal with the dinner crowd trying to get in and out, it's worth it."

"I wouldn't have taken you for a bargain hunter, Serena," she remarked, tucking a forefinger under the collar of my Dior linen jacket. "Your wardrobe suggests otherwise."

In sight of the guards and my peers, this simple act set my soul on fire. She was being outwardly flirtatious with me in broad daylight. Not wanting to neglect a boon like this, I touched her wrist gently. "I splurge on the stuff that matters. No one sees where I get my oranges from, and to be frank, this wardrobe and my modest income demands some frugality somewhere."

She laughed again, turning toward the entrance. "I'll meet you in the parking garage, eighth level, space eight-oh-seven, when we're done here. Sound good?"

"Absolutely," I replied, hot on her heels.

* * * * *

Parked in space eight-oh-seven was a brilliant red Audi coupe, two-door and outfitted in gunmetal leather. I approached curiously. I'd never seen Su drive anywhere, always favoring walking or taking a taxi, but this was unmistakable her style. The foxy little ride was dashing, eye-catching, and sleek, descriptions I'd use for her even on her worst days.

"Punctual as always," I heard her voice call out over my shoulder.

I turned back to see the white-clad executive stroll to me like she was born mine. Before I could think better of it, I draped my arms around her middle. "Looks like you survived another day wholly unscathed."

Her fine lips touched my cheek. A burst of white-hot energy exploded in my belly. Her words were muted as she lingered close to my ear. "I'm glad it's over. Let's get out of here."

I nodded and reached for the driver's side doorhandle, relieved to find it unlocked. I swung it wide and watched as she slid onto the smooth leather with feline grace. Once she was safely tucked inside, I closed her door and made my way around to the passenger door. Inside, she was sneaking off her pale stiletto pumps, trading them for a pair of navy ballet flats. I tucked my bag between my knees and fastened my seatbelt as the engine purred to life.

Wordlessly, and with impressive finesse, she slid on a pair of oval-lensed sunglasses, checked her face in the mirror, and set us off. I was learning more about her every minute and felt honored to do so while being shown a level of pomp and luxury I'd only envied before.

* * * * *

Two hours later, with her coupe's tiny trunk laden with sundries, she pulled away from the market's garage. On the congested streets, she deftly guided us back to the gated garage behind AH's corporate headquarters. Once the car was stopped in her assigned space, she turned to face me. "Mind helping me get all this stuff inside?"

I lifted a brow. "Here? Why not at your place?"

She slipped her sunglasses off, setting them on the dashboard. "This is my place. I moved in late last year."

My jaw dropped. "No way. The head of HR, the one who insists on work-life balance, lives at the office?"

She sighed and shot me a dismal look. "It's true. I've got a loft upstairs. I've spent too much time here over the last year to justify paying three grand a month for a condo. Everything I need is within a few blocks of here, Drew assigned me this parking space, and honestly, it's been easier than I thought it would be. If you'd stuck around a little longer Saturday, you'd have seen it."

Blood rushed to my cheeks at the mention of our liaison. "Right. I, uh-"

"I understand," she interrupted, laying a palm over mine. "It escalated quickly. I just want you to know I didn't think it was a mistake. I still don't. You are special, Serena. Now, let's get all this inside. We've got all night to trade war stories."

In that moment, a strange realization set in. I'd never understood genuine heartfelt affection before, the kind that knits your stomach muscles and makes you crave another dose instantly after the first. I hesitated to use the word that was so often flung about when affection, respect and trust mingled, a four-letter one that brought anxiety along for the ride, but for the first time, it felt within reach. The whole concept felt achievable, attainable, and terrifying tempting.

I was in deep, deep trouble.

She led me to an elevator I hadn't known existed, tucked in the back of the parking garage. It was labeled for freight only. We ascended a dozen levels, our arms burdened with paper bags of infused oils, produce, and baked goods, before the doors opened to reveal a darkened hallway. Unadorned slabs of dingy concrete formed the walls. The hauntingly quiet passage stretched down fifty feet, with metal doors breaking up the expanse every ten steps or so. She paused at the last in the row. Keys were tugged loose from her shoulder bag.

"This is the place." She told me, twisting the key in the simple lock. "It's nothing fancy, so don't get your hopes up."

I edged in behind, dropping the bags to my feet with a dull thud as awe overtook me. The broad, open floorplan of the twenty-foot-square corner studio stunned me to silence. Lofted ceilings crossed with steel beams glowed in the reflected light from nearby skyscrapers. The enchanting radiance entered the space through the same floor to ceiling windows the executive offices downstairs boasted. The far walls were entirely glass, casting shadows over the plain plank flooring. No curtains barred the view beyond. She could see the William Penn statue atop City Hall and the art district beyond. I wandered hopelessly toward the windows, stepping around the simple bedding on the floor and the traditional Japanese garment box positioned nearby.

"Holy," I murmured, setting my palms on the cool pane of glass between us and the city. "This is incredible."

She giggled, stepping up alongside me. "It's the only perk to being here full-time. Fortunately, if I have a place for my clothes and someplace to sleep, I don't need much else."

"The night sky is absolutely beautiful from up here," I told her. *"Comme un réve, et comme toi."*

She smiled. "You're very kind. It is like a dream, but I'm not nearly as beautiful as this sparkling skyline."

"Sure, you are. You are just as breathtaking as any night sky I've ever seen."

"Dreams are best on the darkest nights, *mon ceil du nuit.*"

I'm her night sky, and she's my dream. How is this real?

I'd nearly overlooked a simple fact; this woman was real, with a heartbeat and the basic needs humanity shared. She'd shown me her true side, letting the erudite, prudish visage fall away so I could see the grace below. Gone was the flowy language of the CXO, the stiff prudence the world assumed was her true self, and in its place was a beautiful, splendid creature. What little of her heritage she retained was reflected in the sleeping mat by my ankles, the kimono robe hanging on an adjacent door, and the tea set resting on her simple, knee-height table.

"Where do you cook?" I asked, taking in the rest of the loft space before pointing to an adjacent door. "I'm guessing that's your bathroom, but there's no kitchen here."

She smiled, gesturing to a few shelves across the room. "Whatever I need gets stashed over there. I have a portable stove. There's a kitchen downstairs in the executive wing, and you already know how much I enjoy a fine meal out on the town. I get along just fine."

Before I could fetch the groceries I'd so carelessly dropped by the door, her arms were around me. "Serena, before we worry about that, there's something you should know."

I froze, letting my palms settle on her hips, though I was silenced by her intense gaze.

She continued after releasing a breath. "I'm worried about you."

I narrowed my brows. "What? Why?"

She exhaled again. A dimness settled over her expression as she contemplated, no doubt questioning her next words. "I can't say exactly why. I just know you're headed down a dangerous path."

Lizzie began to panic while Serena fought to maintain control.

Wait. How much does she know?

"I... I don't know what you mean," I managed. "I'm nothing special. There's no reason to be worried."

"Serena," she repeated, a little more grit in her tone now. "You're more than you seem. You're more than you portray to the world. I know it. It won't be long before others know it, too. I need you to be careful."

No way. She's bluffing.

"Su, I really have no idea what this is about. Why can't you tell me? You clearly know more than you're letting on. Just tell me what's up."

"I..." she trailed off, stepping back and letting her arms fall. "I can't. My hands are tied. You just need to believe me. You're in danger. I'm not sure when the hammer is going to drop. I'm scared it's going to be soon. Just," she paused again, eyeing me intensely. "Just be good. Don't do anything else. Please."

She turned her back to me, then took three steps away, her shoulders hunched under a weight I couldn't see. Nothing scared me more. Whatever was happening, it was beyond my comprehension. On shaky ground, working with a split personality against an unseen adversary, I was at a total loss.

* * * * *

I left her apartment earlier than I'd planned. At the market, she'd mentioned staying until morning, but after her mental breakdown and ominous threat, hunger evaded me. I made my way home around dusk, glad to find half of bottle of single malt Scotch in the cabinet. I downed it all, straight from the bottle, before crawling into bed. Sometime shortly thereafter, I passed out under the weight tossed onto my shoulders by my beautiful boss.

The next morning, I made my way to Supremo, equally hoping she'd be there and not be there. I wasn't sure how to proceed. If she did know my ulterior motive for being in Philadelphia, she could've said so. She'd been explicit about her own involvement and her hands being tied. I couldn't help thinking that she was a victim. Was she being blackmailed by the one seeking to out me? Was I even at risk of being outed? The more I considered the possibilities, the more none of them made sense.

A minute later, she appeared on the sidewalk. Her dress was the same cherry red as the coupe she'd driven the night before, and while she appeared in good spirits, I couldn't help remembering the dour sag of her shoulders the night before. I only hoped she'd slept better than I had.

"Good morning, Serena," she called as she approached. "It's a pleasure to see you."

"I was afraid you wouldn't be here," I told her, reaching for the doorhandle of the café.

She laid her palm over mine on the doorhandle, tugging it into her own before I could pull the door open. "Give me a moment. I owe you an apology. My behavior yesterday was completely uncalled for."

The erudite stiffness was back. It scared me, but she was here. I puzzled over her words but wasn't given much time to consider them before she plowed on.

"I hope you can forgive my outburst, and that we can move on in a positive direction. Today is a new day, after all, and we're here to conquer it."

There was an uneasiness in my soul, a quake that shook my foundation in a way I hadn't felt in decades. That phrase, the trite use of it at AH, and the implications behind it, brought bile to my throat. Instinct told me to run. Impulse told me to stay. She awaited my decision with unreadable ambivalence.

"Let's get today done with, then," I replied, reaching for the door again.

She didn't stop me this time. We stepped inside together, silence between us as we waited. I wanted to ask how she was, to engage in normal weekday banter, but it felt wrong. She'd jumped the gap back into "boss territory" after we'd so casually migrated to way-more-than-that days before. In the back of my mind, I knew Bryan would be working on that encrypted file in a matter of hours. That file, belonging to this woman, would certainly clear up the ambiguous threat she'd issued the day before. If she was associated with Interpol, for better or for worse, there was more here than I could've hoped for.

Coffees were passed to us. As we made our way to the door, I heard a gasp and a splash. Glancing over, I saw Su wilt, her cup missing from her palm and her pale shoes now stained sienna brown. Without thought, I handed her my cup, stepping to the counter to retrieve a palmful of napkins as the barista eyed the scene with thinly veiled frustration.

"I got it, no worries," I told the worker before crouching by Su's feet to sop up the remnants left behind. "It happens to the best of us."

"Many thanks, Serena," I heard her say, still as a saint while I went to work. A minute later, the mess was tidied. She passed my drink back to me before taking a freshly made replacement off the counter. She followed me to the door, deflated a bit by either the attention or the setback, I wasn't sure which.

"I know you've got another pair of exquisite sandals to replace those, and the dress is fine. Let's get going before I drop mine, too."

"No, I hope you don't. Be careful with it."

I walked at her side. Conversation was strung together with more pleasantries than normal. It felt like we went back in time, as if the past months of getting to know each other were deleted from our memories. When the building came into view, she ascended the steps without pause. I followed behind, watching as she made her way wordlessly to the escalator. Our normal farewell didn't happen. She never looked back at me.

Disappointment washed over me like an acidic wave, burning my soul more than I wanted to admit.

In the elevator, I took a long pull from my coffee. It was little more bitter than usual. It could've been the work of a harried barista or my tastebuds struggling from the Scotch the night before. This day was bound to progress a little too slowly. I already regretted not calling in sick.

At my office chair, I dusted off the rest of my brew, logged in, and began the menial task of sorting email. AH had signed on six new clients in the last week, mainly social media content creators and personalities. They had plenty of skeletons to dig up. If I found any, it would be taken upstairs for judgment. AH's reputation couldn't be sullied by the misspent youth of its client base.

The misspent youth of its employees was apparently not that big of an issue, though. I snickered at the simple fact. I'd infiltrated the very structure I was now protecting. It was almost poetic.

My stomach roiled a few minutes later, gurgling more than I would've expected so far away from lunch. The boiling turned to nausea and dizziness a little too quickly. I retrieved some mints from my shoulder bag. With one settled under my tongue, I sought to distract myself with mindless tasks. I opened a new client's contract, perusing the fine print for pitfalls. Within a few paragraphs, my vision began to blur.

Panic set in before my mind could control it. I stood a little too quickly, my office chair toppling over with a clang as a dozen eyes focused on me. I touched my forehead with fingers that'd turned icy in an instant. My heart rate doubled as I stepped back from my monitor, debating whether I'd make it to The Red Room's bathroom or if I should just throw up in my trash can.

Before I could decide, a familiar gray tunnel came into view. Darkness overtook me as I collapsed.

* * * * *

"She's coming around. Bummer," I heard a female utter sarcastically by my knees.

A second person's sad sigh followed from over my shoulder. Then the mocking voice resounded again before me. "See? Calm down. She'll live."

My vision brightened a little at a time. I was seated in an office chair atop thick, pale carpeting. I had no idea how I'd arrived here or what prompted my arms to be so difficult to lift. I struggled anyway, realizing a little too slowly that I was restrained.

"Don't fight it, Serena," I heard the same belittling voice say. "The police will be here soon. It's all over."

My gaze lifted from my lap to the origin of the feminine voice. A crop of blonde hair came into focus, her gaze narrowed judgingly as she towered over me. I heard another sigh behind me. Turning to check was impossible with my palms tethered together behind my back.

"What the hell?" I managed in a strangled tone. "This is ridiculous! I can't be detained like this."

"Yes, you can. You're an international criminal. All I did was keep you from running off until the cops get here."

"I'm a... Wait, no! Come on. That's crazy! What's happening here?"

Joy's tone was deeper and heavier than I'd ever heard. "Oh, Serena, you delusional thing. You really thought you'd get away with this, didn't you?"

"With what? I have no idea what you're talking about!" I struggled again, feeling the heavy chair shimmy under my weight. I tossed my full weight to the side, only to have Joy push the chair back into place with firm hands. "Seriously, let me go! You can't hold me like this. It's in my contract!"

"You're going to lecture *me* about *your* contract?" Joy asked incredulously. "I wrote the damn contract. You passed out at your desk. Per contract language, you were to be removed from your workstation. On your desktop was clear evidence of your crimes. And to think you'd risk your dirty work here, on office property? It's despicable."

Bullshit! How is this happening?

The voice behind me sighed again. It prickled the hair on the back of my neck. Baffled, panicked and frantic, I continued to fight against my restraints. Whatever I was tied up with didn't budge.

"Stop fighting," Joy told me again. "It's over, Serena. I knew you'd hang yourself eventually. I just had to give you a noose and wait. You didn't disappoint, kid."

I glanced up in time to catch a serpentine grin, one with the same nefarious nuance I'd caught a glimpse of in my probationary review. It revolted me to the core. I fought the urge to spit in her face. The coward lingering behind me was my only hope.

That hope was dashed when the figure stepped around my left and into view. The sight of her black mane, white sheath dress, fisted hands, and dour expression made my eyes clamp shut. I'd seen enough.

The intercom on Joy's desk exploded to life. Greg reported admitting the police into the lobby downstairs. They were on their way to us. Joy crossed her arms proudly while Su paced, wringing her hands and holding her tongue. I, on the other hand, had nothing to lose.

"Su! Say something!" I screamed. "This is a con job! I'm not some international criminal! This is fucking insane! Tell her!" I glared at Joy, who only smiled at me in return. "Tell her the truth! I'm innocent!"

"No," Su replied with a tiny voice and forlorn eyes. "No, you're not."

I fought against the restraints once more as the office door burst open. Two armed officers in stark black crossed the carpet on hurried steps. One perched by my chair, his judging eyes trained on me, while the other approached Joy. His haggard face was skeptical and impatient as he crossed his arms.

Joy's tone took on a breathless quality, like she'd waited an eternity to confide. "Officer, this is an international cyber-criminal. I have all the evidence you need. She needs to be apprehended immediately. She's dangerous."

"And why is she restrained?" The officer asked her while his partner untied my wrists, replacing the rope with a pair of cuffs.

Out of the frying pan and into the fucking fire.

"She passed out at her desk. When we tried to revive her, she started swinging. I can't risk harm to my employees. This seemed like the only option."

The heavy-set officer grasping my cuffs dragged me up. I stood shakily, the fog of lethargy haunting the corners of my vision. I knew not to argue or fight at this point. I'd been arrested back in Whitehall, but for a much less impressive charge, one that'd been thrown out the following day. Phil had saved my bacon. This time, though, I felt Joy's noose tightening with each passing second. I was without a pocket ace this time.

The second officer, apparently finished with Joy's recounting and the paperwork she'd handed him, approached me. "Serena Hunter, you're under arrest for crimes including but not limited to espionage, phishing, and breaking and entering. You have the right to remain silent. Anything you say can and will be used against you in the court of law."

The Miranda Rights continued as I was dragged across the room to the door. The last thing I witnessed was Su stepping beside Joy, her expression remorseful and ashamed as Joy lifted a palm to wave goodbye. Her lips twisted into a mocking grin as she disappeared behind the closing opaque office door. On the HR rep's wrist was a tattoo, a taunting little black star.

Undisclosed, 2023

I awoke with a start, a lingering scream echoing around the block walls. I'd had the same nightmare a thousand times. I couldn't shake it no matter how far I fled. Every time I relieved that humiliating moment, I wished I'd done something different in the days and months before. My biggest regret in life was not spitting in that harpy's face.

I sat up, rubbing my eyes as they adjusted to the pitch blackness around me. Habit forced me to draw the curtains, though I knew it made no difference. This time of year meant weeklong periods of darkness this close to the Arctic Circle.

An alpaca-trimmed blanket nestled against my torso as I grabbed for my brand-new phone. The latest model was the same as the one before, though the price tag jumped a few hundred bucks. Under the guise of providing better photo quality, safer data transfer to the cloud, and improved functionality, they foisted these overpriced, refurbished computer chips wrapped in plastic to a tech-obsessed and oblivious public. If I didn't need to keep up with the nonsense, I'd have stuck with my two-thousand-fourteen dinosaur phone.

What a shamelessly brilliant racket.

Bitterness eked its way up my throat. I could've gotten into the cell phone business in its infancy. I remembered Motorola's meteoric rise and Apple's foray into portable tech like it was yesterday, though contemporaries in my chosen profession hadn't been born yet.

That fact made me cringe and laugh aloud simultaneously.

My first dose of caffeine was overdue. Whether my clients woke me or my nightmares did, meaningful rest continued to be a fleeting fantasy. Melancholy haunted me nowadays. At the root of the desperation was the fact that I hadn't visited Mom in years. I'd be risking life and limb venturing back to Whitehall. Though I'd been acquitted of the charges back in twenty-fifteen by a stellar lawyer with an incredible rock voice, I was guilty of every one of those crimes now.

Search engines revealed that my dutiful brother and his sliz of a wife had added not one but two heathens to their brood. He posed with them, polyester smiles slapped on their white bread faces, in the most recent picture posted to the Jasper County tourism website. His time in local law enforcement and his wife's heiress status led to an endorsement deal. They were the faces of Whitehall's growing commerce and potential. Scotty and Caleb, the nephews I'd never meet, posed behind desks in another pictorial for the county's only grade school. I sincerely doubted they occupied those desks day-to-day. Phil's "better half" no doubt forced her holy terrors into a private, prestigious charter or some religious school to keep up appearances.

The coffee was smooth as silk as I sipped it down. My bitterness spoiled the brew when it splashed in my belly.

I continued perusing. The same countries were fighting with each other. The same governments were exploiting their citizens' short-sightedness and self-involvement for their own gains. I grew tired of the monotony almost instantly, heading over to more industry-specific news sources for worthwhile stories. At the very top of the one I referred to most for valuable scuttlebutt, a brazen headline and a photo of a cuffed man caused Mom's spoon to slip from my fingers.

Prominent Executive Arrested on Espionage Charges

Son of a bitch, they got him.

In the picture, Bryan was being led down the front steps of Midas's Boston headquarters. Though wrinkles tugged down his mouth now, and his designer suit was rumpled, it was unmistakably the face of my oldest friend. I grinned at the screen, thoroughly impressed with the article's synopsis and thorough analysis of the alleged escapades.

He's guilty of all these crimes. Well done.

I sat back with a deep exhale. It was the end of an era. I was surprisingly okay with leaving it behind. I'd changed a lot since twenty-fifteen. He had, too, but he'd clearly grown sloppy in his work. He'd always criticized me for my haste and ambition. Turnabout was fair play in this case.

He didn't have a quintet of saviors like I did, nor did he have the kind of legal resources and ill-gotten cash I was privy to. He had no chance at redemption. I wouldn't give him any. I'd have pitied him if I felt like he deserved it.

Just desserts.

I dusted off the last bit of black magic after closing the browser. I'd seen enough news for one day.

Inexplicably, quiet persisted another hour. Requests were caught up, email notifications stalled, and my phone laid still beside the empty mug. With a shrug, I rose to find a way to occupy my mind and hands. I'd already spent too much time in my own head this morning, analyzing memories and trying to discern how it'd gone to shit so fast. Another minute of this torment would have me neck deep in a bottle of bourbon before breakfast.

Travelling from room to room, I wiped a shammy over every flat surface. I had precious few knickknacks to contend with, the broad expanses of unadorned countertop and gleaming wood rewarding me some peace of mind. My need for possessions diminished during sequester. What I hadn't been able to carry over the icy expanse was left behind. Precious few chachkas were tucked inside dresser drawers, closet boxes, and cabinets.

The dusting cloth paused over my desk's bottom drawer's face as I recalled the illicit document inside. It'd been years since I'd placed it there.

What harm could it do now?

I released a deep breath as I tugged a letter envelope out from under a surplus stack of pristine copy paper. Its corners were dogeared from years of relocation, the once crimson scrawl of ink on its face now faded to a dull pink. Tension furled my knuckles as I squeezed it into a crumpled mess.

This could do a ton of harm. What am I thinking?

I stashed it back and slammed the desk drawer. That time in my life was over. I was someone else now. I was on the right track after years of floundering, chasing an enigma that ended up ruining my life. What little life I had left couldn't be squandered on remnants like this one.

With a huff, I plopped onto my chair. A text from the big boss illuminated my cell's screen. A single word appeared at the very top.

Congrats.

My eyes snapped shut automatically, denying myself misspent tears. I unlocked the screen and replied with quick thumbs once my pulse recovered.

`No need for all that. Bygones.`

I refilled my coffee, then returned to my chair. According to the computer's clock, it was just after two in the afternoon. The widget on the top-left of my main monitor assigned the correct time to every zone across the planet. I pinged her phone with my own. The boss was in England, just outside Glastonbury, at a top-notch hotel. She was supposed to be closer to her rural English manor home by now. I released a slow breath, knowing where this was headed. A deluge of work was no doubt about to drench me.

Sure enough, my left computer screen flashed to life. The web call program's blanched notification screen displayed her profile photo, a stunning charcoal vignette hand-sketched by her brother-in-law of sorts. The immaculate blonde's eyes were the only color, popping in stunning violet against the smudged lines of dusky gray.

I took a deep breath, rubbing the residue of misery and sleeplessness from my eyes before accepting the summons. The image of the caller switched from charcoal to still life, her torso fully captured by her phone's camera. Wrapped in sheer black lace with an emerald bralette below, her skin dewed with sweat, she'd clearly just walked offstage. Winded and distracted, she huffed and panted at a few voices outside my sight before finally turning her attention to me.

"Catch your breath," I told her. "It's four a.m. there. What the hell happened last night?"

She chuckled, sitting back, and dabbing her brow with a cotton towel. "The closing act bailed. Rumors are already swirling. You're on watch starting immediately."

I was already digging into the Glastonbury festival's details and occurrences, scouring social media for mentions and hashtags. "The current sentiment is a sudden, unnamed illness."

She downed an entire bottle of water before speaking again. "We were halfway back to London when the call came in. The organizers already called the other closers from previous nights. I was the only one that answered."

I couldn't help chuckling, my eyes skipping over dozens of lines of code. "Samaritans at every turn."

"We cobbled together another set list on the ride back. Three hours later, after begging the roadies from the act before to drag our shit back out, we were playing another session to the same crowd. They were practically rioting by the time we made it out on stage. They'd threatened to sue for refunds or trash the place if no one closed out the show. The organizers panicked. So, yeah, it's four a.m. and they owe us big."

"You're a hero," I read directly from a festival attendee's social media comment. "It says so right here. There are hundreds of positive comments. I'll scrub the not-so-great ones. No one should be criticizing a band swap. It says right here in the ticket contract. 'Performers are subject to change at any time, for any reason, at the organizer's discretion.'"

"Ambiguous contract language benefits the party who didn't write it," she told me. "Besides, the next passage states that the organizers were required to disclose changes in a timely manner. They were too busy covering their own asses to bother with the crowd."

I wasn't surprised that my boss-slash-counselor knew that contract inside and out. I set to task wiping social media clean of all criticism, replacing anything untoward with memes and cat videos. "I'll make short work of this. How long before you've got a statement to release?"

"I'll write it now. There'll be another in the next few days. Our Armenian momma is ready to pop. She's the real victim here."

"She was due three days ago. Tell me those incompetent organizers at least offered her a gurney to give birth on if she dropped the kid mid-set."

A snort escaped the boss's nose. "She's not speaking to me right now. We'll all be her best friends again once the epidural's on board."

"What else do you need?" I asked, my fingers skipping across the keyboard.

"I'm forwarding an email to you," she told me in a suddenly arched tone, her eyes locked on the screen as they flicked right to left. "I just got this. It's clearly not for me. How'd she..."

The shock in her voice scared me. My fingers froze over the keys.

A chime rung out from my right monitor as the email appeared at the top of the stack. The boss's name was perched above the email's subject. "FWD" was followed by an expanse of blank space on the narrow bar. I gasped as the words came into focus in the app's right panel.

```
Em, get this message to her. I know she's alive.
Tell her it's done. The paperwork's turned in.
```

They're both on short notice. I'm headed home. Extradition is a godsend compared to what I'd get in court stateside. Please, just tell her I'm sorry. Tell her I never wanted this. I don't expect forgiveness. I can't take any of it back. I can't make it better. She already knows the truth. I don't know why I bothered with this. Just take care of her.

There was no signature, no sign-off, just a wish that was so sincerely "her." I turned off the webcam before some long-held tears edged over my lower lashes.

Damn her. How dare she? What truth do I know? All I know is that she betrayed me.

"What's the truth?" I heard the caller ask me. "Are you really es-"

"No," I interrupted. "No, and I never was. She wasn't, either. I told you the real cracker's identity. I don't know what the hell this is about."

"Apparently you know the truth. As your attorney, I'd love to know it, too. And, as your attorney, I also think it's best that I stay in the dark."

"I gotta go," I told her. "Get the docs to me."

"Bye," she responded simply, the call disconnecting immediately after.

I launched off my chair, tearing open the bottom drawer of my desk and fishing out the long-neglected envelope. Before I could run from the truth again, I ripped the envelope open and pressed the single sheet of folded, rumpled paper flat against the desk blotter. To my surprise, tucked inside the letter was also a two-inch square photo. As I analyzed the convivial scene on display, I realized a simple truth. I thought I'd known the truth already.

I'd been dead wrong.

Tween versions of Su and Joy stood arm in arm with two men who closely resembled each other. Joy's hair was deep brown here, her eyes unrecognizably amber. The hue matched that of the man on her left. Su's dark hair and almond eyes were as I remembered. She was Japanese, surely, but I'd always known there was more there than pure Asian blood. The photo I remembered from her AH desktop was her new family. The man on Su's right in this photo shared his height and faintly olive skin with her. Clearly her mother had dalliances of her own in the years before the Kyoto politician came along.

The letter's words came into focus when I slid the photo aside.

Lizzie. This is the only chance I have to explain all this. I just hope you believe me after such betrayal on my part. You don't know her real name. It's Felisa Hernandez. She changed it the same way you did when the black star came into being. She left a trail of breadcrumbs for you, her starving protégé. I don't blame you for falling for it.

I've been in her pocket for years. My mother threatened my father. She was finally going to have a real future with Kenzo. She'd be a spoiled housewife. He couldn't come forward with the truth of my birth. It would cause irreparable damage. He did, Lizzie. He did talk. Kenzo had him taken care of. Uncle Diego found out. Kenzo took care of him, too. Diego's daughter had taken to programming by that point. She was a savant. She threatened to take down my new family. I did what I had to. I shouldered it. I did whatever she wanted. What she wanted was a scapegoat. She'd known about you for a long time. The rest was your friend's doing. I'm so sorry. I'll make this right if it kills me.

I read the words twice before glancing back to the photo. I felt nothing, but I watched a wet drop fall, landing with a sickening smack on the aged image. I didn't want it to be true. It made us all victims. It made my former idol a soulless monster, and it made my entire existence prior to twenty-sixteen a complete farce.

I collapsed into my desk chair. The only silver lining was that she was true to her word. She did make it right. I knew of one arrest. I'd likely never hear about the other, as *esTre11aN3gra* was too high profile and the investigators made too many mistakes in her apprehension already. The bumbling fools arrested a dozen red herrings, me included, for the social engineering they were light years away from understanding.

I opened my web browser again, intending to continue my work for the only truly honest women I'd ever known. With their smiling faces now set as my desktop background, I was reminded of my life's true purpose; to give the worthy a chance to live the carefree life I'd been denied.

Chichester, PA, 2015

The bail officer escorted me over the cracked sidewalk to the garden apartment's door. The complex was decades older than I was. Aged cinnamon and umber bricks towered forty feet above, studded with drafty windows displaying mismatched curtains within. A few discarded Independence Day fireworks shells littered the ground around the stained navy dumpster. The landscape was verdant, though, with trees baring fluffy leaves overhead and overgrown grass underfoot.

This was the closest thing to freedom I'd felt in months. It was a refreshing type of hell.

The officer, a trim, dark-skinned twenty-something with a holster at his hip, swung open the apartment's door and made his way inside my new home. I knew it was a temporary stop, one I had to deal with, but I gritted my teeth at the idea of the law seeing my place before me, and without my permission.

I waited in the doorway, my palms on my hips. These dress pants fit looser than they had months before, the prison diet bona fide in its efficacy. Sweat made the thin cotton of the state-issued tee cling to my back, the brutal humidity stymying any airflow through the complex's tangle of buildings. I wanted nothing more than to hole up inside, out of the sun's blazing rays, but I had to wait for the lackadaisical officer to finish his rounds.

Before I could complain, he returned to the doorway. "It's clean. Stay here. Your bail arrangement says no visitors of any kind, for any reason. Your lawyer's supposed to let us know of any in-person meetings. We good?"

That very same attorney arranged this ankle bracelet-free stayover. They were my liberator in every sense. I had no intention of betraying their trust or hard work. "Crystal. Can I go inside now?"

He stepped aside, allowing me passage into the scarcely decorated apartment. The kitchen's best amenity was a fridge better suited for an RV, and the dining room was a vacant expanse. A simple futon with a lumpy tan cushion huddled against the far wall. Through an ajar door on the back wall, stark blackness awaited. It wasn't farfetched to assume the bedroom was as empty as the other dank spaces.

His voice interrupted my thoughts. "This is a privilege. Don't screw it up."

"The state calls a dump like this a privilege? I'm shocked it has indoor plumbing. Hell, I hope it does, for everyone's sake."

His arms crossed. "Funny. I'll be back for you in three days. You've got food in the cabinets and your stuff's in a box in the bedroom. Don't get daring. Call me if you need something. Oh, and lock the door. This neighborhood sucks."

No fucking kidding.

I nodded at him as he closed the door behind him. Incredible, breathtaking, and relieving silence followed. The weeks of slamming doors, intercom wakeups, and screaming inmates around me at all hours were finally in the past. Here, in this lackluster den, I could finally unfurl.

I couldn't wait to bathe by myself. The thin plastic curtain fluttered like butterfly wings as the dollar store showerhead spewed water everywhere. Without a towel, I was left to shake off and dry myself with the two threadbare dishrags I found in a kitchen drawer. If I wasn't allowed to leave or accept visitors, I'd need my attorney to bring me some damn towels and pillows. This was ridiculous.

I tugged open the box of my worldly possessions once I'd showered off the stink of incarceration. Inside were remnants of a prior life, one so mercilessly tugged away by a charlatan. The linen blend suit jacket was in desperate need of dry cleaning, the jewelry I'd worn on that day months ago was missing, and only a melted lipstick and half-eaten pack of gum remained from my purse's contents. Two tee shirts, worn and wrinkled, rested with a pair of simple jeans in the top dresser drawer. As I'd suspected, there was no bed to be found.

I hesitated to open the kitchen cabinets, knowing the state's law enforcement hadn't bothered to provide real nutrition. Sure enough, one glance at the supply left me cringing. Processed carbs, frozen slabs of nondescript meat, and foiled-lined bags of salted snacks were my only forms of sustenance.

The sound of a ringing phone pulled my attention from the meager rations. I wandered across the apartment, shocked to see a wall phone in the dining room. I hadn't seen a rotary phone since the farmhouse, and I couldn't believe the things even worked anymore. With nothing to lose, I lifted the transceiver.

"Hello?"

My attorney's voice rung out from the handset. "Hello there. I'm glad you made it. How are your living quarters?"

"Dismal, but somehow still better than the SHU," I told her. "Some necessities are missing. What are the chances I can get some tech in here?"

"Not great. A condition of your bail is no internet access. I can get you a tablet, but no WIFI, unfortunately. The phone you're on is the only one you've got."

"And it's monitored," I assumed aloud. "If it is, I hope they hear this. It's ninety-four degrees outside. The metal cage around the AC panel means I can't adjust it. It's currently off. I have two changes of clothes and no way to launder them. I'm going to smell like a wet dog at my next hearing. That's bad news if you're responsible for cuffing me."

My lawyer sighed. "These are temporary, I assure you. I need you to be strong until I get the legal work done."

"What about a TV? Is that considered tech, too?"

"I'll find out. You're not to receive any visitors, so anything issued to you will arrive by officer. Those are the rules for now."

I glanced down at my feet. "I guess this was the trade-off for not having an electronic anklet or a cellie."

"Stay put," the advisor told me. "Oh, and I managed to find that antique you mentioned to me."

I gasped, reminded of her prowess. "Mom's spoon?"

"It's safe with me," she told me before the line went dead.

* * * * *

Loopholes were discovered. Arrangements were made. Rules were "worked around." I waited as patiently as I could. So, when strange packages started arriving in the middle of the night, unprompted and unmarked, I didn't complain, especially considering their contents were desperately needed.

Artisan coffee and a French press arrived first in a plain, carboard box. Over the following week, one by one, little pieces of my former life were left on my doorstep. I used kitchen cabinets to hide the sundries, never knowing when the fuzz would drop by. They were probably busy with more troublesome cases, but I wasn't risking this newfound fortune.

Clothing from my Philadelphia closet arrived in sealed plastic bags from a Center City dry cleaner. Fresh produce, the likes of which I hadn't seen in months, came delivered in a bushel basket. A laptop, basic but efficient, came next, complete with instructions on how to tether internet connection to the neighbor's broadband. The following night, a smaller parcel filled with burner phones arrived. Within an hour, one of them rung, reflecting a phone number I didn't recognize. A search engine revealed the call's origin to be central Wyoming.

I pressed the green button but didn't speak a word, moving the earpiece to my cheek. Without prompting, a female voice muddled with heavy modulation echoed in my ear.

"I see your gifts have arrived. That's a relief."

"Who is this?"

"That's not important right now. I'll fill you in later once you've helped me out. We're in similar situations. I believe we can mutually benefit each other. As you can see, I'm interested enough to risk my neck in getting those packages to you. Do you want to hear more?"

Sure, hot stuff. Whatcha got in mind?

"I'm not sure I have a choice," I told the caller. "This cloak and dagger routine is hilarious, though, considering you know where I live and seemingly a whole lot about me. You must know I pose no threat to you. I'm under house arrest. I can't show my face outside this four-hundred square foot shithole. What in the world can I offer you that you can't get elsewhere?"

"Discretion," the called replied. "We're acquainted. I'll leave it at that. You had the chance to expose me. You didn't. I have more evidence on you than the feds do. This makes us uneasy allies. We're both broke, without resources or options. If you want to keep working, to keep flexing those skills I know you have, I can make it happen."

"I'm listening."

I perched on the edge of the futon, listening intently as this nefarious creature detailed an elaborate online vigilantism scheme. She'd supply leads. I'd work them for insider info. We'd share the proceeds. She'd launder the funds into international accounts and bitcoin. It'd run like clockwork.

She was more informed on clandestine finances than I was, and I found myself impressed and terrified at once. The whole endeavor was almost too good to be true, assuming of course that it was a genuine offer and not some trap.

"All right, so," I replied once her explanation came to stop. "I'm going to need a gesture of good faith here. The gifts are nice and all, but this is my ass. One false move and I go under. Believe me, I'll take you down, too. You're not nearly as hidden as you think, especially once I start digging."

"Oh, I'm aware. Like I said, I'll tell you my identity in time, once a few jobs are complete. And as for good faith, I think that apartment is proof of that. That famous attorney of yours was happy with a hotel room. I insisted on better, on a private residence that just so happens to be surrounded by former colleagues of mine. I can pull the plug on that apartment in a moment. I don't want to. Your neighbors are good resources. Don't fuck this up."

Oh, you sneaky vixen. Way to tip your hand.

I released a slow breath, my heart beating out of my chest. Here was an opportunity, though shady, to retake control of my life. Thrill mingled with terror as I contemplated real vigilante work alongside this unlikely ally. I wanted nothing more.

"I'm in."

Philadelphia, PA, 2015

I snapped up in a sitting position, cuffed to a chair in a plainly painted room. The events of the morning flooded back to my mind in technicolor. As astounded as I was infuriated, I struggled against the restraints as a guy in a blue button-down and khakis exploded into the room from a door alongside a massive rectangular mirror.

"Finally, Sleeping Beauty's awake," he scoffed, approaching the table situated between us. "That tranq's good stuff, isn't it? You finally ready to talk?"

The scene was the archetype of interrogation, complete with the two-way mirror and the thin, metal table and chairs. I'd seen enough movies to know the routine and had no intention of playing along with the farce. My lips stayed sealed as he pulled his seat out, spun it around, and sat backward on it. Tawny eyes fixed on mine below a tight crop of matching hair. Fine lines extended above his eyebrows and around the corners of his narrow mouth, revealing his age to my discerning eye. His forties were in the rearview mirror. He'd have been better off not dyeing his facial hair. Embracing the salt and pepper would've given his lackluster face some character.

"And what are you staring at, hmm?" He asked, interrupting my thoughts. "Busy analyzing me like one of your targets? Don't bother. You're the mystery here."

I sat back, laying my hands on my lap and tipping my head slightly.

"Now," he told me, setting a manila folder down on the table and opening it. "Perhaps we should start with the formalities. Is it Serena Hunter, or do you prefer Elizabeth Cushing-Daly? Or is there another one we haven't dug up yet?"

I couldn't help the reflex. My eyes widened just a touch. He saw it. The grin gave him away.

"Let me say, whoever you are, that you're going to have quite an impressive rap sheet once we're done here." He flipped a few pages while I watched, keeping as neutral an expression as I could manage. "Domestic and international espionage, extortion, data theft, breaking and entering, phishing, intellectual property infringements, identity theft, tax evasion, blackmail, plus a half-dozen cybercrimes I've never seen anyone charged with before. I'm impressed, and I'm a tenured detective. That's quite an achievement, let me tell you."

I exhaled, holding still with an exhausted expression.

"The FBI's digging through your work, and Interpol's got a laundry list, too. I can't wait to see the morning papers. The biggest cybercriminal of the past decade's been apprehended right here in our fair city, in her Monday to Friday office, in front of everyone. What a shame to fall so far so fast."

You absolute moron. Your precious cybercriminal's still at large, and she's done more good deeds for this world than you ever will. Wait, why am I defending her? She's why I'm here!

"I want my lawyer."

"Oh, so you do have a voice." He crossed his arms, the badge on his belt glinting as he turned toward the mirror.

An aging man in a decades-old gray suit entered. I wasn't reassured. The lack of briefcase or documents in his hands meant he wasn't here to help in any kind of meaningful way. His voice was a hollow drumbeat and his mature face was a sea of worry lines. "I'm Gary Maroney, your public defender. Apologies for making you wait. I was only notified an hour ago."

I turned impatient eyes to the detective, who only shrugged. "A doodle on your cell wall doesn't count as a request for representation."

The lawyer turned to face him. "I need a moment with my client."

The detective took his sweet time leaving, snickering the whole time. As the door slammed shut, I released a breath. "Gary, was it?"

He nodded once. "Before you start, you should know I'm only here temporarily, to represent you until your attorney arrives. Were you aware that an attorney has been retained for your case?"

My jaw dropped open. "No, who…"

"You've still got a friend on the outside," he replied. "I'll sit here today while the detectives do what needs doing, and I'll type up the report for your counsel. Apparently, they're delayed until tomorrow. You'll just have to make it that far."

I watched as Gary moved a chair alongside mine, then turn the detective's documents around on the table. He methodically ran his finger along the lines of script, his lips moving though no words emerged. Pages flipped as he continued. Five solid minutes of silence persisted between us. Finally, he glanced up to me.

"This whole thing stinks," he finally surmised. "I'm not saying you're pristine, but this is a mockery."

For a split second, I prayed my hired attorney was as shrewd as this guy. I managed a small smile. His supply of trust and confidence softened the hardened crust around my soul.

He sighed, sitting back to rub his eyes. "All right, here's how this is going to go down. They've got a lineup of witnesses, people who'll say what needs to be said to get these charges to stick. Keep quiet. If there's something you want said, say it to me. Anything they claim, I'll notate. Your attorney can review it tomorrow."

I edged in close to his ear, my voice a bare whisper. "Do you know who's here?"

He shook his head almost imperceptibly as the door reopened, the generic detective reappearing in the chasm. He stepped inside, leaving the door open. "Shall we begin?"

"Not until you uncuff my client," he told the detective. "She's not going anywhere, she hasn't officially been charged with any crimes, and she's already demonstrated control in all the confrontational situations you've thrust on her. Uncuff her or I call for an injunction."

The detective tucked his head back behind the wall between us, uttering a few words outside my hearing. A moment later, his shoulders dropped. Dejectedly, he stepped around the table, brandishing a key to release my hands from their shackles. I instantly nestled the freed wrist in my other palm, rubbing where the cold metal had been.

"Better," my attorney snapped. "Now, let's get this circus underway."

The detective laughed aloud as he turned to the door. "Eh, it's your funeral. Bring in the Sheriff."

My gaze narrowed on the door instantly.

Sheriff? Oh. Oh God, no. Anybody but him.

My morale crashed like a jetliner as my stepbrother emerged from the adjacent room. He was taller than I remembered, and more imposing, with his muscled shoulders concealed by a narrow, navy athletic jacket. It was embroidered with his badge and title over his left chest. In pressed black trousers, dress boots, and sporting a heavy watch from a mid-level department store, he was an impressive sight, one I'd hoped to never see again, and certainly not like this.

"Damn it," he cursed under his breath. "What a disaster this has turned out to be."

I wanted nothing more than to agree, to call him a shit stain like I had years before, but it felt callous now. My attorney angled his chair toward me, his heavy brows lowered.

Phil continued before my representative could get a word in. "You should know what's up, Lizzie. I've reviewed the accusations and the proposed charges. While I can't get my head around why you'd do all this, I don't put it past you. What I want to know is why."

I released a breath, meeting his gaze firmly. As advised, I stayed silent.

Gary rested his forearms on the table. "How about an introduction, though my client seems to know you?"

"Apologies, Mr. Maroney. I am Phillip Daly, Sheriff of Whitehall, South Carolina, and elected State Representative for the Fourth Congressional District. I'm here, and not where I should be on a workday, to formally identify the accused. I have no idea what moniker she's been using, nor what she's been up to since moving to the Philadelphia area, though I am intimately familiar with her behaviors prior to her leaving Greenville County."

"Intimately?" Gary repeated, lifting the pen sitting on the manila folder. "You've shared these behaviors with the investigating detective?"

Phil nodded once. "All of them, and I've pledged to cooperate in any ongoing investigations and criminal proceedings. I'd apologize to my sister, but she knew about these consequences. She has shown no shame or remorse in the past. I don't expect to see any now."

"Thank you, Sheriff Daly," my attorney replied in the wake of my silence. "I'll be asking the detective for your complete deposition, so please be prepared to be questioned again. And, for the record, my client is only being tried for current crimes. Details or testimony you provide that is immaterial to the pending charges will be thrown out. She is not on trial yet, and certainly not for any crimes allegedly committed between siblings, nor any for which she was not found guilty prior to this arrest. I appreciate your unbiased account of her recent activities only."

The Sheriff's lip curled. I knew that expression. I'd seen it a million times before, whenever I'd argued a finer point he'd neglected. It was equal parts outfoxed antagonist and impressed recanter. "I'll do what I can. There is someone else who wants to say hi, though. She's here on my invitation. It turns out my sister ruined her investigation with one of her own."

Gary eyed me curiously and I shrugged. It could've been any number of people I'd inspected back home. I had no intention of opening my mouth, no matter who strolled through the door. Phil had been a punch in the gut, but I'd made it through.

How much worse could it get?

As the scent of honeysuckle infiltrated my senses, my luck thoroughly ran out.

In stepped a svelte, ruddy blonde I never thought I'd see again, also in an embroidered sports jacket bearing a badge on the chest. Hers, however, was red, and had "Det. Winston-Salem PD" below a name I didn't recognize.

I knew her as Georgia Harris. The jacket identified her as Stephanie Adelaine.

"Good afternoon, Ms. Daly," the newest arrival murmured. "It's a pleasure to see you again, and here, specifically. It's about time."

I'd forgotten she existed. Gary sifted through the paperwork in the bland folder, fruitlessly searching for a legal name I never knew. All I could do was lean toward his ear and whisper as quietly as I could. "I knew her as Georgia Harris, a shop owner back in Whitehall. She and I hooked up once. I never saw her again after that. I thought she vandalized my property, so I took it to the Sheriff. It was a stupid kid that did it, but I did break into her house thinking she was inside and potentially hurt or worse. She'd fallen in with a known shyster. I wanted to talk it out. I guess she was out to get the shyster all along."

"Undercover," my attorney whispered back. "Gotcha."

"Oh, see? She'll talk now that you're here," Phil mocked from the doorway, snickering at Detective Adelaine before disappearing. The lovely detective crossed her arms and cocked her head to the side, her firearm knocking against her narrow thigh.

Gary peered at the table, gathering his thoughts before gazing up at the new arrival. "Sheriff Adelaine, I assume you also knew my client prior to her relocation to Philadelphia?"

She nodded confidently, a smirk pulling her pink lips up. "I did, very well. I pressed charges against her before she fled the area, namely breaking and entering, though she did tamper with official documentation at the crime scene. Months of work came crashing down due to your client's negligence and ignorance, not to mention her impatience with due process."

"With all due respect, Detective," the attorney replied pertly. "As is the case with Sheriff Daly, my client is here for current allegations, not historical ones."

"Ah, but Mr. Maroney, perhaps you're familiar with character witnesses? Ill-placed family loyalty may cause the Sheriff to back away from such a testimony, but I assure you, I have no interest in protecting this client of yours. If I'm called to testify on your client's character, I will do so, unabashedly, truthfully, and unapologetically. In the meantime, Ms. Daly, enjoy your stay."

With a swish of ponytail and twist of hip, she was gone, leaving us in her wake. The door shut and there was a moment of silence before Gary turned to me.

"So far, so good. You all right?"

I managed an appreciative snort. "Yes, sir."

"Good. Let's see what else they've got for us."

Next was Avery, all tears and sympathy, though he begged for me to come clean and admit I'd been casing his workstation and tapping into his system since the very beginning. Of course, I gave him no response, sitting still with blank eyes until he finally gave up. After Avery left, the detective escorted in a parade of other Red Room representatives. Even Vera made an appearance, seemingly disgusted by the lack of sanitation protocol in the questioning room. Gary was stoic the whole time, jotting notes as each performer implored me to own up to crimes I hadn't committed. Even the detective's routine of half good guy, half bad guy didn't work. I held my tongue like a diligent lantern carrier in a squall.

Two hours later, I was exhausted. I'd slept two hours the night before, and the unconscious transport to the police station hadn't exactly been restful. I was growing tired of this nonsense. No doubt, that was the detective's intention.

Su had warned me. I'd been too stubborn to listen. Memories of her and our good times together were enough to give me a second wind, though I knew it was short lived. I just needed to get through the last inning intact.

A six-minute delay made Gary lean toward my shoulder. "Maybe they're done."

I murmured to him. "They're just trying to make me sweat."

"Possibly, but you've been cool as a cucumber so far. Let me take a closer look at these docs."

I racked my brain. There were a few folks I hadn't seen yet, but none I figured would make an appearance. Gary's gritty tone cut through my thoughts. "Who's Bryan?"

I turned to face him, my expression shifting to shock. "He's in there?"

I was so careful. Damn it. Don't let him get wrapped up in this, too.

"He's the SVP of Cyber Security for Midas International, yes?" My lawyer asked.

"Yep, and he's been my best friend since college."

Gary hummed in understanding with eyes narrowed on the pages in his hands. They passed over lines of texts as the wall clock ticked relentlessly. Seconds turned to minutes as he perused, wearing my patience down to a nub. Finally, I turned to him, trying in vain to keep my tone low, cordial and calm, but failing miserably. "Jesus, Gary. Tell me what it says!"

He turned the pages to face me. "See for yourself."

My world came crashing down, narrated in twelve-point Times New Roman.

Bryan Landry, SVP, Midas International, issues the following statement:

I, Bryan Landry, do swear that I have willingly and voluntarily contributed to the behaviors and apprehension of Elizabeth Cushing-Daly, a.k.a. Serena Hunter, a.k.a. *esTre11aN3gra,* by committing the following actions: providing access to Midas International's internal systems and software to enable Ms. Daly to commit cybercrimes on behalf of herself and Anderson-Hilliance; coordinating and encouraging illegal behaviors; obscuring the reality of the investor/investee relationship between Midas International and Anderson-Hilliance for the purpose of deceiving Ms. Daly; providing necessary technical and professional support in order to educate and encourage Ms. Daly to continue her behaviors; and allowing the use of my personal and financial data to continue her pursuits as *esTre11aN3gra*. My actions were conducted solely for the purpose of aiding legal channels in apprehending Ms. Daly, and in cementing her subsequent conviction. I appreciate the consideration given to this deposition.

Sincerely, Bryan Landry, SVP, Midas International.

A shallow breath squeezed from my lungs as I eyed his childish, indigo signature at the bottom of the paper. I fought the urge to rip it into shreds, instead dropping it to the table. My attorney laid a palm on my shoulder, and for the first time in my life, I didn't shrug it off.

"He's angling for a plea deal, and to be the hero of this whole mess," he told me.

I swallowed back bile, keeping my tone quiet and my body pointed away from the mirror. "He's been my partner for years. We started hunting together. He knows I'm not *esTre11aN3gra*. I... I'm so angry, I could flip this fucking table."

Gary squeezed my shoulder with a calm exhale. "Keep it together. They're floundering. This house is built on popsicle sticks. Any attorney worth their salt will get you off, including yours and this one over here. Keep it together."

I met his stare, his patience and decades of experience resonating in them. He wasn't panicked, despite the endless interrogation I'd faced so far. He'd clearly seen worse in his years at the bar. I fed off the quiet calm I saw, praying to a god I didn't believe in before releasing a slow breath. I faced forward on my chair, steeling courage that was waning by the second.

I'll get through this. This is all circumstantial. He's right.

A few more minutes of silence persisted before the door swung open again. There, in the threshold, wrapped in a linen suit and silk scarf, was my dream girl. Her onyx irises were full of restlessness, guilt, and shame. I waited, stiff as a board, while she took the seat across from mine. It wouldn't have surprised me to know she, too, had contributed a statement for my prosecution. I was batting a thousand when it came to honorable friends.

"May we have a moment, Mr. Maroney?" Su asked my attorney.

He turned his attention to me. I nodded once. He wasted no time in seeing himself to the door. "Five minutes, no more, and everyone's listening." He closed the door behind his fleeing frame.

Su's eyes never left mine as she swept her scarf from her shoulders. "I... I don't know what to say. I know you can't say much anyway."

I lifted my brows slightly, hoping she knew me well enough to interpret.

Her tone dropped an octave as she continued. "I'm not here to contribute to the investigation. I'm here to give you an update. I assume Mr. Maroney informed you that an attorney is inbound. That's my doing."

Well, that answers that question.

"Your attorney, she's a genius. I met her at UCLA. She was brushing up on law to pass the bar. She showed up half the professors with whom she mentored. She takes no prisoners. When all this started happening, I made the call. It'll take some time to get this straightened out, but I'm covering the legal fees. Don't fight me on this, and don't fuck this up."

I sighed, my eyes closing slowly. I'd sweated the idea of a high-profile attorney and a drawn-out court case. Su's intervention was a welcomed shot in the arm, and her advice was poignant, though a little too late.

Maybe she and this attorney buddy of hers are the only prayers I've got left.

Su's voice turned erudite. "She'll angle to have you released pending trial. I'm working on a safe place for you to go. This, and the attorney on retainer, are the least I can do. I know you don't care about my conscience, but I feel like I should come clean."

My gaze shifted to my lap. Of course, she wanted to talk. It was her worst quality. She spoke the most when no words were needed.

"I'm going to leave a letter with your attorney. I hope you read it. Every word of it is true. And I'm sorry. If I'd just-"

I interrupted her sorrowful song with an impatient slap on the metal tabletop. My palm stung, but the sudden racket halted her blubbering instantly. She regarded me curiously as I scowled. Without another word, she rose and made her way to the door. With scarf replaced around her neck and head, she escaped into the room beyond.

Gary made his way back inside, retaking his seat, reassembling the paperwork, and closing the folder. "We're done. I've called an end to this nonsense. If your attorney doesn't show tomorrow, call me." He handed me his business card and a sealed envelope emblazoned with a bold, scrawling signature in red ink. "This is from Ms. Iruma. You're allowed to retain this document during your stay here. Don't let anyone take it from you. Any questions?"

All I could do was shake my head.

* * * * *

Seven hours after I was roused by the ear-piercing squeal of the breakfast cart, a navy-uniformed officer, as rotund as he was impatient, appeared through the flap on my cell door. I lifted my eyes. I knew I looked like shit. He confirmed it wordlessly.

"You've got a visitor. I'll give you five minutes."

Four passed before he returned to me. Along with him was a stout, dark-skinned battering ram of a woman with tight braids and crow's feet. Outfitted with cuffs and shackles, I was wordlessly dragged out of my cell. As I proceeded down the narrow tier to the steel staircase with the scowling female a step behind and the porker a step ahead, walking backwards, I contemplated my luck, or lack thereof. I'd slept maybe an hour on the hard bed chained to the wall. I'd refused to use the utilitarian aluminum toilet, and I'd pushed away the tray of gray sausage links and quarter-inch thin pancakes that had been delivered before daybreak. Though I'd been told I was fortunate for a cell on a quiet tier, I begged to differ. My definition of quiet didn't include snoring in adjacent cubbies, or the routine shouts of officers over the intercom.

Through two sets of heavy metal doors was a wider hall. A broad mauve stripe at waist height guided visitors down the gulley to unadorned rooms, their doors labeled with single digit numbers. Gordo nudged the last door open.

"Far seat's yours."

A simple square of white-painted cinder block awaited me. Twin aluminum chairs flanked a three-foot square table, dead center in the sterile space. The officer watched from the door as I settled, the chains I wore clanging against my rickety chair. I sat back as silence settled between us. I appreciated the isolation. This was shaping up to be the best part of the stay so far.

A moment later, my stomach rumbled audibly, echoing off the stone and making the officer chortle. "Maybe you'll eat eventually, or maybe you'll die of starvation. I guess we'll see."

I rolled my eyes. "I'd be one less body to count."

"Eh, the paperwork's a pain in the ass. Try not to die on my shift."

While I appreciated the retort, I wouldn't give him the gratification. He slammed the door, trapping me. A plate glass window straight ahead revealed a cloudy view of the outside hall, and of the stout officer, watching me from a distance. Unwilling to give him the satisfaction, I gazed around listlessly, awaiting my unknown visitor. The day before had been a string of unfortunate cameos. I didn't dare guess whose presence was next.

It took a few minutes for the hallway door to swing wide, but when it did, I gaped openly. A pert and professional golden blonde, all grace and elegance in a three-piece cobalt suit, strolled in on lofty pumps. She was as impressive in person as she was on stage. She settled into the seat opposite mine, scowling openly at my chains before shouting over her shoulder. "The injunction has been filed. Get the restraints off my client."

The overweight officer's face disappeared from the window. A second later, he was inside the room, undoing my shackles. They slid to the floor with a dull clang. His voice was a mumble. "They go back on for transport."

"I know, I wrote the injunction," my rockstar attorney replied flatly. "Thank you, Officer."

He shook his head in irritation, showing himself out, and retaking his place beyond the hazy pane. Left face to face with my physically and intellectually impressive lawyer, I felt like a child for the first time since Mom died.

Her face brightened just a touch at my shocked silence. "Good afternoon. Sorry for my delay. Before we go on, what name are you using these days?" She asked, popping open her impeccable Italian leather attaché to retrieve a familiar looking manila folder. "I've got three names on this one document."

I hadn't regained my breath yet, but I managed a single word. "Whatever."

"Let's go with Beth," she replied, her amethyst eyes twinkling ever so slightly. "Now, tell me how the hell you ended up here, will you?"

⊕

Printed in the USA
CPSIA information can be obtained
at www.ICGtesting.com
JSHW021933200924
69982JS00001B/1